Still Life
with Husband

Still Life
with Husband

A Novel

LAUREN FOX

ALFRED A. KNOPF
New York 2007

THIS IS A BORZOI BOOK
PUBLISHED BY ALFRED A. KNOPF

Published in the United States by Alfred A. Knopf,
a division of Random House, Inc., New York, and
in Canada by Random House of Canada Limited, Toronto.

www.aaknopf.com

Knopf, Borzoi Books, and the colophon are
registered trademarks of Random House, Inc.

Library of Congress Cataloging-in-Publication Data
Fox, Lauren.
Still life with husband : a novel / Lauren Fox.—1st ed.
p.   cm.
"This is a Borzoi book"—T.p. verso.
ISBN: 978-0-307-26491-6
ISBN: 978-0-307-27737-4 (pbk.)
1. Adultery—Fiction.   2. Marriage—Fiction.   I. Title.
PS3606 095536S75 2007
813'.6—dc22   2006047394

Manufactured in the United States of America
First Edition

For my parents

Still Life
with Husband

IN THE MIDDLE OF THE NIGHT I DON'T KNOW WHO HE IS, this man lying next to me, his leg brushing against my leg, arm draped over my hip. And that's when I want him. I keep my eyes closed and turn toward him, stroking him softly, fingers skimming over his chest, his thighs, feathery touches light enough to wake up just the parts that matter. He responds, and we both know what to do, how not to talk, not even to whisper, letting our bodies move together in the dark. This is a man I picked up in a bar; this is a man whose name I don't know; this is searing, anonymous sex with a stranger, and I'm using all of my senses and none of my heart. He rolls on top of me, heavy and hard, not kissing, hot hands all over me. I grab a condom from my night table and hand it to him.

"Emily," he whispers, crashing rudely into my dream, breaking the rules of 2:00 a.m. sex. "Please?"

"No," I say, my eyes still closed, arching toward him now in spite of myself. "Shhh." I know what he wants, and I'm not prepared to give it to him.

"Baby," he breathes, and I open my eyes to the face of my husband hovering over mine, earnest and needy, the man I have known since college, the man I share a bathroom with, the man who cried during *Little Women,* who thinks I don't know that he plucks his nose hairs, who's afraid of raisins because they remind him of mouse droppings. "Baby," he whispers again, and I sigh, fully here now, fully awake and resigned to it. And this is how we finish, knowing everything about each other, completely together, naked and silent and half-satisfied in the middle of the night.

"I'M THINKING ABOUT STARTING AN ALL-GIRL BAND," MEG says to me as she flips through an old *People* magazine, stopping at a large photo spread of a popular boy band. " 'N Secure. What do you think?" She points to the last blueberry muffin under the plastic cake cover. "I'll have that one, please," she says to the girl behind the counter. She looks at me, smiles, turns back to the girl. "And a decaf cappuccino. And a bran muffin." I've already ordered my tea and my own (pumpkin–chocolate chip) muffin. You might as well be eating cake for breakfast, is the word on the street about muffins, but I don't care. I would *happily* eat cake for breakfast.

"A bran muffin instead of the blueberry?" The exasperated teenager plants her hands on the counter, refusing to continue until she gets this order straight. She is annoyed at us for talking, for reading magazines, for not concentrating on our transaction. There is a tall glass next to the cash register stuffed full of bills. The ominous sentence, "TIPS is SPIT spelled backwards," is scrawled on an index card and taped to the glass. I imagine the tip money must have either come from her own pocket, or that customers envision her spewing into their lattes and drop their money so she can hear it.

"Both," Meg answers. "I'm having *two muffins*." Meg is eight weeks pregnant, and says she feels as if she has a tapeworm. "None of that pansy-ass morning sickness for me!" she says. She started out about twenty pounds overweight, and, like most chubby girls, she doesn't usually eat much in public. Now she has no choice, motivated by the hungry alien growing inside her. "It forces me to do things I would never normally do," she admits, "like finish my whole meal at a restaurant." Meg told me that a waitress at an Italian restaurant once actually discouraged her from ordering lasagna, telling her, "That's fattening!" Shocked, Meg answered meekly, "Okay, I guess I'll have a salad. . . ." And then, a split second later, as the insult took full effect, she added, "Bitch!" and stormed out. Her hapless husband left five dollars for the bread and Cokes they'd already had, and followed her. Meg is my closest friend, but I'm a little bit scared of her.

"I'll be the drummer," I say, "for 'N Secure, but I'll just drum really quietly. And after every song we can kind of sidle up to the microphone and say, 'Was that okay?' "

"And our first song can be, 'Will You Be My Friend?' "

"Or, 'Do These Jeans Make My Butt Look Big?' "

Meg is a grade-school art teacher, but she's been on sabbatical since the beginning of the year, freeing us to meet for breakfast twice a week at White's, our favorite bookstore/coffee shop. The reason for the sabbatical, she tells people, is that she simply needed some time off to regroup. She and Steve, her husband, had been trying in vain for two years to conceive, and, after undergoing invasive diagnostic tests and humiliating procedures ("Think of this as preparation for the humiliation of giving birth," one female doctor told her cheerfully, shoving an ultrasound camera up inside her), Meg decided, she tells people, that she needed to remove the stress and chaos of the job from her life for a while. The real reason she left was that she couldn't bear the thought of one more seven-year-old sticking a pipe cleaner up his nose, one more fourth-grader trying to impress her friends by eating paste, chalk, and/or modeling clay, one more parent bitterly complaining that, by preventing precocious little Ashleigh from exploring the medium of gluing the unpopular boy's pants to his chair, Meg was stunting the development of a budding genius. Pregnancy or no pregnancy, she'd had it.

"We were trained not to scold children, to respect their individuality, their autonomy. Which I agree with!" Meg told me this summer. " *'You need to make better choices, Michael.'* But when I found myself wanting to tell small children to shut the fuck up, I knew it was time for a break. Half the reason I wanted to get knocked up in the first place," Meg admitted, "was for the maternity leave."

In July, Meg and Steve squandered their savings on a trip to Paris, where Meg promptly got pregnant.

Now, she licks her fingers between muffins and looks me in the eye. "Maybe you and Kevin need to take a trip to Paris." We had always said we wanted to have babies at the same time, Meg and I, to be new moms together. We thought it would be a kind of combination life-changing event/girls-only road trip. We imagined ourselves meeting every morning at the playground—our same witty, edgy selves, but now with tiny new accoutrements. Meg is disappointed that she'll be going on this voyage alone now, and, I think, she's beginning to realize that the whole thing might be slightly less charming than we'd imagined. She'd like nothing more than to drag me into this procreational mess with her.

Kevin, too, has been trying to convince me for a year now that it's time for us to start a family. But it seems that my biological clock is a cheap knockoff, a ten-dollar Rolex sold by a guy on the street wearing a trench coat. Every time Kevin turns to me with that melting-ice-cream look in his eyes, every time he sees a baby in a stroller on the sidewalk and starts cooing uncontrollably at it, I have to squeeze my hands into fists and clench my teeth to keep from running away screaming from my darling husband. I think that this is probably not a good sign. In fact, we fought about it last night, for the millionth time. Kevin cornered me as I was getting out of the shower and rattled off a list of advantages to starting a family now (my favorite: "I want to have three kids, and you're not getting any younger!"), and I railed, "Do you think you can *sell* me on having a baby? Do you think it's like changing our long-distance company?" I pulled my towel tightly around me and shook back my dripping hair. "Once we switch over to Sprint, I'll wonder how we ever managed without it?" Kevin, as usual, retreated into silence, the gears and cogs in his brain spinning silently. True, we had periodically spoken about having children—but vaguely, never with any particular time frame in mind. It was part of our plan, but then, so was buying a sailboat someday and sailing around the Great Lakes. Maybe it would happen when we were older; in the meantime, there were movies to see, books to read, camping trips and cheap vacations to enjoy. I've always wanted to take a pottery class, too, but I'm not rushing out to register for Beginning Wheel Throwing.

I don't know why I find myself repulsed and scared witless by the idea of having a baby right now, but I do. Small children used to be part of the landscape to me, not really registering, benign, like sidewalks or awnings or squirrels. But lately I see them around, fat babies flailing about, imperious toddlers riding around in plush strollers, and they look abnormal, like sinister, shrunken aliens; I imagine them secretly communicating with each other in a language we can't understand, plotting—succeeding in!—global domination.

Mostly I'm struck by the amount of space they inhabit. It's as if they appear on the scene and just announce their demands, like Zsa Zsa Gabor, like a million tiny Zsa Zsa Gabors. Just the other day I watched as a little girl *deliberately* chucked her orange plastic cup out of her stroller, then screamed with rage because her distracted mother didn't notice. Why would a woman—and it seems like it's always women—do that to herself? Why would she invite chaos into her life like that? The idea of it terrifies me. There is even a part of me that secretly wishes Meg weren't pregnant. I feel like we get closer every day to the moment the baby is born, when I will lose her for good. Of course I can admit this to no one.

"I don't think I need a vacation. I'm a freelance writer with a part-time job. I'm *on* vacation, more or less," I say. I'm picking the chocolate chips out of my muffin, lining them up on the side of my plate. "The other morning, I played computer solitaire for two hours. Besides, Kevin would never take the time off." I stuff a huge chunk of muffin in my mouth.

"That's bullshit," Meg says. "First of all, Kevin needs a vacation. Anyone can see that he spends too much time in front of a computer. He's as pale as a fish. And you," she pronounces. (Other people say things; Meg pronounces.) "You don't even notice how stressed-out you can get. You're stressed about work when you have work, and freaked out about not working when you're not working. You need more structure. Your lack of structure *is* your stress."

"Meg," I say hesitantly, "your baby will be glorious. And you're ready to welcome it. But I'm just not ready yet." *Yet*. It feels like a tiny lie, like I'm purchasing Meg's understanding with this untruth; what I want to say is *I'm not sure I'll ever be ready*. I slurp my tea with great concentration.

Meg leans in close to me. I can smell the cucumber-melon soap she uses. I look up from my mug, wondering if she'll try to argue with me, to convince me again to be her traveling companion on the highway to motherhood. "Don't look," she whispers, "but the guy across the room is totally staring at you." She looks down at her bran muffin and giggles. This is Meg's and my default mode, the screen saver of our friendship: acting as co-conspirators in a battle against adulthood.

"Nobody's staring at me," I hiss. I glance around the coffee shop. Nobody is even remotely looking our way. And if anyone were, he'd be staring at Meg. Even though she wears a size sixteen, even though she sports a shiny wedding band, even though she rarely wears makeup and often doesn't bother to brush her hair, men make passes at Meg constantly. She's beautiful, tall and curvy with long, thick, straight blond hair, light brown eyes, and a perfect cupid's bow of a mouth. It's ridiculous, really. She's like the sun. Men are blinded by her light and will do anything to get close, at their peril; she, of course, spurns them with glee. Even women—even straight women—can't keep themselves away from her. When we were roommates in college, she was always coming home with gifts given to her by strangers. Once, she walked in with a bag of bagels from the deli. "We have so many!" the old lady who owned the place had said to her, pressing the sack into her hands. "Take just a few home with you, darlink!" Another time, at the mall, the Clinique lady gave her a bag full of samples, just because, she said, Meg's skin was so radiant. I'm a good sport. I have to be. I've spent countless accumulated hours sitting at tables in restaurants, coffee shops, bars, as guys come up to talk to her and ignore me. I used to pretend not to mind, secretly loathing myself for not being gorgeous, loathing the men for ignoring me, loathing Meg for being beautiful. Then, years ago, when we were still in college, I had it out with her. We were at the park, and she had just convinced a guy who was trying to pick her up that she was from the Eastern European country of Slovatarkia and didn't speak English. "Nie! Nie!" she had said to him sadly, shaking her head, shrugging her shoulders. When he finally gave up, she turned to me, ready to burst out laughing, surprised to see me staring back at her, my mouth tight with fury.

"Do you have any idea how I feel right now?" I had asked her coldly, surprising myself with the degree of my anger. "Do you know what it's like to be your closest friend, when every single time we're out together, some guy is ready to fall at your feet in adoration? Do you have any idea what it's like to be the moon to your sun?" While Meg had been pretending to be Slovatarkian, I had been practicing my speech. "You make a joke out of it every time," I said. "A comedy routine. I don't want to be your goddamned straight man."

Meg was shocked, and defensive. She told me I was being crazy, oversensitive, and mean. "You go on as many dates as I do!"

she'd insisted. "How about that guy in your Shakespeare class who's obsessed with you?" (It was true; there was a skinny, somber sophomore who kept trying to get me to come watch him perform at the Renaissance Faire and who had, in fact, once written me a sonnet.) Then Meg ticked off a list of all the boys who'd ever asked me out, and, for emphasis, a second list of all the favors she'd ever done for me. "And I've never gone out with any guy you've been interested in!" By then even she knew she had missed the point. "You're my best friend!" she finally said. "I would never do anything to hurt you. I thought . . . these creeps . . ." She waved her hand around at an imaginary assembly of all the skeezy guys who'd ever wanted her phone number. "I play it up so that you and I can laugh about it," she said softly. Then she started to cry. Then I started to cry. Then we hugged, and, although in the ensuing years Meg has not grown less beautiful, and I have not become a man magnet, the issue settled between us into something chronic and manageable, less like an angry rash and more like a minor bunion. And besides, we each grew up, fell in love for real, and got married. The things that matter when you're barely in your twenties seem ridiculous, childish from the other side of thirty. Still, certain patterns in a friendship hold true. What's more, in a coffee shop with my best friend, without my husband, certain other, harmless feelings can be indulged.

"Nobody's staring at me!" I say again. "What are you talking about?" But then I see him, the young, dark-haired man sitting alone across the room. He is unshaven in a sexy, can't-be-bothered way (but also potentially in an unemployed way); he's stuck a pencil behind one ear, and a thick book lays open in front of him. Surprisingly, he is staring at me. There's no doubt about it. I look away and my hand darts automatically to my mouth. I wipe nonexistent crumbs from my lips. "Is there something hanging off my face?" I whisper. "A *booger*?" I rub my nose surreptitiously.

"No, Em!" Meg stage-whispers back. "He's staring at you because you're a babe!" In fact, I get the ones who are interested in faces with "character." I've been described as dramatic-looking, striking, interesting, and once, "Venezuelan." I have a mop of shoulder-length curly brown hair that is often more frizz than ringlets, dark brown eyes, and a large nose with a bump on the bridge. I get the ones who want exotic-lite. I get the ones who, for whatever reason, don't want Meg.

As I glance back at mystery man, he flashes a shy smile and turns back to his book.

"He's blushing," Meg says. "You're making him blush!"

In spite of myself, I'm loving this. I have no qualms about harmless flirting, and I would never do anything beyond it. If a situation like this, which is rare for me to begin with, progressed past smiling and blushing and a little small talk, I'd cut it off. I think about Kevin and what would humiliate or embarrass him if he knew about it. In the unspoken code of ethics of our marriage, that's as far as I would go. I presume Kevin behaves the same way, and I don't mind. After all, he lives in the world, too. I'm glad that we're both young, that we can attract attention. It makes us more attractive to each other. Not long ago I idly mentioned to Kevin that a guy at the library had asked me out. We were in the middle of cooking dinner. Suddenly, Kevin was all over me. "What did he look like?" he asked, pressing himself against me from behind, nuzzling my neck while I chopped carrots. "What did he say to you?" He ran his hands up and down my sides, reached around for my breasts. Is it some alpha-ape thing? The idea must flip a primal switch in a man: if other apes want my female, then I am the prize-winning baboon. For my part, I think about Kevin's young female coworkers, how they must nurse terrible crushes on their shy, handsome young colleague, and it excites me, too. After all, they don't get to have him; I do. Maybe that makes me some kind of territorial monkey, too.

Meg takes things a half step further than I do, but that's it. She, for example, would accept a man's phone number if he gave it to her. But she wouldn't call him. Steve is the most mature of us all; utterly devoted to Meg, he pays no attention to the writhing world of human sexuality that still breathes around him. It's as if it disappeared when he met her. I can understand that, actually. But it's boring.

"I'm going to get a refill," I say, grabbing my cup. "Want anything?" Meg is working on her second muffin. She shakes her head and winks at me. "Did you just wink at me?" I ask. Meg is laughing as I walk up to the counter.

I wait in line as surly-girl takes her time with another order. After a few minutes, I sense someone behind me, a rustle of clothes, soft breathing. I know it's him, and my palms actually begin to sweat. He clears his throat, and I turn around.

"Hey," he says, meeting my eye for a second and then looking down. He's adorable up close, darker than he looked from across the room, and a little bit younger: no older than twenty-eight.

"Hey," I answer. It's all I can think to say.

"I, um, I've seen you here before." This is awkward and, at the same time, it feels scripted. But I haven't acted this part in a long time. "I come in here some mornings," he continues, "for a break from work."

"Oh. What do you do?" I'm trying to act interested but not too eager, cute and mature, but not too mature, all at the same time. But it's taking up all my energy, diverting the blood flow from my brain.

"I'm a writer," he says, loosening up. "I'm a reporter for *The Weekly*. Have you heard of it?"

"Of course I have. I read it all the time." Right, *this* is how you do it.

His face lights up. "I write the 'Local Beat' column, and I write the cover story about once every two months or so, and I fill in as features editor."

"Well, that's . . . So you're . . ." I'm trying to picture the byline underneath his column, but I can't. The truth is, I only occasionally glance at the paper. We pick it up mostly for movie listings.

"David," he says. "Keller." He offers me his hand and I have to shake it, which ruins my advantage, because my palms are still sweaty.

"Emily Ross," I say, sounding more formal than I mean to. "Actually, I'm a writer, too." He's staring at me now as if I'm telling him I've just won the Pulitzer and, in my spare time, have worked up the cure for cancer. "But freelance. For magazines. Women's magazines." Oddly enough, although this fact embarrasses me, it seems to impress him.

"Wow, that's a hard market to break into, I've heard. Which ones do you write for?" We're like old friends now. Except that we've just met, we're having an incredibly awkward conversation, and if I weren't married, I'd want to sleep with him. I mean, I *do* want to sleep with him, or at least kiss him, but I *am* married. It's the strangest thing.

"Hi!" Without warning, Meg has appeared at my side. I hadn't noticed her approach, I'd been so wrapped up in our brief conversation. She's smiling at us, but it's not the same conspiratorial smile as before; she seems slightly irritated, so very slightly that only her best friend could read it. "Emily, sorry to interrupt, but didn't you say you had a meeting at ten today?" It's nine forty-five. I don't, of course. I give her a little shrug. She narrows her eyes back at me.

"Oh, hey, yeah, I do. Thanks." I set my mug down in one of the gray tubs reserved for dirty dishes. "David," I say, as we maneuver awkwardly, the three of us, away from the counter and back in the general direction of our tables, stopping in the middle of the coffee shop like a disoriented herd of elk. "This is my friend Meg." They shake hands.

"So, Emily," David continues, still focused on me; I'm completely sucked in. He reaches into his front pocket, pulls out a pen and a scrap of paper, and scribbles something on it. "Here's my number and my e-mail address. Give me a call sometime. Or send me an e-mail. It'd be nice to talk more. And, if you're interested . . . we don't pay as well as what you're probably used to, but maybe you could write for me. For us. For the newspaper." He's blushing again. I take the paper and our fingers touch. I pull my hand back fast, as if I'm recoiling from a flame.

"Thanks," I say. Meg takes my elbow and leads me toward our

table, where we gather up our things and head for the door. Suddenly, my long-lost bat radar is activated; I know that he's watching me as we leave. Fortunately, I have excellent posture.

Outside, Meg is quiet. We start walking back toward my apartment, where her car is parked.

"Well, that took an odd little turn," she says finally, halfway down the block.

"What do you mean?" I keep my voice light.

"Emily, that was . . . you were . . . I heard you. That guy asked you out and you basically said yes."

"Meg! That is not what happened. First of all, he's a writer for *The Weekly,* and we were talking shop. That was harmless flirtation!" I stop for a second, turn and face her. "Do you really think I'd . . . what are you thinking? It was *harmless,*" I repeat. "Why are you being so judgmental?"

"Sorry." She starts walking again, links her arm through mine as a peace offering. "There's a line, you know, and it seemed like you crossed it. But I guess you didn't. Sorry," she says again.

If I wanted to, I could take this further, make it escalate. Look who's talking about line-crossing! I've seen you take men's phone numbers lots of times before! But I don't. "That really was nothing," I say instead. "I would *never.*" We walk in silence for the next few steps. "Why didn't he notice my wedding ring, I wonder."

"Because you're not wearing it, sunshine."

I unhook my arm from Meg's and stare down at my left hand. It's true. I'm not.

LAST YEAR, KEVIN AND I TRAVELED BY TRAIN FROM MILWAUKEE to Minneapolis to visit my sister, Heather. On the way over, Kevin sat in the window seat, and I took the aisle. We sat across from a couple, about our age; the woman also sat in the aisle seat, and her husband had the window. After about an hour, as we rattled through the Wisconsin countryside, both Kevin and this man (Marcus, I learned later) had fallen fast asleep, lulled by the rocking of the train. So, leaning across the space between the seats, the woman and I began to talk.

Amy and I became fast, if temporary, friends, and we exchanged our stories, the way people do who vaguely look alike, who carry the same brand of handbag and wear the same kind of shoes, who know they will have pretty much in common. Still, we were astounded by just how specifically our lives resembled each other's. Amy and Marcus had met, just as Kevin and I had, at school in the Midwest. Marcus was from a small town, just like Kevin, studying architecture in Chicago. Amy, who was from Ann Arbor, had changed her major six times before she finally settled on political science, mostly because her parents had threatened to cut off her tuition money. Right after college—quickly, too quickly, Amy said—they had moved in together, and, because they'd been in such a rush, they ended up struggling over when to get married. But then they did get married, and now, Amy confessed in a whisper, they were busily trying to get pregnant, which immediately and unfortunately caused me to picture them having sex. Marcus was building a reputation for himself as an architect in a large Chicago firm, and Amy was an assistant to the assistant director of a small nonprofit consumer advocacy foundation. They went to Nebraska every summer, she told me, to visit his family.

Naturally, we overdisclosed to each other. It was as if we had met the physical manifestations of our own private diaries, and we knew that, for the next four-and-a-half hours, or at least until Marcus or Kevin woke up, we could divulge anything to each other. Anyway, try as we might, we weren't the sort of girls who had all that much to reveal. We told each other about our families (both overprotective, both loving), our jobs (unfulfilling), and we giggled about ex-boyfriends (I tried to make the most out of my three dull former relationships, one at the end of high school and the other two in college). We cast glances at our sleeping mates as we told our secrets.

After an hour and a half, near Tomah (the Cranberry Capital), we started to wind down, began to grow a little bit bored with each other, as much as we were probably both a little bit bored with ourselves, and our conversation circled back to when we first met the men who would become our husbands. I was trying to remember what it felt like to know that Kevin and I were going to be together. I was thinking, trying to call up the emotional details of it, from our first kiss (which was unspectacular and concluded with Kevin telling me he knew I'd had onions for lunch and me not telling him that tongues were not meant to be used as plungers), to the first time we said "I love you" (which was somewhat more spectacular, and involved fireworks, occurring as it did on July Fourth).

"I always thought I'd get married," Amy said, interrupting my daydream, "to whatever man I happened to be dating when the time felt right." She glanced again at her sleeping husband, but affectionately, not surreptitiously; if he happened to wake up and hear this, she obviously wouldn't have minded. "I thought I'd be twenty-five or twenty-six, or maybe a little bit older, be involved with a guy, someone decent and nice enough, and it would be time. And we'd get married." She took a slow pull from the bottle of iced tea she'd been nursing for the past two hours. "But what I never predicted was that I'd fall so crazy in love. In college! I never thought I'd meet my soul mate." She laughed, a little embarrassed, turned again to still-sleeping Marcus. "I never even believed in the concept. But there he is." She paused, waited. Was I supposed to say something now? "You know what I mean," she said. It wasn't a question.

"Sure!" I said. "Definitely I do," and I cast the same puppy-dog look at Kevin, who, in his sleep, had maneuvered his long legs halfway across my space. But I didn't. I had no idea. Of course I loved Kevin, and more than I'd ever loved anyone. But crazy in love? My *soul mate*? It wasn't that, like Amy, I didn't believe in the concept. It had never even occurred to me.

The next moments were slightly awkward, as the rhythm of our conversation had concluded. We each made a few chatty comments, an observation about the scenery, a compliment on a sweater, but neither of us picked up on them. And finally, we stopped talking entirely, only smiling when we happened to catch the other's eye. As I mused uncomfortably on Amy and Marcus's crazy love, the impossible depth of their connection, I thought about what Kevin would say if I told him. He would argue against her claim that such an enviable state of love could exist. And that would make me feel better. So did that mean we were soul mates after all? Soul mates who were too analytical to believe in the idea? I didn't suppose so. But I decided it wasn't important. Kevin muttered in his sleep, and I rested my arm against his. I hoped it didn't matter, after all.

. . .

When I get home from my breakfast date with Meg, the apartment is empty. Kevin has scribbled a note and left it on the kitchen table: "MT B LT 2NT," meaning, he might work late tonight. I pick up the scrap of paper and toss it in the trash, annoyed, despite myself, at his perfunctory communiqué; from someone else, I think, I would at least get a complete word, if not a "See you at eight, sweetheart," or even a "Love you!" I feel a twinge, a prickle of something at the back of my neck, and I think, unbidden, *He takes me for granted*. And as quickly as it appeared, the thought is gone. I find my wedding ring on the bedside table where I leave it every night and I slip it back on. It feels bulky, unfamiliar, as if meeting David Keller has created a chemical reaction in the plain gold band, changing its diameter, slightly altering its smooth surface. *Crazy,* I think, rubbing it against my middle finger, twisting the ring around and around. *Overly symbolic!* I think, and twist, twist, twist it.

I have no deadlines today, nothing pressing to do, so I finish an article proposal: "Exploring the Great Indoors: The Things You Can Learn by Staying Inside." I am an expert on the subject. I've accumulated years of important, detailed information, gleaned from the hundreds of daytime hours I have spent in my pajamas. For example, if you stare long enough, you can be a part-time naturalist, with your front-row view of the urban wilderness outside your window. I once watched ants on the windowsill having sex, it looked like, in what I was pretty sure was the missionary position. I witnessed an autumn love affair between two squirrels, one of whom would get despondent whenever his lover wouldn't appear at their designated tree, and would end up chewing nervously on his own arm like it was corn on the cob. Even your appliances have a thing or two to teach you: milk in the refrigerator has a tendency to freeze if you leave it too close to the edge, whereas Fudgsicles will melt in the freezer if you don't put them close *enough* to the edge. I don't expect that I will get this assignment, but I seem to have reached a critical point where I have exhausted all of my seriously good ideas, my brain like a diabetic's pancreas. I'm fresh out.

I call my sister. But it's the middle of the day and, like most people, Heather's not home. I check my e-mail. There's a note from Louise Aslanian, my old college adviser. Louise is a depressive lesbian poet who publishes slim volumes of verse every five or six years with a tiny local press. She writes a lot about getting old and dying, and about her mother dying, and sometimes about how she is becoming her mother and will soon die. She taught until two years ago, when she decided, at fifty-five, to fulfill her lifelong dream of moving to Wyoming and working on a ranch. I don't even quite know what a ranch is, but Louise and her supportive partner, a painter, sold their house and did it. Now she's a depressive, lesbian cowgirl poet. Last week I had mentioned to her in an e-mail that I was short on inspiration, knowing that she would have words of real wisdom for me.

"Dearest Emily," she writes, "A prolific writer I once knew had a debilitating stroke several years ago. He lost the ability to speak, so he and his longtime companion worked out a system whereby this writer would communicate by blinking. He wrote his last book in blinks. Then he died. Take heart, my friend. Fondly, Louise."

My perky friend Sara has written to me, too. She lives in Dallas and is married to the CEO of a large software company that's been in the news recently for refusing to hire a well-qualified dwarf. She's written to tell me that she is pregnant with her second child. "We're hoping for a girl this time, but we'll take whatever we get!" Except a dwarf, I think, and turn off my computer.

By the time Kevin comes home, not late, as it turns out, but earlier than usual, I've spent the entire day fuming and have officially worked myself up into a foul humor. I hear his key jiggling in the lock. He bounds cheerfully into the apartment like a big puppy dog.

"Emily!" he calls from the hallway. "Flopsy!" Flopsy, along

with Mopsy and sometimes Cottontail, are his nicknames for me. I hate them. I'm slumped on the sofa, where he finds me and climbs on top of me, practically licking my face. "Surprise for you!" he announces.

"Mmmhmmm," I say, pushing his head away from me. He climbs off my lap and sits next to me, pulls my feet into his lap.

"We're going to Lake Geneva this weekend." Lake Geneva is a resort town about an hour from Milwaukee. My interest is piqued, but I'm too cranky to let on. "Hasting's holding a conference for their tech writers," he says happily. Kevin works for Hasting Electric, writing instructional manuals for their small- and medium-sized electronics and appliances. He's amazing at his job; his manuals are always receiving company-wide acclaim and being circulated in-house as examples of superior work. Kevin experiences actual inspiration as a technical writer. Where others slog away over "insert tab A into slot B," Kevin finds elegance, economy, even humor. He can wax lyrical on the difference between "click closed" and "snap shut"; he's responsible for rewriting the gauche "hold on to the appliance's plastic base before taking the coffee grounds out and disposing of them" to the graceful "grasp handle before removing filter." His finest hour is the warning tag he crafted, now prominently displayed on all Hasting hairdryers: WARN CHILDREN OF THE RISK OF ELECTRIC SHOCK! I had that one framed for him for his last birthday. Kevin, God help him, was born to be a technical writer. "They're updating their entire line of small appliances!" he says gleefully, rubbing my toes. "Dermott asked the guys from engineering and some of the folks in legal and all of us tech writers to attend. I figured, a fancy hotel, free meals . . . You know," he adds quietly, "maybe this weekend, maybe this would be a good chance for us to talk more calmly about things. We could talk some more about buying a house," he says, deftly dodging one issue and pressing down on the bruise of another one. Kevin has recently decided that, in addition to starting a family, we're ready to buy a house. In the suburbs. *More bang for your buck in the 'burbs,* he likes to inform me. He's done his research. "We could think about a timeline, and about where we might want to move."

"Where *you* might want to move," I say.

"Yeah, well, Emily, then we don't have to talk about it." He presses his lips together and releases a puff of air from his nose, the first indication that my surliness is getting to him. "But I told him we'd definitely be there."

"Did you ever think that I might have plans this weekend?" I ask.

"I'm trying here, Em."

I pause, glance over Kevin's shoulder at the news on TV for a few seconds. "Fine."

"Good, then. We'll go!"

ONCE WE'RE ON THE ROAD TO LAKE GENEVA, HURTLING AT TOP speed away from our lives, I have the sense that I can breathe again, although I hadn't realized I had been deprived of oxygen before. I think Meg was right; I think we *do* need a vacation. Maybe this trip will be Paris, without the interesting architecture, great art, or fabulous food.

We cruise through rural Wisconsin, a landscape of autumnal rusts and oranges. Kevin has brought all of my favorite CDs, and has gallantly consented to listening to bluegrass—my pickin' and grinnin' music, he usually calls it—for the past forty-five minutes. He's probably done this to appease me, and it's working. When we arrive in Lake Geneva, we drive past our hotel's wooded entrance, take a quick spin through the town for a look at Main Street's several Ye Olde Fudge Shoppes and all manner of Aren't We Cute Boutiques, then U-turn back down the road and into the sprawling compound, littered with golf courses, that comprises the resort. I resolve to come back later for fudge, one of my favorite foods. Kevin says that he plans on skipping as much as possible of the actual conference in favor of the whirlpool and the free cable. He raises his eyebrows at me lasciviously. "I know how we can keep busy this weekend."

"HBO?" I say.

One hand on the steering wheel, he reaches across the seat and gropes my chest. "Not quite."

I know that he means it, that at this moment he sincerely plans on a weekend of fun and debauchery, but I also know that as soon as he sees the registration desk he'll start salivating, and his wild, reckless sense of responsibility and duty will take over.

We park and haul our bags inside. Kevin sets his on a big pink lounge chair in the lobby and motions for me to do the same. Poking out of a pocket of Kevin's suitcase, I notice, is the book he brought to read during his free time: *Sound Investments for the Careful Planner.* I feel a familiar pang of love for my steady, staid husband. He's like a brick wall you can lean against when you're tired—immobile, rutted with predictable grooves, always there. "Emily, can you hang out here for a minute? I guess I'll just go register and check out the main conference room. I'll get myself sorted out and I'll be right back."

Twenty minutes later, I'm lugging all of our bags up to our room. Kevin has decided to sit in on the first session ("Window and Floor Fans: A Better Blade, a Better Breeze"), but he promises that he'll meet me in the room in a half hour. I should unpack, he says, and relax. He grabs one of the room keys and dashes down the wide hall, waving to someone in the distance.

By the time Kevin comes back, I have unpacked both of our bags and hung up our clothes, showered, watched the news, flipped through the forty-two channels three times, watched an episode of *Sabrina, the Teenage Witch,* unwrapped all of the drinking glasses, turned down our bed, pored over the room service breakfast options, called the front desk to request more shampoo, wandered up and down the hallways, and still had forty-five minutes to spare, sitting at the little desk and trying to read, but stewing, instead, about all the time I'm already spending alone. When Kevin walks in the door, guilty and on the defensive because he has left me alone for two hours, I am beyond testy.

"I'm sorry, I'm sorry, I'm sorry, baby," he says, plunking his new conference bag onto the chair. His voice is of a subtle caliber between edgy and placating; my response will determine its course. "I got caught up in the session, and then I had to mingle afterward. I couldn't get away. Have you been having fun? What've you been doing?" He stands next to me and anxiously rubs his hands together, looks over my shoulder at the novel I'm reading.

"I just don't want to be on my own for the next two days," I say sulkily.

"I do have to attend some of the conference," he answers evenly. "I mean, I suppose I can skip the early morning address on can openers, but I *will* probably have to spend most of the day tomorrow in the small-group small-appliance sessions. . . . And tonight I do have to go back downstairs for the evening program. They're unveiling their new bread maker. It's half the size of the old one, with the same bread-making capacity!" Clearly, the man can't help himself.

"Great. Great, I'll just watch TV for the next forty-eight hours. Or maybe I'll swim by myself in the hotel pool. That should be fun. Or, no, I know, I'll go back down to the lobby and just wait for you in that big pink chair until Monday." I'm escalating. I can't seem to stop myself. "Why did I come with you? What am I even doing here?"

"Emily, for God's sake," Kevin says sternly. "You're out of control!" I hate it when he accuses me of this, even though at the moment it happens to be true. It makes me sound like a lunatic, and him like an emotionless reptile.

"No, I'm not!" I shout. "I just wanted to go on a little weekend vacation with you, and now I'm going to be all by myself for the next two goddamn days!"

In the rhythm of our smaller-scale fights, this outburst indicates that we have just hit the zenith. Kevin wheels another desk chair around next to mine and takes both of my hands in his. "You won't be alone," he says. "I promise. I'll skip out as much as I possibly can." He rubs my knuckles with his thumb. "I promise, baby. Come here," he whispers, moving his hands up my arms and around my back, drawing me toward him. "Come here." He stands and pulls me up with him, presses his body to mine. He starts kissing my collarbone, my forehead, my lips. I feel him grow hard against me. He's unbuttoning my sweater and covering my neck with kisses. His breath is hot on my skin, and I start to respond, to kiss him back. He's murmuring in my ear now, and moving us together toward the bed. I had forgotten how excited he gets at conferences! He stops at the foot of the bed and kisses me again, slowly, his hands reaching inside my shirt. Heat begins to radiate from my center. My insides are turning into lava. I know that what we are doing is an avoidance of the issue, of my feeling abandoned, but what the hell; I don't feel abandoned now. He guides me down onto the bed and kneels over me, unbuttoning my jeans. He slides his hands down my stomach, my hips, grazes the tops of my thighs, back up to my breasts. I'm pulling off his shirt, kissing him as he lowers himself onto me. We're moving together, still partially clothed, with something halfway between urgency and familiarity, the particular landscape of our lovemaking. I'm letting myself be submerged in the easy waves of this, before I realize: a condom. We need a condom! Did anybody bring condoms?

Kevin is on top of me, we're both naked now, and I can feel his penis like a divining rod knocking about, searching for me. I run my tongue along the edge of his ear, lick the side of his neck. Is this Kevin's sneaky way of getting me pregnant? Nod intently when your wife tells you she's not ready for a baby, then seduce her? He moves his lips roughly against mine, his tongue inside my mouth. So do I stop this, abort the passion, force the issue? I need to say something. Does he remember what we talked about? Was he listening? He begins to move, slowly, slowly, and I forget what it is I was about to say.

I do spend virtually all of the next two days alone. On Saturday, Kevin and I eat an early breakfast together in the hotel restaurant, during which he sips coffee and scans the day's conference agenda, muttering to me about food processors. I spend most of my day in a chair in our room, like a retiree, reading and napping and watching mindless TV, and then at nightfall we meet for dinner in the main conference room, where he wears a name tag and I am his wifely appendage. He's distracted, focused outward, socializing with his comrades, introducing me—sometimes actually forgetting to introduce me—and then getting wrapped up in discussions about the legal ramifications of appliance-related warning labels, or about the pitfalls of too much punctuation. I listen in, and it's like I'm in an episode of *Star Trek;* minutes go by and I have absolutely no idea what has been said, or whether or not I've actually been present at all. There's a good chance I've been temporarily whisked off to an alternate universe. I do seem to be nodding at appropriate moments, though. I hope that my eyes aren't rolling around in my head.

During the brief times we're alone together, early in the mornings and late at night, we're polite to each other, extremely cordial, but tense. We fall asleep with the television on and wake up to the chipper squawking of the early morning news anchors.

On Sunday I drive back into town and wander around, poke my head in and out of the shops, and it's warm enough, even though it's early autumn in Wisconsin, to sit by the lake and read for a while. I buy some fudge. I buy a pack of condoms from a disapproving pharmacist at the Old Tyme Drug Store. ("I'm married!" I want to say to him as he hands over the package, frowning. "I wouldn't even need these if the pill hadn't made me so irritable and bloated. Seriously!" But I manage to stop myself.) I order a grilled cheese sandwich in a dimly lit diner, and I have ample time to consider just why it is, despite how much I love Kevin, despite how much he loves me, just why it is that I am going to get in touch with David Keller when I get home.

It's for work, I decide.

KEVIN AND I MET DURING OUR SENIOR YEAR AT THE University of Wisconsin–Madison, at a political protest, sort of. Several days prior to the demonstration, a hapless employee at the most popular coffee shop on campus, Sludge, had noticed a couple locking lips at one of the front tables. After it became clear that their panting was disturbing the other customers, he approached them, asked them to cool it, and offered them free refills on their lattes. When they refused and instead cranked their make-out session up a notch so that the people sitting nearby began to pack up and go, the young worker asked the couple to leave, which they did. The problem was, they were lesbians, and they called it harassment. They rallied their troops, and three days later, Lesbians Involved In Political Struggles To Improve Campus (LIIPSTIC) had organized a massive kiss-in at the coffee shop. "All are welcome!" their posters read. "Even breeders!"

It was early April; who didn't want to kiss someone? I went to check it out and found the place mobbed with students eager to protest intolerance based on sexual orientation and/or suck face with a cute stranger. I barely noticed the skinny blond guy stand-

ing next to me until the organizer of the protest, a gorgeous lesbian famous in Madison for converting straight girls and then
breaking their hearts, announced that it was time to show the
community that we wouldn't stand for discrimination, that everybody had a right to cop a feel in public with whomever they chose.
"Now grab your lover or the nearest stranger, and *kiss*!" she yelled
inspiringly. That's when my cute, scrawny neighbor turned to the
girl on his left and swept her into his arms for a passionate embrace.
I stood there staring at them. He bent her lithe body over his arm
and leaned down to her, and long after everybody else had stopped,
they just kept kissing. I felt myself blushing and wanted to turn
away, but I couldn't. When they were done, the girl stood up,
straightened her T-shirt, and shook his hand. Then she smiled and
walked away. I was mesmerized. The blond guy turned to me and
said, "I hope she doesn't have a boyfriend."

"Or a girlfriend," I added helpfully. He looked flushed and
satisfied. I felt embarrassed and drawn to him. He was like a filled
doughnut, conventional on the outside but full of possibilities.

"Yeah, I don't think she was a lesbian. It's funny," he continued. "I was just in here for a cup of coffee. Who knew?"

"Who knew?" I echoed.

"Can I buy you one?" he asked.

Buy me a lesbian? I thought. "One what?" I was confused and
couldn't quite remember where I was or what I was doing there.

"A cup of coffee." He jammed his hands into the pockets of his
jeans and shrugged. I wondered how many times in his life this guy
had passionately kissed a stranger and then asked another girl on a
date. I would later find out the answer: none. But I didn't know
that yet. I didn't know that at all.

We sat on a bench outside and talked for the next two hours.
Kevin walked me home in the early evening, and at the door of my
apartment building, he took my hand and brought it to his lips,
lightly kissing it, leaving me wanting more.

. . .

On Monday morning I wake up earlier than I need to, with a sparkly, electric feeling zipping through my body. I feel like I've had good dreams all night, although I can't remember any of them. I bound through my morning routine and I even arrive at work before nine, something I've never managed to do before. Along with my freelance work, I'm the part-time assistant editor at *Male Reproduction,* a medical journal devoted to the study of the male reproductive system. I love this job, and not just for the opportunities it presents for rude jokes. One of my bosses is an elderly academic researcher named Dick. He says he went through life being called Dick, and he wasn't about to change his name just because he took up the study of the penis. He's paternal and dotty, and he treats me kindly, as if I'm his clever granddaughter. I'm not as fond of my other boss, Dr. Miller, a thin, nervous, exacting, workaholic urologist, but he's rarely around, always removing gallstones or reversing vasectomies at one of his other two offices, so it doesn't matter.

This morning, Dick is rifling through my desk when I walk in. I suppress the urge to ask him what he's doing rooting around in my drawers.

"Emily, love, would you have a quarter to loan me?" He looks at me, wide-eyed. "Does the vending machine take quarters?" he asks. "I am desirous of a cola this afternoon!" It's actually 8:54 a.m., but I don't tell him that.

"Dick," I say, hanging up my coat. "I was just thinking the same thing. I would love to buy you a soda." I dig around for change in my purse. "How was your weekend?"

"Lovely, lovely. The wife and I took care of the grandchildren on Saturday. They really kept us on our toes. Elizabeth just runs around like a cyclone. . . ." Elizabeth is the name of his thirty-six-year-old daughter, not his granddaughter.

I want to hug him. Instead I just nod. "Mmmhmmm. Little kids can be exhausting." I grab my wallet and head around the corner to the vending machine for two sodas. Our offices are on the second floor of the chemistry building at the university, and the dank hallways always smell vaguely putrid, like a dead frog, or an experiment about to go terribly wrong.

I'm feeling efficient this morning, and I realize as I plug quarters into the machine that, although we usually chat for ten or fifteen minutes when I arrive, now I want Dick out of my office. I have six manuscripts in my in-box waiting to be logged and assigned to reviewers, and several rejection letters to draft left over from last week. I've been meaning to update our mailing list, and I have to send an e-mail to our publisher in Omaha. And I have two articles to proofread, a process that can take hours, scientists being notoriously subliterate. I'm inspired, and as I make my way back to my office with our two Cokes, I'm wondering how I can gently encourage Dick to meander back to his own office across the hall.

"Emily, you'll enjoy this," Dick booms as I walk in the door. He's standing in the middle of the room, surrounded by filing cabinets, his thumbs hooked into his belt loops like he's a potbellied cowpoke. "Were you aware that turtles develop as males or females depending on the temperature at which they incubate?"

"I wasn't! That's fascinating." He told me this last week.

"It's common knowledge in the field of reproductive and spermatological studies, of course," he mutters. "But how was your weekend, my dear?"

I hand Dick his soda. I consider the hours I spent wandering around Lake Geneva on my own. I think about the vast amount of TV I watched by myself, about the cold pasta at the buffet dinners where Kevin spent his time talking about blenders with his colleagues. I think about the conversations we decided not to have. I think about our unprotected sex. "We went to Lake Geneva," I say. "It was . . . it was fun." I sit down at my desk and begin to sort through papers, separating manuscripts into piles.

By the time Dick finally leaves, I am aware that what I have mistaken for my just-born work ethic is really an urgency of a different sort. My skin is prickly because I want to send an e-mail to David Keller. The scrap of paper he gave me at the coffee shop is somewhere in my bag. Although I haven't looked for it, the knowledge that it's there has been swimming around in my brain like a happy little fish since he gave it to me three days ago. It only takes me a second to find it: a torn-off corner of notebook paper, his number and e-mail address written in black ink. These are the first things I know about him, it occurs to me as I examine it: his phone number, his e-mail address, and his handwriting. His penmanship is legible but not neat, small and slanty, boyish. David@the-weekly.com. David@the-weekly.com. David, David, wasn't there a decade a while back when every boy was named David? But not so much anymore. A name really dates a person. For example, you don't meet many babies named Jennifer these days, but twenty years ago, all the girls in my grade school were Jennifers. Jennys. Jens. The boys were Davids, or sometimes Jeffs or Scotts. But really, not so many of those anymore. Emily is a timeless name, my mother likes to brag. But Heather, my sister's name, is not. Why is that? David I could see coming back into fashion, though; it's solid, with a nice biblical resonance.

And what am I doing?

If you think too much about a thing, it's no longer innocent, even if, in truth, it began that way. So I will stop thinking so much about this thing. I could call him, but that would be too personal, too much like I want to go out on some kind of a date with him, which of course I do not. I'm going to stop thinking now. I will dash off an e-mail to David Keller, and then, tonight, I'll tell Kevin that I did. This is, after all, a way for me to make progress in my writing career, a way to get an article assignment from one of the editors at *The Weekly*. Nothing more. And if I admit it to Kevin, that's all it will be. A spark between two people does not mean a fire will necessarily ignite. Not at all.

Hi, David—
Just wanted to send you a quick "howdy!"

DELETE

Dear David,
You gave me your number at the coffee shop on Friday.
I'm the girl with the brown curly hair standing in line in
front of you. We chatted. I was with my friend Meg. I was
wearing a red sweater. Actually it was more pinkish. Possibly you would call it salmon-colored.

DELETE

Hi!!
I was telling my husband about you last night, and

DELETE

Hello there,
I'm sitting here in my office at *Male Reproduction,* a journal devoted to the study of the penis and its related
anatomical structures.

DELETE

Hi, David—
Remember me? I've been thinking about writing for *The
Weekly.* Any chance we could talk about it? It was great to
meet you the other day.
—Emily

SEND

"HOW DID WE END UP IN A *FOOD COURT*?" MEG SAYS, looking around at the sea of tables, the hordes of people inhaling fast food in the middle of Shorebrook Mall.

"And doesn't it always make you think you've done something wrong, nutritionally?" I add. "You're under arrest for overeating, ma'am. See you in *food court*."

Meg snorts at this, and drops a tiny bit of her kung pao chicken onto the front of her shirt in the process, causing a mother and her three kids to turn to us simultaneously and stare. After the woman and two of her children return to the business of eating their lunches, the littlest kid, wearing army fatigues—why do they make them that small?—whispers to Meg, "You're crazy." Meg crosses her eyes at him and lets her tongue loll out of the corner of her mouth, pretending to gag. The boy glares at her and turns back to his McNuggets.

"Nice," I say. "Good example to set for your future child."

"Good thing my future child is the size of a Rice Krispie and can't see me. Are you going to finish that pizza?"

Writing an e-mail to a man on whom you might have a small

crush, which would be not only forbidden, but would also be disloyal to your marvelous husband, does wonders for weight loss. I haven't been able to eat since I hit "send" two days ago. I slide my nibbled-on slice of cheese pizza across the table to Meg. I want to share this dieting insight with Meg, but I can't. I haven't told her about the e-mail.

I have, however, *checked* my e-mail once an hour over the past three days. I've received another chirpy message from Sara, one from an old high school friend who lives in Syracuse, several solicitations for MIRACLE BREAKTHROUGHS IN BREAST ENHANCEMENT and/or PENIS ENLARGEMENT, but nothing from David Keller.

I want to tell Meg. I feel guilty, and can't bring myself to admit what I've done. Which is *nothing*.

"Do you remember what it was like, getting together with Steve?" I ask.

Meg pauses at my non sequitur, wipes her mouth with a napkin, and dabs at the front of her shirt. "Of course I do," she answers, puzzled. She and Steve met at a dinner party four years ago, and I was privy to every detail of their courtship. She'd call me after their dates, and we'd scrutinize each moment. We figured out together what it meant when Steve spent an hour on their second date talking about his ex-girlfriend: misguided confession on his part, but not fatal. We discussed whether or not she could call him, and the optimal time to do so: yes, and two days after their first date, if he hadn't called her by then. We analyzed why, after their first kiss, Steve backed away and didn't call for a few days, and we celebrated when their relationship began to take off. I recall practically as well as she does what it was like, Meg and Steve getting together.

"I mean, do you remember the feeling of it, of knowing that you were falling for him?" I ask, my voice quiet under the echoey rumble of the mall. "That time when you're all sparky and flushed, and everybody tells you how pretty you look and asks you if you got your hair cut?"

"Well," Meg says, beginning to get into it, "I absolutely

remember the exact moment when Steve first took my hand. We were walking down Farwell toward the movie theater, and he just sort of grabbed it, mid-arm swing, and I remember thinking, 'This is the happiest I've ever been,' and then I remember simultaneously stuffing that thought away, because it seemed so melodramatic, but so true at the same time, and I was scared of it, scared of feeling that good." She folds her napkin, absently arranges the plastic fork and paper detritus of her meal into a pile on the tray. "And then I remember thinking that I would tell you about it later." She stops fidgeting and rests her hands in her lap. "Did I?"

"I don't know," I say. "I mean, I don't remember that particular detail." I notice that the food court is beginning to empty. The throng of diners is down to a medium-sized mob, and the tables around us are littered with food. I'm suddenly aware of how nasty it smells in here, as if every molecule has been dipped in grease and batter fried. The midday sunlight streams in through the skylights, illuminating the disgusting details of our surroundings. "I don't think I'll ever feel that way about Kevin again," I admit. "Or anything close to it." And then I start to cry.

Meg is looking at me with such surprise and sweet concern that I start to cry harder, and before I know it I'm blowing my nose into a napkin and swatting at my tears and trying to make sure that nobody notices me, which is probably not working since I'm flapping around like a bat. I'm just starting to get myself under control when Meg says, "Sweetie, what is it?" and then I'm crying even harder.

When I can finally speak, I say, "It's nothing. It's PMS." I blow my nose one more time and then I smile at Meg and say, "Now let's go get you some maternity clothes." I stand up and take my tray over to the garbage can. Meg follows me, and when I turn back to her, I can see that she doesn't believe me for a second.

That night, the e-mail comes in. It's short and sweet and it makes my heart thump in a sick and irregular way.

Emily,
I was glad to get your e-mail. Want to have coffee with me? I was thinking Friday, 10:00, at White's. Does that work for you?
—David

Of course it does.

Later, in bed, it occurs to me that maybe a lie is composed not of the substance of what you tell someone, and not even of its intention, but of the amount of stress it causes you to tell it.

I'm lying awake, thumbing through a magazine, waiting for Kevin to join me. Lately he's been staying up reading, sometimes until one or two in the morning; I'm half-hoping he'll come to bed long after I've fallen asleep, half-hoping he'll slip in next to me in five minutes.

I didn't tell him about the e-mail. I never found the right moment. Now I want to tell him that I have set up a meeting with an editor at *The Weekly*. I want to mention idly that I met this person at a coffee shop. I want everything I say to float out of my mouth like cartoon musical notes, like the way a comic-book bird would whistle. I want to tell Kevin, casual as can be, but I'm nervous; I feel like what I'm about to tell my husband has the portent of a life-changing moment, a choice I am making to tell a lie to the man to whom I've pledged my honesty, to mislead him, if only about the directions of my emotions. This doesn't feel casual. I flick through the pages, but I can't concentrate. I reach over to turn out the light, and then I just wait in the dark for Kevin.

After a while, as I'm beginning to doze off, I hear him come in. He's trying not to make noise, so I say softly, "I'm awake."

"Good," he whispers, climbing in next to me. He fidgets for a while, settling his body under the covers, making the mattress jiggle. He clears his throat and takes a sip from the water bottle he keeps on his night table. I hear the gurgle of the water moving down his throat. "Um," he says softly, "I don't know if I mentioned, Doug Wetzel and his wife had a baby yesterday." Doug Wetzel is one of Kevin's gregariously cheerful, endlessly procreating colleagues, always inviting us to attend another Sunday cookout where the men grill meat and talk about golf and the women discuss the sleep habits of their children while doing the dishes. I spend my time at these events drifting between the two crowds, reminding myself to breathe, carrying around a handful of pretzels or nuts and nervously shoving some in my mouth every time someone is about to ask me a question. I like Kevin's coworkers; they're kind and generous and they always try to make me feel like I belong. But they are an exotic species of toad to me.

"That's nice. By the way, I have an appointment the day after tomorrow with an editor at *The Weekly*. I met him at White's the other day with Meg," I say, deliberately using the word "appointment" and including the safe fact that I was accompanied by my girlfriend. "We started talking, and he probably wants me to write something for the paper."

"Hey, that's great," Kevin says, his voice thin with tiredness. "Do you know what he wants you to write?"

"No, not yet. That's what we're meeting to talk about."

"What's his name?"

"Actually, I don't remember," I lie. And there it is, the first one.

"So, you have a date on Friday!" Kevin laughs. "With a nameless editor. Very mysterious. Is he cute?"

"Please," I mutter. "I'm a married woman."

We're silent for a long time, and then Kevin rolls away from me and says, very softly, "Doug and Wendy had a girl," probably thinking that I'm already asleep.

KEVIN AND I BROKE UP ONCE. WE HAD BEEN TOGETHER for almost three years, and for the last two months of it, a particularly bleak and cold winter, things between us had been wilting. Gradually, we had both been backing off, calling less frequently, spending a Friday or Saturday night doing other things, just because other things seemed more interesting. Sometimes, during those weeks before we called it quits, the phone would ring, and I would think, "I hope it's not Kevin," and then I'd brush that thought away and answer the phone. But we both knew what was happening. We were sliding away from each other like melting slush.

What surprises me now about the breakup is how civil it was, how lacking in drama and emotional strife. One Sunday morning in January, we met for breakfast. It was unseasonably warm that day, and raining. We hadn't seen each other for several days; the night before, I had told Kevin I was busy, and then I'd rented *Terms of Endearment* and watched it by myself, moistening my popcorn with satisfying tears. I dressed carefully that Sunday morning, in a dark maroon turtleneck sweater and new jeans. I spent some time

on my hair. I had a hunch, as I was getting ready, that a certain pro-
tocol was necessary, but I didn't quite know why. We met at Nel-
lie's Deli near my apartment and ordered two large stacks of
pancakes. While we waited for our breakfast, neither of us spoke.
We just watched the rain stream down. It was bound to make a
person melancholy, the warm weeping of the gray January sky,
after such a bitter few months. That night, a freeze would descend
on Milwaukee and it wouldn't lift until March. The huge puddles
that were just then in the process of forming would turn the entire
city into one gigantic, treacherous skating rink. Every day for
weeks, cars would slam into each other; people would slip and
break their ankles on their way to work; old ladies would refuse to
leave their homes. Of course, we didn't know that then. We just
watched the water fall and fall, streaking the glass, blurring the
lights.

We ate in silence. Against character, Kevin was the one who
finally spoke. Halfway through his stack of pancakes, he took off
his glasses and slowly cleaned them, then took a gulp of water,
wiped his mouth, and said, "Emily, I think maybe we should see
other people. I think maybe we should. I think we should take a
little break."

Since my very first boyfriend, I had not responded well to
those words. I had been dumped three times before, and each time
I had wept copiously, had tumbled into pits of despair twice, had
once embarrassed myself in a restaurant by throwing a glass of ice
water at my ex and storming out, had once begged the boyfriend
in question to reconsider, had once, briefly, turned into a stalker.
This time, with Kevin, with the man I would later marry, I felt
very little: a twinge in the stomach, maybe, but that could have
been the pancakes; perhaps a small palpitation, a skipped beat of
my intact heart. I smiled at him, not because I was trying to prove
that I didn't care and that I was in control of my emotions, but
because I didn't, and I was. "Oh, I think you're probably right,"
I said, nodding, spearing a couple layers of pancakes and dunking them in syrup. I sniffed the dripping forkful, then stuffed it in

my mouth. My appetite was unspoiled. "I'm really glad to know you, though," I said, reaching for more syrup. We finished our breakfast in companionable silence, then split the bill and hugged good-bye.

"Can I call you?" I asked, meaning it. "Can we still hang out?" Kevin nodded and hugged me again. It *was* sad. But not in an irrevocable, Debra Winger's character dying and leaving her children behind kind of way: more like in a Hallmark Hall of Fame Sunday night movie presentation kind of way, more like in a *Sarah, Plain and Tall* kind of way. Our years together were coming to a close as the skies wept in fond commiseration. We said good-bye in the rain. I bought a pint of Triple Chocolate Chocolate Chocolate Truffle ice cream on the way home and ate it that night for dinner.

Two weeks later, Kevin called me. I was so happy to hear his voice, I had to sit down. But I had recently moved the overstuffed chair I kept next to the phone, so I ended up falling on the floor and dropping the phone. When I picked it up, I heard Kevin saying, ". . . and you have to understand, Emily, that I'm not the world's most passionate man."

The Kinks song immediately started playing in my brain. "What? Sorry, what?" I had spent the last two weeks sleeping and eating ice cream, missing Kevin, shocked that I missed him so much, trying to pretend that I didn't miss him; I had passed the nights lonely, the days wandering around my apartment with various utensils in my hand, a fork, a pair of pliers, wondering why I had picked them up in the first place. I knew as soon as I heard his voice that we would get back together.

"I said I miss you. I miss you so much. I know I can be boring, but I'll really try to be more spontaneous, if there's any way you would consider getting back together with me, Emily."

"Kevin," I said, "I love you just the way you are," as long as we were quoting songs from the oldies station. And I meant it. I really did.

WHEN THE PHONE RINGS BEFORE 8:00 A.M., IT'S NEVER good news.

"Emily," someone says on the other end, in a voice I don't recognize. I glance blearily at the clock. It's 7:46.

"Yes, this is Emily," I say. I have been jolted awake, but I quickly activate my customary I'm-a-professional-and-I've-been-up-since-six-thirty voice.

There's sniffling and then silence, and I'm about to hang up when a soft, hoarse voice says, "It's Meg." And I'm suddenly wide awake and alert.

"What's wrong?"

Another long pause. "I'm—I'm bleeding," she whispers.

At first I think she means she's cut herself, and I imagine her bathroom spattered bright red with her blood. I picture a sliced artery, an arc of blood pulsing like a geyser, Meg drifting into unconsciousness on the tile floor. "Bleeding? What—where are you? What happened?"

"I just got up and Steve's already left for work and I . . ." More sniffling. "I went to the bathroom and there's blood. I'm bleeding. I just got back into bed and I'm not . . . I think I'm having a miscarriage."

As usual, I'm a mess under pressure. My stomach goes tight and my mind lurches to a full stop, and I can't think of what to say or what to ask her, or what I should do. I close my eyes, try to think, but it's like someone has pushed the pause button on my brain.

"Emily, are you there?"

"I think we need to get you to the emergency room," I finally say. Is this the kind of thing you call an ambulance for? I don't know. I can't even quite remember my name. "I'll be right over, okay?"

"Okay."

When I get to Meg's, fifteen minutes later, she's sitting on her front step waiting for me. From the car, she looks fine, normal; it looks like I'm picking her up for a movie, like she's ready for a fun outing. I park the car and run over to her. She doesn't move. She's waiting for me to help her stand up. As I approach, I see that she's wearing a sweatshirt over her pajamas, and her face is as pale as I've ever seen it. She looks bloodless. There are dark, yellowish circles under her eyes, and her skin has an ash gray undertone that scares me. And as I reach my friend, I know that she has lost her baby, or the Sea Monkey–sized bundle of cells that would have become her baby. Now it won't be. In a flash, I know this, and I also know that I will reassure her, tell her that everything will be okay, that probably lots of women bleed a little during their pregnancies, that it doesn't even necessarily mean anything. I'll say this, as I wrap my arm around her and help her to the car; I'll tell her to be hopeful, as we speed toward St. Joseph's Hospital. But I know. It's already gone.

I have fond memories of hospitals. The particular sensory combo platter of glaring fluorescent lights and disinfectant that evokes, for almost everyone else on the planet, sickness and fear and bad memories, for me has a comforting effect. When I was a junior in high school, my grandfather had a stroke. He spent five weeks recuperating in the rehab wing of St. Mary's Hospital, and I used to visit him after school. I would drive over to the hospital, grab a snack in the cafeteria, and then I'd take the elevator up to the fifth floor to hang out with him. We usually watched reruns of *Little House on the Prairie,* or afternoon game shows. *Wheel of Fortune* was our favorite. They were happy times, and the whoosh-whoosh of soft-soled shoes down hospital corridors reminds me of them. He died when I was in college.

Meg and I are sitting on mushroom-colored plastic chairs in the waiting room, surrounded by people who are either coughing or bleeding. The lady at the admissions desk gave Meg a sympathetic smile and then handed her a thick volume of insurance forms to fill out, and told us that it would be at least an hour before a doctor could see her. Steve is on his way over. In the bustle of everyday life, I never think about the fact that awful things happen to people all the time: teenagers die in car crashes; regular people get cancer; pregnant women have miscarriages. Looking around at this waiting room full of people in the throes of illness and the aftermath of accidents, I want to say this to Meg. But of course I don't.

I never know whether to touch people who are having emotions that have nothing to do with me. I'm never sure whether to hug friends who are crying about their boyfriends or their breakups. I don't know if I should hold their hands or keep my distance and let them at least retain the dignity of their personal space while their suffering spills messily out of them. I contemplate this for a while, then drape my arm over Meg's shoulders. She doesn't pull away, but seems to relax into me a little bit. We don't talk, just stare at the television that is mounted high above us and is blaring a big, bad Jerry Springer fight, as if to remind us, the sick and the wretched in the ER waiting room, that there are people sicker and more wretched than we are.

The fact is, I wished this on Meg. From the moment she first told me, radiating happiness, I felt a twinge of disappointment. I hid it, but I did. I wanted my pregnant best friend not to be pregnant. I wanted to keep her for myself, not to share her with a baby, not to lose her to motherhood. I wished for this, in a way—not *this,* but there's no denying it, I wasn't entirely joyous about her pregnancy. And although I'm not crazy or narcissistic enough to think that I caused her miscarriage, guilt crawls up my spine and reaches its spindly fingers around into my chest. I can feel it: the uncomfortable pressure of selfishness, the realization that my own personal ugliness extends its tentacles and connects to the world, to my best friend.

"Can I get you a cup of hot chocolate?" I ask. "Or tea?"

She shakes her head. "This is bad, Emily. I know it."

"You don't," I say. "You don't know anything, and all we can do right now is wait for the doctor." A woman two seats away from us begins to cough, hard. Even after she stops, her thin body seems to vibrate from the effort of it.

"I'm starting to have cramps," Meg whispers, hunching over a little bit. I just squeeze my arm around her more tightly. "I thought I'd be coming to this hospital to have my baby, not to lose it," she says, staring straight ahead. I don't know how to answer that. And anyway, it's not a question.

When Steve arrives, Meg has just gone into an examining room with a stern young doctor. She hadn't wanted me to come with her. She'd asked me to wait outside for Steve, but I think that she needed to hear the bad news on her own, to let it sink in before anyone else found out, to mourn in private, even if only for a few moments.

Steve and I spot each other at the same instant. He plows through the sliding doors and races toward me. Steve is a pediatric dentist and a slob. He's still wearing his white coat, which is wrinkled and flapping open behind him as he walks. His child-friendly purple tie, decorated with laughing bananas, has a big grease spot in the middle of it, and his shoelaces are not only untied, but shredded. He looks like he slept in his entire outfit, a gray oxford shirt and black pants, and in fact he may have. But Steve somehow makes it work. One look at him and you know that he's not only handsome, which is something that can't be squelched by sloppiness, but sexy, which is something that can be, and would be if he were someone else. But Steve is just adorable, messy because he lives large and uses a lot of ketchup, clumsy except when he's gently tending to the tiny teeth of children. Women want to mother him. Meg does, which is both irritating to watch and perfectly apt. She'll reach over and pluck bits of dirt off his clothes, wipe his face with a napkin. They probably don't even realize they do it. Kevin and I make fun of them behind their backs: "Should Mommy tie your shoes?" "Do you need me to wipe your bottom, snookums?" Right now Steve is in a barely controlled panic, and I actually do want to reach over to him and smooth his hair down. But I just stand up and take his elbow, lead him down the corridor. "Meg's in exam room four," I tell him. "She's been in there for about fifteen minutes."

Steve looks like he's about to cry. Like me, Steve is a wreck under pressure; Meg and Kevin are the calm ones. "Is she having a miscarriage?" he asks me.

"I don't know. She thinks she is."

"But she's going to be okay, right?"

"Of course." I feel like I could easily say something stupid or wrong, so I'm trying to say as little as possible.

Just then, the doctor emerges from the examination room, scribbling something on a chart just outside the door. Fair and blond, he looks like he's about sixteen years old. Doogie Howser takes long strides down the corridor toward us.

Steve introduces himself, and the doctor unceremoniously tells us that Meg is in the process of undergoing a spontaneous abortion. The phrase feels like a knife, cold and sharp and unaccountably mean. This process, he tells us without noticeable kindness, will take anywhere from twenty-four to forty-eight hours, after which Meg should stop bleeding. And if she doesn't, he adds, she'll need to come back for a surgical abortion. The word—he says it again—makes me cringe, implying choice; but here we are, with no choice in the matter. The information that took this doctor eleven seconds to impart will take Meg and Steve weeks, months to recover from.

"Early miscarriages are extremely common," the doctor continues, backing away from us slightly. "They're usually the body's healthy response to a nonviable pregnancy," he says, his words starting to jam together. "Very common. Most women go ontohavesuccessfulpregnancies." He's halfway down the hall; he's gone.

"I'm so sorry, Steve." I say. "Do you want me to stay?"

He looks at me as if he's forgotten I'm there. He nods and shakes his head at the same time, so I let him go into Meg's room on his own, and I lean against the cement wall, waiting. I close my eyes and try to think about what I had planned to do today. It feels like nothing else exists, like there is no other world outside this hospital, this hallway. The heavy door clicks shut behind Steve.

After a few minutes, they come out, arm in arm. Meg blinks as if she is emerging into bright sunlight. Steve looks stricken, but Meg seems resigned.

"Thank you for everything," she whispers, hugging me.

"Oh," I say. "I'm so, so sorry. . . ." I stop talking. I'm about to cry, but I don't want Meg to have to comfort me, so I swallow hard and try to contain it.

"Steve's going to take me home now. I'll call you later."

"Emily, thanks," Steve says dully. He and Meg are leaning against each other, facing me, forming their own tiny constellation. Before I can say anything else, they turn and head off toward the exit, and I'm standing by myself in the middle of the hospital corridor.

I'M SITTING HERE AT WHITE'S, FEIGNING CALM. There is only one outward sign: I have bitten my fingernails down to jagged little nubs, and I've gnawed my cuticles into ripped edges of skin—and all in the last ten minutes. It's disgusting, and as I sit here with my cup of coffee and my book, trying to look as if I am just sitting here waiting for an old pal, trying even to look a tiny bit bored, I resolve to keep my hands hidden from David Keller as much as I possibly can. This will serve a dual purpose, since I'm wearing my wedding ring, and I don't want him to see it right away. I realized yesterday, on my way home from the hospital, that I obviously do need to tell him that I'm married. Meg's miscarriage threw my situation into sharp relief. Life is hard and painful and full of losses we can't prevent. I've been a silly, ridiculous girl. This daydream I've been sucking on like a lollipop has been *poison*. A poison lollipop! Kevin is a loving, kind man, and I have been fantasizing about ruining his life, breaking his heart. I need to confess to David, but in my own time. Because telling him that I have a husband—"husband!," what a strange word!—will nip this in the bud, exactly where it should be nipped; I just need some time to ease my way into this reality. I have to give up my stupid little fantasy, but slowly, because after it's gone, I imagine I'll be a little bit bereft. When I woke up this morning, I resolutely slipped the gold band onto my finger.

Besides, I haven't even seen the guy, haven't talked to him for more than five minutes. It's a little premature of me to conceive of this as an affair, even a gestating affair. How am I going to keep my hands hidden, though? I need at least one hand to drink my coffee. I could drink coffee only with my right hand, I suppose. But I might also want to gesture, perhaps to emphasize a point: the bathroom is *over there.* It will look strange and suspicious if I spend the next hour, thirty minutes, two hours?—how long do two people spend together when they're on a date that is not a date and one of them is married?—sitting on my hands.

My entire body is clammy and sweaty; I feel like I've had six cups of coffee, but I've barely even had two sips of one. Maybe I should just put my ring into my pocket for a while. I know that I would rather tell him, would rather speak the words than let this silly symbol clue him in before I'm ready. I glance up as the door swishes open, and my heart jumps up into my throat, but it's a woman wearing a coat that looks like a cape and pushing a baby carriage. It's 9:50, prime women-in-capes-pushing-baby-carriages time.

Is it going to be all about rationalization from here? Am I preparing to think my way clear to doing something heinous? I decided yesterday: absolutely not. But now, today, as the doors swoosh open every few moments and I surreptitiously look up from my book every time, turning back to it and reading and rereading the same paragraph, as I watch a steady stream of coffee drinkers and scone eaters walk up to the counter and unzip their children's jackets and find their tables and sip their coffees and nibble on their scones and chat with their friends *as if this were any ordinary morning,* I'm not so sure.

But if I tell David I'm married, what will he say? Will he be shocked, indignant? Or will he whisper, *I don't care,* in a voice so sexy and soft that I'll have to move my face mere inches from his just to hear? Or will he nod, unfazed, never having considered me anything more than a potential colleague, a possible friend?

I could barely look at Kevin this morning. He didn't notice, just went about his business, muttering to himself about the hot water situation in the shower. The faucet with an *H* produces cold water, and the one with a *C* provides hot, a glitch that never would have happened if Kevin had written the pipe-installing instructions, and one that periodically sends him into fits of frustration. I spent forty-five minutes in the bathroom, as opposed to my usual five, applying a light coat of mascara and then wiping it off and then reapplying it, and then wiping it off again until there were dark, raccoony circles under my eyes and I had to wash my face and start all over.

Sometimes I think that Kevin and I just wander around the rooms of our apartment. There is something unfixed about our marriage. We're like two planets come loose from their magnetic pull. *Is this it? Is this what the rest of my life will feel like?*

Well, this is true: I wouldn't mind making a new friend. I'd like to have a buddy in the journalism world, someone to talk to about the frustrations and pleasures of writing. Can't I just be here, do that? Can't I just connect with David Keller on that level, maybe start up a friendship, possibly even somewhat of a *charged* friendship, but leave it at that? My mom used to tell me that if I liked a boy, I should just march right up to him and say, "Whaddya say we start up a friendship?" Of course, I scoffed at that, and anyway I always favored the flirt-so-subtly-that-it-was-unrecognizable-as-flirting-and-then-pine-in-vain approach, the nurse-a-festering-obsessive-crush approach, but now, why not? I'm not some kind of hyena, lacking control of my instincts, unable to resist the lure of another pheromone-emitting hyena, for God's sake! I can allow myself to establish a relationship that may even *contain* some physical attraction, that may not include, for example, long discussions about my marriage, without letting that relationship spiral out of control. Yes, I can! I'm too conscious of my motivations to embark on an affair. In my life, one thing never just leads to another. But a friendship? A friendship I could do. A friendship might even be easy.

About two miles from my parents' house, just off I-43, there is a place called Jupiter's Palace of Cheese. In a sea of strip malls, it stands bravely alone and unchanging, set back from the road, protected by the moat of its oversized parking lot. When I was growing up, we would drive past Jupiter's Palace, sometimes as often as two or three times a week—on the way to the grocery store or to Heather's violin lesson or to the ice cream parlor nearby. It's still a regular part of my geography: every time I visit my parents or go to the dentist or do an errand in their part of town, I see it. But I've never been inside. As a child, on every car ride, I would stop bickering with Heather as we'd approach Jupiter's Palace of Cheese, and I'd watch its spires and colorful flags loom closer, tiny in the distance and growing larger, until we'd zoom past, and I'd crane my neck as the turrets and minarets receded in the distance. Jupiter's Palace of Cheese! I pictured a fairy tale world full of dazzling, dairy-rich interplanetary surprises: a fabulous fortress of cheese, soft mozzarella stars gently twinkling in the sky and—naturally— a green cheese moon shining. I imagined a Brie princess trapped in one of the towers, while all sorts of complicated magical passageways paved with dangerous Swiss, or maybe more solid Gouda, led to her prison. And a cheddar king ruled over his fantastic galactic domain with a string-cheese scepter. I was a strange girl with an active internal life and many imaginary friends with whom I conversed under my breath and exchanged complicated jokes.

We never stopped at Jupiter's Palace of Cheese. We could have, easily; my parents would have been happy to indulge me in this, as they did in every other way. But as a child, it never occurred to me to ask. It was as if I knew, on some level, that Jupiter's Palace wasn't real, and not just the universe of otherworldly cheese, but the part I could *see,* with my own eyes. How could anything so wonderful be true? And then, as I got older, I developed a nostalgia for it, even though it continued to exist, even as we continued to drive past it on our journeys. I realized that Jupiter's Palace of Cheese would probably turn out to be a tacky little store, a flimsy prefab hut full of displays of cheese molds in the shape of castles and, well, I couldn't bring myself to conjure what other fantasy-killing products would be plied there. Martian Muenster? An assortment of cosmic jams and jellies? These days, I pass by it with a pleasant longing: I both want to, and never want to, step inside. Jupiter's Palace of Cheese has become for me the one fantasy I can harbor boldly because it will never bludgeon me with its lumpy reality. Jupiter's Palace of Cheese is all the things that will never disappoint me, all the things I will never do.

But what if I do, someday, venture inside? Who knows what will greet me? It may turn out to be everything I dreamed of. That's the thing. The shiny mystery of it.

David Keller walks through the door and unwraps his long scarf from his neck. He's tall. His longish dark hair flops just a little bit in his eyes. He looks like someone I've known forever. I close my eyes for a second. My hands are in my lap. I slip my wedding ring into my pocket, and then I wave.

"Hi!" he says, before he's even made it all the way over to me, and a wide smile colonizes his face. Something inside me gives way—like a mudslide, like when you are very happy, or about to throw up.

"Hi!" I say back. I feel goofy, overcome. He stands near me, pulls out a chair and drapes his blue wool jacket over it. He smells like outside, like air, like wind. I have never, ever felt like this before: I'm collapsing in on myself. I'm the universe, expanding, contracting. I see him in front of me, and at the same time I see myself in his arms, feel his rough cheek on my neck. God, I want him inside me; I want to be inside him. I want to wear him. What *is* this?

He sits down, then bounces right back up, nervously. "I'm

going to get a cup of coffee. Can I get you one?" he asks. I smile, tilt my head toward the cup in front of me. "Oh, right, you have one. I'll be right back."

I have always fallen for guys the way smart girls do, the way not-beautiful girls do, with my brain. My first boyfriend was a revelation. We met at the end of high school, at the Southeastern Wisconsin Regional Debating finals. His team was in favor of the death penalty, ours was against it. When we talked on the phone, late at night, after our parents were asleep, we whispered about our SAT scores and the AP classes we were taking. In college, the first boy I loved sat next to me in Pre-Eighteenth Century Lit, and he asked me out after reading my essay on the Wife of Bath (the First Feminist!). A year later, I met boyfriend number three, the one before Kevin, at a political rally. Mark and I leafleted against our local Republican councilman together and argued politics before, after, and sometimes during sex on the single futon on the floor of his bedroom at the co-op. And Kevin, well, Kevin. This is different from that, different from love, of course, but different, too, from the brainy entanglements of my past.

David sits down across from me. He takes a sip of his coffee, puts his cup down, and meets my eyes. We look at each other for a long second. As my brain seizes up, I realize that I should have prepared something to say.

"I'm really glad you e-mailed," he says.

I have a husband. "Thanks," I say. "Me, too." Now that that's finished, we stare at each other in silence again. I look down at my hands, my pale, naked hands. I have a flash of Meg in the hospital waiting room, the way she looked drowned, wrung out. I called her yesterday and left a message. Nobody answered, but I'm sure they were home.

After a few moments, David finally breathes life into the dead air between us. "So, what kind of writing do you do?" I want to lick him.

"Well," I say, wondering what will come out of my mouth, "I write about relationships, I guess, and I happen to have just finished a short piece for *Me,* the magazine *Me,* not *myself* me, on hats . . . but really what I try to do, when I can, when I have some free rein, is show evidence that the world is as weird as I think it is." I'm a tiny, strange bird, chirping nonsensically at the sky. For some reason I hear myself continuing to talk. "I wrote a review a few months ago of this new book that argues that your astrological sign determines your interior decorating style." I stop, abruptly, mortified at the stupidity of it all.

David laughs, but gently, I think. "I'm a Taurus," he says. "What does that say about my living room?"

That I am suddenly imagining us on your plush sofa, you on top of me. "You're into natural materials and natural colors, like sky blue, and textured fabrics. You're tactile." I feel myself blush immediately. Tactile! I might as well just have asked him to run his hand up my thigh!

He smiles. "It's true, actually. I am kind of tactile! But, you know, my decorating style is more old stuff left behind by former roommates than anything else. Well," he continues, "if I'd ever given a second's thought to it, I guess I *would* be into textured fabrics."

"I think it's really great that you can talk about interior decorating without feeling that your manliness is compromised," I say, and wait three long, horrible seconds before he laughs.

"Yes, I'm very secure that way. I could go on for hours about flower arranging, too."

"Not many guys can say that."

"What's your sign? What're your interior decorating inclinations?"

"I'm a Leo, and actually this really fits. We're supposed to be all about bright colors and creative decorating." I have a vision of Kevin's and my bedroom, of the abstract print I bought at the museum last year, all splashy purples and greens. Hanging above our bed, our bed that is covered with a sunny yellow quilt. "It's true," I mumble. "I really go for bright colors."

"I had an aunt who was an astrologer," David says. "I used to spend summers with her. Until she started baking birthday cakes for her plants. But, before that, she was really into all of it, astrology and tarot, and she made it seem very legitimate. Almost scientific, in a weird way. Or, prescientific, but somehow valid."

"That's funny. I have an aunt who always says, 'I don't believe in astrology, but I'm a Sagittarius, and we're very skeptical.' "

David looks at me and laughs again and all of a sudden I know, if I had any doubts before: the deal is sealed. He's gazing at me like I'm the cleverest person he's ever met, like I'm a jewel he's discovered buried in the sand. I see it in his eyes, and it turns me into liquid. Whatever this is, I'm going to have to face it.

"How did you get into this racket?" I ask him, a traffic cop of conversation. Yield! Avoid intimacy!

"My degree was in journalism. After college, while my friends were becoming Internet zillionaires, I decided to go the *really* lucrative route and write a novel," he says, still not dropping his eyes from mine. "It was a comedy about three unlucky mercenary soldiers in Central America. I wrote a hundred-fifty pages of it before I realized I knew nothing about mercenary soldiers or Central America. Although I had been to El Salvador for a week in high school. But . . . oh, and I called it, *Soldiers of Misfortune*. I could actually see it on the *New York Times* best-seller list. That was how I'd lull myself to sleep at night, visualizing it. Number one, three weeks running. Sometimes it was number two, if I didn't want to seem greedy. Anyway, I was having these vivid fantasies about my success, but I was living on ramen noodles. I woke up one morning and realized it was time to call it quits."

"And then what?" I ask, enthralled. David's career search mirrors mine, and makes me feel legitimate. In spite of himself, the example set by Kevin—disciplined, rigorous, career-oriented Kevin—has always made it seem like you either have what it takes or you don't. No in-betweens.

"I got a job at a suburban paper in Chicago. I was living in the city, and it was a ninety-minute commute. And I sat through more school board meetings in three years than most school board members did. But then this came along five years ago, so I moved here."

"Do you ever wish you'd stuck it out with the novel?"

"Sure. Sort of." He sips his coffee, which must be cold by now; mine is. It doesn't seem like he cares. "I wish I'd been able to persist and write a *good* novel. *Soldiers of Misfortune* wasn't. But, I figure, I'm young. There's still time."

If you walked into White's Bookstore/Café on this particular chilly Friday morning and you saw us, David Keller and me, sitting at the table in the corner near the window, both of us occasionally sipping from big green mugs, talking, laughing, our bodies leaning forward, dark heads close together, you would see a small solar system, closed, impenetrable; you would see two people on a date—possibly, you would muse, a first date; undoubtedly, you would think, an excellent date. Unless you knew me, of course. Then you'd think, *What's Emily doing with that guy who's not her husband?*

We talk for two hours that feel like ten minutes. We divulge silly, intimate things to each other. David blushingly admits that his favorite thing to do is to watch Woody Allen marathons and pick out all the references to Bergman. He tells me that he's been researching Irish history, planning to take a walking tour of the country someday. I confess that I'm a closet fan of cheesy science-fiction novels, explaining in detail the plot of my favorite one, about two modern-day sleuths who time-travel to ancient Peru. We tell each other our life stories, magnified and heightened for maximum punch—*I fell off the jungle gym when I was seven and broke both wrists! My sister convinced me that she and our parents found me in a junkyard one day when they were getting rid of their old refrigerator!* I can practically feel sparks shooting off me and landing in his lap. And then, without warning, David glances at his watch and actually jumps.

"Oh, no! Emily, I was supposed to be back in the office an hour ago. I have to go!"

"I'm sorry," I say, wondering if he blames me, if he's going to go all Type A and anxious and fly out of here.

Instead he rolls his eyes and smiles and says, calmly, "Do you think my boss will believe me if I tell him I was interviewing a confidential source?"

"I don't know. What kind of story are you working on?"

"A history of the Nirvana Chocolate Company."

"Any chocolate-related scandals that would require top-secret interviews?"

"There was the hot fudge debacle of 1957."

"Really?"

"No. . . ." He shifts in his chair. I've managed to pass two hours without mentioning Kevin. I edited him right out of my life story. I never lied, never said I was single, but I sure as hell sinned by omission. "But, look," David continues. "Before we go, I should tell you something."

Shit. He has a girlfriend. A serious girlfriend. He's married! He's not even wearing his wedding ring! I can't believe this! I'm crushed. I concentrate on keeping my face impassive. He looks embarrassed. Well, he ought to, the jerk!

"I hope you don't think this is weird, but I Googled you." He blushes and looks down for a second. "I checked out some of your work. I read an article you did last year on Internet dating, and something a couple of years ago on holiday guilt. I talked about it with the editor-in-chief, and I think you should be *The Weekly*'s relationship expert. You know, an article every week on the ways people meet and date in Milwaukee. . . ." He scratches his stubbly chin and pauses. "I think you'd be terrific for the paper."

I'm overwhelmed with something like relief (which almost manages to squelch the absurdity of David's idea). It's accompanied by a rush of excitement: he Googled me! And he likes my work! Followed on its heels by something very much like guilt. Here's my chance. It has to be done. A sudden, surprising tidal wave of love for Kevin washes over me. I feel him in my head, which is where he lives when we're not together. Everything I have thought, for the past nine years, I have sifted and sorted and filed away in the Tell Kevin Later folder. "I'm no relationship expert," I say.

"No?"

"I mean, I'm . . ." *Tell him.* "I'm just no expert."

"Will you think about it? I think we'd be lucky to have you."

Oh, God. "Okay. I will think about it."

"Can I see you again?" he asks softly, as we both stand up to go.

"Yes," I say, hot with shame and self-loathing. Yes.

I'VE DONE NOTHING WRONG. WHAT HAVE I DONE WRONG? Nothing.

What's more, I'm looking forward to seeing my husband. I am guilt-free (for the most part) and I've done nothing wrong! And I'm looking forward to having dinner with my husband, Kevin, and telling my husband, Kevin, about my day, including my appointment with this editor, and my new assignment. Relationship expert! I am looking forward to discussing it all with Kevin. Because I have *free will,* and I will keep not doing anything wrong. It's not that I regret seeing David Keller, or even liking David Keller, which, let's face it, I do; I can't help it. It's more like, I'm a juggler. These balls I am juggling are in the air, flying in fast circles above me, but I catch them and toss them; I am in complete control.

Only, when Kevin finally comes home, just as dusk is casting a dim, gray blue light through the rooms of our apartment, he forgets to ask me about my day. He's distracted, throws off his jacket and plops down on the chair in my study where I've been trying to proofread a manuscript on male-pattern baldness in chimpanzees.

"Interest rates are going up," he announces with a look of scolding disappointment, as if he's just found out that Alan Greenspan secretly calls me for advice. I raise my eyebrows at him. "Housing prices are on the rise, and interest rates are going up, and I was just doing some calculations, and if we want to Buy . . ." (these days Kevin says the word "buy" with a portent, a heft that clearly means he's not talking about shoes) ". . . if we want to Buy in Deer Park or Lakewood, our salaries would have to increase by twelve percent this year, and I don't know about yours, but mine's not about to. Emily," he says in a panic, barely stopping for breath, "that means, a house we can afford today will be beyond our means six months from now! If we don't get on the ball here, we're going to be priced right out of our first-choice suburbs!"

"The polar ice caps are melting faster than scientists had predicted," I say, stacking my chimpanzee pages on the edge of my desk.

"*Emily.*"

A few months ago, when Kevin first announced that make-wife-move-to-the-suburbs was the newest addition to his to-do list—*the suburbs are the best place to raise a family, of course*—I listened quietly, without much reaction, and then later picked a random fight with him. "You always make our weekend plans without consulting me. It's disrespectful!" I shouted, blindsiding Kevin as he was pouring himself a glass of milk. "It's *piggish!* Also," I added, in full shriek, "you ate the last orange! You could have at least told me you were going to eat the last orange! YOU KNOW HOW I LOVE ORANGES!" It took me two days (and one sheepish apology) to finally conclude, with a satisfying jolt of insight, that not only was I not ready to have a baby, but that I didn't want to move out of our little apartment in the city, either—our bustling corner of the city where the sidewalks are crowded with people, and the movie theater, the bookstore, and our favorite restaurants are all within a few blocks. *Phew,* I thought. *Good thing I've figured this out before it's too late. I'll just go explain it to Kevin.*

But my revelation was a mosquito in his ear; he flicked it away.

Since then, Kevin has pressed on in his quest for suburban migration, alternating between ignoring me and thinking he can change my mind by sheer persistence. He receives weekly listings from a real estate agent and leaves them in the bathroom and on the kitchen table where I'm sure to see them, and he schedules regular viewings for us. "This one," he says every time we pull into another freshly paved circular driveway in Valley Glen or Glen Valley, "*this one,* you're going to fall in love with." And I go with him on these odysseys, most of the time—reluctantly, but still, I go. Because how do you tell your husband that the prospect of moving to the suburbs with him sounds like slow death? How do you tell your husband, who wants to take the next steps with you in your life together, to stop stepping?

So now I just look at him as he waxes poetic about thirty-year mortgages, I watch as his lips move, notice that his lovely green eyes seem to darken as his excitement grows. I watch as he gestures and it strikes me, suddenly, how chunky his hands are. How thick his fingers. Like sausages, really. Like beef jerky. How is it that I've never noticed this before, the pink Slim Jimness of my husband's hands?

"I just really think we should get moving on this," he says, waving his meaty fingers. "Get on the ball. Stop dawdling."

"Yeah," I say. "I guess we better get on the ball."

He nods, satisfied by my apparent acquiescence. He leans forward, rests his elbows on his knees, and then he just sits there, gazing slightly past me at the wall behind my head; I look down at my feet, at the off-white carpeting that needs to be vacuumed. For a minute we're just sitting, silent, frozen, a portrait. Then suddenly Kevin says, "Hey! I'm starving. Have you given any thought to dinner tonight?"

So I will keep my secret about David Keller, for now, and I will keep my thoughts to myself, and, without the need for discussion, we will order a mushroom and green-olive pizza from Alfredo's, the way we always do.

MEG LOOKS EDGY, HER FEATURES SHARP. IT'S ONLY BEEN A week, but she is a few pounds thinner, and I think, when I take my first look at her, that five pounds of happiness have been drained from her. She's wearing nice charcoal gray pants, work pants— except that her work pants used to be paint-splattered jeans—and a lavender cashmere sweater set, which is very strange, since she told me on the phone that she's barely left her house in a week and doesn't have any plans to go anywhere. It's like I've walked into Meg's bizarro-world, where she's an office manager at a medium-sized accounting firm instead of a grade-school art teacher on sabbatical. She's wearing makeup, too, which is another flashing neon sign that things are not right. She seems somehow fragile but hard, breakable, like glass. It's the first time I've seen her since her miscarriage, and, although she is my best friend and we've supported each other through romances and breakups and various disappointments from minor to major, we've never seen each other through grief. Therefore, I've baked chocolate chip cookies and brought them over to her house. I invited myself over this morning, after I finally realized that she wasn't about to initiate a visit, that we weren't just going to pick up our semiweekly breakfast dates quite yet. Which is actually okay by me. I'm not ready for my suddenly disparate, suddenly self-conscious worlds to collide.

"How are you?" I ask, handing her the paper plate of cookies and bending to untie my shoes in the doorway. I picked out my approach on the drive over, like I was shopping for accessories: solicitous and tender, but also cheerful, at least until it became apparent that another mood was required. I thought I ought to be prepared, since I am out of my league here.

"I'm okay," Meg answers, rushing the words together so they sound like one, "Muhkay." Their house smells, as usual, like cinnamon gum, although neither Meg nor Steve chews it. She bustles about, sets the cookies on the coffee table, takes my coat, tosses it over a chair, picks the cookies up, carries them into the kitchen. I follow in the wake of all of her swift, unnecessary movement. "Want something to drink?" she says, turning. "Tea? Or I could make sandwiches. . . ."

"Let's just sit down and eat cookies," I suggest, and pull out one of the solid kitchen-table chairs. "Pass them here."

"Thanks for bringing them," she says, her voice flat, unrecognizable.

I figure I should just wait for some kind of cue from her. "How's Steve doing?"

"Okay." She begins to nibble on a cookie, so clearly uninterested in it, so obviously eating it for my benefit, my heart breaks a little.

But I can't wait. "And you? How are you, honestly?"

Meg narrows her eyes and gazes into the space beyond me, past the kitchen doorway, at something that isn't there. Against her newly pale face, her lips are red as blood. "Honestly?" she asks. "Half the time I'm all right and the other half I'm so mad I want to scream and break things and—really, Emmy, I see something solid and I want to destroy it. I had no idea I could be this angry. I'm exhausted, just from holding it in. Pretending to Steve that I'm sad but recuperating, like a normal person would be. Pretending I'm going to be okay . . ." She turns back to me with a little start, as if she's surprised to see me. "But I don't think I am going to be okay," she says. "I know that women have miscarriages all the time, and then they go on to have healthy babies. And I was only eight weeks pregnant. Barely even pregnant. I was hardly even used to the idea. But you know what?"

She stops talking, but I'm not sure why. Is she waiting for me to guess what "what" is? I shake my head.

"I don't believe it's ever going to happen for us again," she says. "I don't know why, but I think that this baby was our one chance, and now it's gone. It sounds stupid. But I know it." Before I can argue with her, she's off and running. "You know what else? What the hell am I supposed to be doing with myself now? I'm on this break from my job, and it was like, being pregnant was my job. Retro, huh?" She exhales, a gravelly whoosh of air. "But now what the hell am I supposed to do?" This would be the time I would expect my best friend to be crying. But she just looks at me, her lips pressed together, her eyes steely. She smooths down the front of her sweater with trembly hands.

"Meg, oh, I don't know what to say to you," I admit, pretense gone. "I don't know how to make you feel better. That's all I want to do."

"How can you?" she asks. "This kind of thing definitely qualifies as a girl's own private hell."

"Well, do you know anything else concrete about the miscarriage?" The word unexpectedly embarrasses me, like "vagina." "Did they say why this might have happened, or what might come next?"

She sets the practically untouched cookie down on her napkin. "The doctor said that these things sometimes just happen. It probably doesn't mean anything, especially so early. It's not uncommon and it's likely that I'll carry my next pregnancy to term. That's what they say, blah, blah, blah." She sighs.

We sit in silence for a while, awkward silence, I think, but maybe Meg is so deep in her sadness that she doesn't feel the discomfort. To compensate, I eat three cookies. "Want to go for a walk?" I ask, brushing crumbs off the table and into my hand.

Meg and Steve live across the street from an elementary school, and, naturally, just as we step outside, thirty five-year-olds emerge en masse from the building for recess, a carnival of brightly colored, puffy parkas and monkey-house screeches. I look over at my friend, who is watching the chaos intently.

"It doesn't matter," she says, turning back to me. "I never imagined it as a five-year-old. As a baby, yes, and even sometimes as a toddler, but I never envisioned an older child."

"Well, still and all, let's move away from here," I suggest, crunching through a pile of brown and red and yellow leaves.

"I haven't been out much since it happened," she continues, as if I hadn't spoken, and from deep inside this other place she seems to inhabit, "but every time I do go somewhere, all I see are pregnant women and little babies in strollers. You just start to think of yourself as someone who's about to enter a new phase of your life, and then all of a sudden you're not." Meg chops her hand through the air, a gesture of finality. She's moving just the tiniest bit faster than I am; she probably doesn't even notice it. I take a quick extra half step, adjust my speed to hers.

We walk along in silence for a while longer. The day is brilliant blue and warm for October in Wisconsin. We're both wearing coats, but we hardly need them. I want to make a comment about global warming, which is one of my favorite subjects, but I decide not to. All around us birds are chirping wildly. I've never understood why people say that birds sing; to me it always sounds like they're fighting. Which it turns out, of course, they are.

Meg slows down as we reach the end of her block, and her speed becomes more companionable. "God, I've been so wrapped up in myself . . ."

I cut her off. "Of course not."

". . . I haven't even asked you about yourself. What's been going on with you?"

"Hmm. Not much. A little work, this and that." A few more

steps. Our coats flap behind us. A slow, dulled-by-autumn bee buzzes around us and then careens away; it will be dead in a week, I bet. I make a split-second decision. And then just like that, there it is, my little private gem, the jewel I've been hoarding, exposed: "There is something."

For the first time, Meg brightens. "What?"

"Well," I say slowly. Now that I'm about to tell this story, I don't know how to arrange the details. Not that I've done anything wrong . . . Still, isn't a thing like this all in the telling? Especially given Meg's strange tendency to leap to judgment about this issue. "Um, remember that guy we met at the coffee shop, the editor at *The Weekly*?"

"Yessss."

"He e-mailed me. I mean, actually I e-mailed him. Because I decided that I might want to do some work for him. Things have been a little light on that front lately. We met for coffee yesterday."

Meg laughs. "You did what?"

Encouraged by her laughter, I continue, "Yeah, we did. He asked me to meet him. We had a great time together. He wants me to be the paper's 'relationship expert.' I'm going to have a regular gig with the paper. And it turns out he's very cool; he's a very interesting person," I say, a little breathless. "He likes to travel. And he's smart. He knows a lot about movies. Films. He gave me all these suggestions of old obscure ones, a couple of Hitchcocks I've never even heard of, and Bergman, I can't believe I'm thirty and I've never seen a Bergman movie! Have you?" I hear how I must sound to Meg, but I can't stop myself. "I have to tell you something," I say, turning to look at her. "I have a little crush on this guy." And Mount Everest is a little hill. "Not that I would ever do anything about that," I insist; the strength of my assertion makes me believe it. Of course I wouldn't.

"Wow," Meg says, visibly perked up, a facsimile of her old self for the first time today. "Crazy. What else did you talk about? Was it mostly professional? Did he blush?"

"Oh, yeah. The whole time."

"Emily!" Meg stops, grabs my elbow. "Did you tell him you're married?"

I try to keep walking, to pull Meg along, but she's holding tightly to my arm. "Well, it . . . well, I was going to, but . . . no. I didn't." Meg is standing stock-still, about to say something, but I'm determined to plow through, to make her understand. "Look, here's the thing. You know this has never happened to me before. I like him. We could be friends. But I like him. I felt this attraction to him that was . . . intense. Do you think we could be friends?" I feel a knot inside me coming loose. Meg, my friend, will help me sort this out.

Meg pauses, considers my question. "Do you remember Peter Johannsen?" She says it with a lilting Norwegian accent, *Pay*-ter Yo-*han*-sen? Before Steve, Meg's last serious boyfriend was Craig, a sweet, curly-haired social worker who played the trumpet and adored her. He used to write songs for her. He'd give her a print-out of his poetic lyrics and play the tunes on his trumpet, being obviously unable to sing and blow the horn simultaneously. Although apparently once he did try. After about six months, Meg started complaining to me that she was bored. Craig was sweet and loving, but things had grown predictable. She knew precisely what he'd order at the two restaurants he felt comfortable fre-quenting, exactly how he'd respond to every movie they saw. All his songs started to sound the same, she said, and romance seemed to be more or less incompatible with the brass instruments. Then eighth-grade social studies teacher Peter Johannsen entered the scene, a brawny Scandinavian from Minnesota with a surprisingly biting sense of humor. They met in the teacher's lounge and started hanging out, going out for beers after school on Fridays, meeting for walks on Sunday mornings. Meg insisted that they were friends. Until they slept together. Craig's heart was broken, Peter Johann-sen turned out to be a commitment-phobic, anal-retentive control freak, and Meg was alone. For about ten minutes. But still. It was an ugly time. She learned her lesson.

"Ja," I say.

"I don't know, Em. I suppose it's possible." She turns to face me. "But I love Kevin. I love you guys. If I thought you were about to squander your happiness with him for something so . . . superficial, for a thrill, I'd tell you never to let another e-mail from this guy darken your in-box again. If you think you can handle it, then, yeah, I suppose you can have a friendship with what's-his-name. And, you know, word to the wise. I'll regret what I did with Yo-*han*-sen for the *rest of my life!*" She says the last part with such unexpected emphasis that a little spray of spit escapes from her mouth.

"But, first of all, we were twenty-five when that happened. And second of all, that was you, not me," I remind her, discreetly wiping my cheek where the splash landed.

"I'm just saying."

"I know, but, do you think men and women can't be friends?"

"Sally, you know that's not what I mean," she says. "I'm just saying, watch yourself. Don't get carried away by excitement. And don't think that an affair is going to be the answer to some kind of creeping marital malaise."

"Well, Harry, don't you think married people develop crushes on other people all the time?"

"I'm sure they do," she says. "The question is, what are you going to do about it?" She's picked up her pace again during the course of this discussion. I'm practically jogging to keep up with her. I don't answer her question. I wonder if Meg's hormones are out of whack, postmiscarriage. Why else would she be so adamant? I can handle this. I'm resolved.

Being married is like reading the same novel over and over again. You might discover new subtleties of language on the twenty-millionth read-through, a metaphor or two you'd missed before, but the plot is always the same. Kevin is in a bad mood, and there's nothing I can do about it: chapter six.

We're driving home from Madison, where we spent the day

visiting old friends of ours, Michelle and Tina. Michelle is a law professor and Tina stays home with their six-year-old son, Zack. Tina gave birth to Zack, but his actual conception is a mystery to us, and Michelle and Tina refuse to tell. One of Michelle's male relatives? Sperm bank? Friend? We'll never know, although we've tried for years to trick them into divulging. "Which family member does Zack most resemble?" I'll ask, or Kevin will casually mention an article about sperm-donor babies who grow up and locate their biological fathers. They just roll their eyes at each other, then at us. Zack calls Tina "Mommy," and Michelle "Momichelle."

We walked around town, the five of us, made our way slowly up and down State Street, poked in and out of various stores full of various colorful trinkets, stopped for lunch at an Indian restaurant, ate orange chocolate chip ice cream at the Memorial Union . . . all in all, a lovely day. Except that, while we were all eating our *dosas,* while I was regaling Zack with fascinating details from my latest freelance editing assignment, a children's book called *Everything You Ever Wanted to Know about Hamsters,* Tina said something to Kevin. Kevin was telling her about his job, about the latest set of instructional pamphlets he was working on, and Tina said, "That sounds so *dull*! How can you stand it?" And then she threw her head back and laughed like a hyena and changed the subject. It was rude, but Tina's like that—blunt and jovial, and she takes it as well as she dishes it out. And Kevin does have the tendency to go on about his work, oblivious to his audience's eye-popping boredom. But he's a fragile beast, which Tina knows: they've been friends since college. They even dated for a while, until they both realized that Tina was more interested in their young female English professor than she was in him.

I heard the exchange between them at lunch, saw the knife inflict the mortal wound, but I was very busy discussing hamsters; Zack is particularly interested in animal-related details these days, and tends to blurt out a thing like, "A hippo can snap a person in two with its powerful jaws!," so I had a captive audience. I was in the middle of explaining to an enthralled Zack that a hamster can carry, in its cheeks, half its body weight in food. I had stuffed my own cheeks full of bread as a visual aid. I couldn't rescue Kevin. And the damage had been done. He retreated into his shell. He kept up appearances for the rest of the afternoon, but I knew how hurt he was; our couple-radar can be quite nicely calibrated. I knew he was sulking, a fact that settled uncomfortably into a corner of my brain for the rest of the day, like a popcorn kernel lodged in a molar.

So by the time we've said good-bye and climbed into our car, headed for I-94 and the ninety-minute drive home, I want to gently ease him out of his mood, but I also want to shake him: he's hypersensitive, an exposed nerve. I wish he would just lighten up.

"You've been upset since lunch," I announce as we turn onto the highway. My voice accidentally sounds a little bit sharp.

"I have not been," he says, hands gripped tightly on the steering wheel, eyes straight ahead.

"I know you," I sigh, "and I can tell when you're upset." I stare at his profile as he drives, his straight nose, his pale cheek, pale eyelashes, his delicate, almost girlish mouth set in a tight line. Sometimes when he's asleep at night I look at him, and I see the same expression on his face, the same tight-lipped, worried grimace: the midnight scowler. "So why don't you just tell me what happened. It was what Tina said at lunch, wasn't it?"

"Yes, but I don't want to talk about it. It was no big deal."

"I know that; that's what I think. But it clearly bothered you, so why don't you please talk to me about it?"

He turns on the radio, tunes in a classical station. "I just need a few minutes of quiet. I'll get over it on my own. I know it was no big deal," he repeats. "Tina can be really harsh. It bugged me."

God, he's such a baby. But I begin to soften. It's not his fault. It's just who he is. "Sweetie, I—"

"—Emily, WOULD YOU PLEASE STOP TALKING? Just leave me ALONE for a few minutes!"

Oh, boy. The car fills up with classical music. Jerk. Asshole. Prick. Jerk asshole prick. My God, am I going to cry? My face feels tingly and my eyes are suddenly pressurized from inside their sockets. But I won't do it. I won't cry and let him apologize and make it all right. I swallow hard, twice. Asshole jerk prick, the nerve of him to yell at me when I was trying to comfort him. I close my eyes, lean back against the headrest, tug at the seatbelt that has suddenly become uncomfortable across my chest. And then the strangest thing happens: the face of David Keller flashes before my closed, not-crying eyes. David Keller's face calms me down.

"Christ. I'm sorry," Kevin says.

"Whatever!" I can be very mature.

"I am sorry!"

He doesn't actually sound sorry. "Now we both need a few minutes of quiet," I say, in what I hope is a flinty tone.

I wonder what this music is. I like classical, even have a few CDs at home, but mostly I can't tell the difference between a moonlight sonata and an unfinished symphony. I grab hold of the idea of David Keller, the object of my crush, the man I barely know. He feels like an option. He feels like a clear light shining through the cloud of my anger at Kevin. My anger, my disappointment in . . . in . . . our relationship, our life, my disappointment in myself.

You say, Yes, yes, yes, and This, then this, then this, and you find yourself: thirty, frustrated, adrift, and married to a teeth-grindingly tiresome man who suddenly wants to handcuff himself to you with both progeny and real estate. Why didn't I do things better, more deliberately, more carefully? Why didn't I think things through more thoroughly? Why am I not where I want to be? Do I even know what that place looks like? I think about seeing David Keller again.

Ten minutes later, Kevin reaches over and strokes my head. *Yes, yes, yes. Okay.* I let him.

I WILL SAY THIS: I'M PROBABLY DOING SOMETHING WRONG NOW. Although, not very wrong. Not wrong like shaking a baby wrong, or cheating on your taxes wrong, or even really betraying Kevin wrong. But I can face the fact that taking a walk with David Keller is more wrong than right. I'm aware of the messy morality of all of this, which, I happen to think, kind of redeems me. Today I'm going to go for a walk with David Keller, which is not the most right thing I've ever done, but I'm going to tell him that I'm married, which will fix everything. Well, it won't fix everything: it won't fix me. But it will repair the situation I've gotten myself into.

There was an e-mail waiting for me when Kevin and I got home from Madison. I knew there would be.

I meant to ask for your phone number, Emily. But I suppose e-mail is a reasonable form of communication for people like us. If I have any hope of impressing you, it's probably by writing rather than talking, anyway.

Can we get together again? Would you like to go for a
walk with me one day this week?
(I'm trying to play it cool here . . . but I have to admit,
I'd really love to see you soon.)
—David

If I hadn't already been over the edge, the words inside those
parentheses would have done me in.

We meet at the War Memorial on Lake Michigan. He's waiting for
me on one of the uncomfortable brown benches, huddled against
the autumn chill. As soon as I spot him, I'm yanked from side to
side like a marionette, flipped upside down and then right side up,
so fast that the human eye can't see it. But I feel it happen.

I told Kevin this morning that I was going to meet a friend for
lunch. I decided that this one lie would be discrete, roped off from
the rest of my life like a room in a museum. It was a necessity
before I put everything right. I decided that it was no big deal,
almost harmless.

Anyway, I seem to be developing the odd ability to compart-
mentalize my life. So while I'm at it, I'll box up this stomachache
I've been carrying around, send it away, or at least ignore it. It has
nothing to do with me right now.

David stands as I approach and holds up his hand in greeting. I
have a brief, blinding vision of him grabbing me by my coat collar
and pulling me toward him, kissing me wildly. I have to snap out
of it, focus, drag my wobbly self back to this planet. "Hey!" I say,
walking toward him.

"I have the day off," he says. "I brought chocolate."

I can tell that he's flustered. His non sequiturs are an advertisement for it. He pulls out a bar of fancy European chocolate from
his coat pocket, holds it flat in his open palm.

"I took a risk," he says, "that you'd be a dark chocolate woman."

"I am," I say, smiling, still facing him, ten inches from him. I take a tiny step closer.

"I was going to buy two kinds, but I had a hunch."

"Impressive." I don't know what else to say. I have turned into a Neanderthal. Ugh. Grunt. Take me back to your cave. He begins unwrapping the bar, breaks off two squares. It's one of those chilly autumn days where the sun is so bright you can see every detail on a person, where every pore on your face is visible. I'm glad I bleached my mustache a few days ago. I'm glad I used the lint brush on my coat. David's hair, which I would have described as dark brown, turns out to have many reddish strands in it. His lips are dry, but not chapped. The chocolate bar's foil wrapping reflects the sun. Everything is heightened, magnified. He takes a deep breath.

"It's really great out today," he says, looking around, squinting. I nod. We are, in fact, strangers to each other. Well, good, I guess; this makes my task easier. I pop a square of chocolate into my mouth, let it melt there.

"Want to walk?" he asks, turning back to me, still squinting against the sun. There are a few lines at the corners of his eyes. He looks a little bit older than I'd first thought he was. Thirtyish? I wonder.

I nod again. Nobody is around. It's colder than it seemed when I left the apartment this morning. I adjust my scarf as we begin to walk. It's almost noon. The day is surreal, and I am not myself.

We walk in silence for a while, awkward, friendly.

"So, what did you do this weekend?" David asks.

"I—I went to Madison on Sunday to visit some friends. You?"

"Oh, same thing I always do. Rented movies, read, hung out with work buddies, did my laundry. Pretty wild." We're walking in rhythm, arms swinging lightly next to each other. "I went to a fish fry on Friday night," he continues. "In my five years here, I'd never done it, and I figured I couldn't call myself a Milwaukeean—not that I necessarily want to call myself a Milwaukeean—until I experienced an authentic fish fry."

"And?"

"It was definitely fried fish," he says. "It was pretty gross, actually. I shouldn't take 'All you can eat' as a challenge."

I laugh. The wind is coming in from the lake. A few clouds blow quickly across the sky. There is an empty park to our left, the choppy water to our right. The word "clandestine" pops into my head, stays there.

"How was Madison?" he asks.

"We just walked around. And ate." I think about "we." "Seems like there used to be more to do there, when I was in college. There was always a protest or a boycott or a sit-in, and it was all brand-new and it felt really crucial." I think about the kiss-in—it was almost ten years ago—and look away from David, toward the lake. "Now the students look like toddlers to me, and State Street feels like a moving walkway between fast-food joints and chain shoe stores."

"Emily!" David says, surprised. "So cynical for someone so young!"

"Is it?" I ask. I hadn't meant it to be. I like how he says my name.

"No, I know what you mean. For me it's not so much that things mattered more ten years ago, but more like I thought I could actually have an effect. . . ." His sentence drifts off.

I nod. "That's it exactly!" I give a little embarrassed laugh. I feel overexposed. I'm letting him see too much of me. I'm flashing my emotional underwear. But I keep going. "I used to think getting involved in politics, protesting, working on campaigns . . . I used to think it all made a difference. I don't know about that anymore." Our hands are so close, almost brushing, hanging there at the end of our arms, bony pendulums. I swallow, take a breath. "But even talking about it feels indulgent. Existential angst is so 1990s!"

I look up at him, nervous; I wait for him to shrug, nod, tell me I'm a genius, tell me I'm an idiot.

And then he takes my hand. He takes my hand in his, laces his fingers through mine. He holds on firmly, but not too tightly. His palm is warm, his fingers smooth against mine.

Is this separate from my life? Can I wrap it up in a package? Is this person me? We keep moving. I don't let go.

We walk, holding hands. My legs are gummy. What if I see someone I know? But there's no one around. David tells me a story about the newspaper, about how his colleagues revolted against the editor in chief two years ago and ousted the guy, about his conflicted loyalties, because this man was a horrible editor, but also his friend. Every molecule in my body has been rearranged. My heart has surreptitiously migrated to my right hand.

I tell him about my job at *Male Reproduction,* about my bosses and how I organize my schedule so that I only have to work with the nice one. I tell him more about my family, my sister in Minneapolis, my mom and dad here in Milwaukee. This is the hand I promised to Kevin, the heart.

"I rented the movie you were telling me about," I say as we pass a cluster of deserted stone benches and almost-bare trees. *"Wild Strawberries."* What I don't say is, "And I felt like I was inside your head, I wanted to become an expert on Ingmar Bergman just to know you better, and if you had told me that dung beetles were your passion, I would develop a voracious interest in disgusting bugs."

David gives my hand a little squeeze. "Did you? What did you think?" He's pleased, flattered. We talk about old movies for a while. I know nothing about the subject, but David acts like my every question is a perfect diamond; he holds each one up to the sun, examines its brilliance.

We make our way slowly down the path, reach the place where it forks off, and turn around. Our conversation has settled into a quiet rhythm, less forced than before we touched. Now that we're connected physically, we let silent currents flow comfortably between us. I'm aware of the sound of the water splashing up against the side of the concrete barrier, of the clean, almost imperceptible scent of the wind.

By the time we're back at the War Memorial, I know three things: that I would like to stay here with David Keller all day; that it's time to go, because you should always leave a party while everyone's still having fun; that he will kiss me. What I don't know is whether I will kiss him.

He pulls me toward a bench, the same one that he sat on earlier as he waited for me. We sit close, lean against each other, the padding of coats between us. The temperature has dropped, even in the hour or so that we've been out here, and my eyes are teary and wet from the wind. I wipe them with the back of my hand, clear my throat, turn my whole body to face him. His cheeks are red. "I should probably go," I say.

He mirrors my movement, rotates himself toward me. "Okay," he says softly. He leans nearer to me, slowly.

Is this what it feels like, just before a first kiss? I can't remember. It's not like riding a bike. I'm tense, perched on the edge of a cliff, terrified. I never thought I'd have another first kiss. I thought that my first kiss with Kevin, nine years ago, would be my last first kiss. That was the agreement, anyway. My teeth are chattering a little bit. My body's trembling from the inside out. I want this. I don't want this.

David is so close to me now I can see the shadow across his jawline, the slight circles under his eyes. His face is beautiful, dark and strong. His nose is a little bit crooked. I glance down. His hands are resting on his thighs. What a strange thing, a body, with its dangling limbs, its movable parts.

"Hey," he says, his voice low, this last second before a kiss. I can feel his breath on my face. It smells sweet, a faint remnant of chocolate. I look into his eyes.

And then my body takes over, acts of its own volition, ignores the hope in my heart, or maybe listens carefully to it; I don't know. I jump up as if I've been shocked, in the split second before it's too late. While my brain valiantly tries to register what I've just done, and not done, I find that I am standing, looking down at David. I feel outsized, gigantic.

"Oh! Okay, well." My ridiculous voice is thin and shaky. "I really should go. Bye!" I turn and leave in a sudden swoop, before David has the chance to digest this, before he can call me back. I'm walking fast and I don't turn around, but I imagine him there, baffled, still leaning forward, mouth slightly open in confusion. I'm halfway up the hill. I can see my little red Toyota, a long half block away. I hate myself. I've never felt quite like this. I am a hideous, pungent concoction of guilt, shame, embarrassment, and desire. I'm hot with it, this terrible new potion coursing through my veins. Betrayal changes a person physically. This is a different me, racing to my car, heading toward home. I have held the hand of, almost kissed, lusted after a man who is not Kevin. Not to mention, I've lied to David and to Kevin both. What I have done has transformed me, like alchemy, only backward: whatever there was in me that was precious metal is now nothing but common elements, gravel, straw.

"I NEED A FAVOR," MEG SAYS. IT'S THURSDAY NIGHT, and Steve has late office hours, so we're sprawled out on their enormous overstuffed sofa, passing cartons of Chinese food back and forth, watching TV. I haven't told Meg about the other day.

"Name it," I say, my mouth full of tofu and pea pods. This is the first time I've been hungry in two days.

She chews, swallows. "I want to go back to work. I want to sub. But . . ." She pauses. "Actually, this is a big favor. But I don't know how else—I really—"

"It's okay," I say. "Whatever you need me to do."

"I need you to come with me. Just for a day or two. It sounds nuts, I know, even to me, but I need to get out of the house, I want to work, but I'm not ready to do it on my own, to be in front of a classroom by myself. I've already gotten permission from Judy." Meg is friends with the principal of her school. "And I'll pay you!" she says, perking up.

"I wouldn't take money from you."

"Of course you would. You'd be my aide, and it wouldn't be easy, so of course you'd take money." She holds out her hand and I pass her the container of cashew chicken. "It's not even going to be art classes, necessarily. I said I'd be available to substitute for anyone, any grade. It could be third-grade math or fifth-grade history. But, the thing is, I need you."

"When?" I ask. I'm not chomping at the bit to spend a few days with Meg helping her teach subtraction to fidgeting eight-year-olds, or scraping washable paint out from under my fingernails at the end of the day, but I'll do it. I'd do it even if I didn't feel secretly guilty for karmically causing her miscarriage.

"Anytime starting next week?"

"Okay. It'll be fun!" I say feebly.

I considered telling Kevin. I thought about coming clean. The term is apt: after my walk with David, I felt as if my body were covered in a grimy coat of sawdust, a light ash created by the friction of attraction sawing back and forth against guilt. I came home. Kevin was at work. I closed the door to my study and thought about confessing, washing away my sins. I began sorting through the books and papers strewn all over my desk: year-old fashion and health magazines that I thought I might want to write for; catalogues; receipts; scribbled, unintelligible notes to myself (what did "tragic beans, not hateful" mean?); junk mail I'd never bothered opening.

But then I thought, *Why hurt Kevin?* I made a "discard" pile on the floor and started randomly flinging things into it, creating chaos: at least the old, messy arrangement had made sense. Why cause him pain, when I'm the one who screwed up, I'm the one who should face the consequences, not Kevin? I stopped looking at what I was throwing out. Anything more than six months old was history. I stacked up enough papers and magazines to fill two brown paper bags. The top of my desk was visible. I began to gather up the mess; the room started to look neater, more organized. I knew I wouldn't tell him. This was my fault, not his. Kevin was innocent.

Innocent and intolerable. Everything he does: not just how he's been ceaselessly pressuring me lately, but the way he chews his food with an excess of lip-smacking; how he hogs the bed, inching over to me, pawing at me in the night; his habit of rubbing his hands together like a lecherous old man when he's nervous or excited. Even the color of his eyelashes irritates me, so pale they're almost invisible. Everything about him sets my teeth on edge. Passionless, uptight, blond-eyelashed Kevin—he's the anti-David.

On Friday night, we go over to my parents' house for dinner. Kevin and I drive silently through the city and then out of it, into the suburbs that open up before us. On a crisp, darkening night like this, it always strikes me that Milwaukee's suburbs were farmland just a few years ago, the subdivisions were cornfields, cows grazed in pastures that are now libraries and gas stations . . . and that what seems enduring may be momentary, fragile, and subject to change. As we approach Jupiter's Palace of Cheese, its lights glowing orange in the autumn dusk, I want to casually reach over and rest my hand on Kevin's shoulder; I want to say to him, "Let's stop here. Why don't we go in and have a look around, maybe pick something up for my parents?," as if this is something we do all the time, a part of our comfortable routine. It would be a relief, to do this with Kevin. It would put the planets back in line. But the words get stuck in my throat, and Kevin's eyes are resolutely on the road ahead, and so we keep driving.

We pull into the driveway of the house I grew up in, a 1950s ranch with beige painted trim. It's a small, flat house with a carport, a sunken living room, a rec room, an electric can opener—all the space-age accoutrements. The three outside lights over the garage, the carport, and the front door all blaze, marking our trail and making this the brightest spot on the block.

"Is there a connection between ranch-style houses and ranch-style salad dressing?" I ask Kevin as we walk up the path. He looks at me, raises one eyebrow, an expression I've seen him practice in front of the mirror.

My mother stands waiting for us at the door, wearing a flowered apron over her clothes, although I doubt she did anything more culinarily taxing than heating up frozen stuffed chicken breasts. She is like an older, shorter, bustier, eyeshadowed me. Her frizzy hair is pinned back with little spangly barrettes that look like ones I wore when I was ten, and probably are. She wears lots of jewelry—big gold button earrings, bracelets, sparkly rings—at all times. She favors loose, tunic-style, silky blouses with sequins on them. "Erica Marchese had twins," she says by way of greeting, giving first me, then Kevin a perfumey kiss on the cheek. "She named them Chloe and Zoe, however." I went to grade school with Erica Marchese, although I haven't seen her in about twenty years. But my mother keeps her finger on the pulse of her thriving, procreating suburban community.

"Chloe and Zoe, huh?" I say, humoring her, even though I don't care. Bright light and the murmur of voices fill the front hallway and spread throughout the entire house. My parents have a habit of leaving electrical appliances on—televisions, radios, lamps. It always seems like there's more going on here than there actually is.

"I bought you some underwear, sweetie," my mom stage-whispers to me. "And some darling earrings. They're on your bed. See if you like them."

I take Kevin's heavy leather coat and carry it along with mine into my old bedroom, which has been preserved as a shrine to me. If I ever wanted to move back in, if I ever wanted to move back to 1992, there's a room in Bay Point, Wisconsin, six-and-a-half miles north of downtown Milwaukee, waiting to oblige me. My one trophy, which I received for being an integral part of the 1990 Bay Point High School debating team, holds pride of place on my yellow bureau. The pink polka-dotted bedspread I picked out to match the light purple carpeting still covers my little twin bed. I enjoyed pastels in the late '80s. The color scheme in here is accidental Easter egg. Every time I walk through the door of this room, I am overcome with the feeling of both safety and suffocation.

"Hiya, sweetheart," my dad says, emerging from the wood-paneled den, where he's likely been watching public television and/or reading about the history of aspirin or of tree-trimming or of Woodrow Wilson's presidency for the past four or five hours. He stands in the doorway to my room, scratching his bald head. He's wearing one of Heather's old sweatshirts, which pulls tightly across his belly, and a pair of light brown polyester slacks that were perhaps in fashion circa 1973. Black dress socks complete the picture. My dad, a retired high school social studies teacher, spends his time reading educational nonfiction or watching PBS. He's a gentle man who seems to inhabit a different planet from the rest of us, near to ours but not quite intersecting, one where the pursuit of facts and knowledge provides infinitely more sustenance than food and oxygen. He blinks a lot, as if natural light surprises him. He has the habit of wandering off in the middle of a conversation to look up a word in the dictionary or to page through an encyclopedia in search of a historical reference. Naturally, he and Kevin get along famously.

Kevin is in the kitchen, helping my mother set the table. I don't know this for sure, but since things unfold in the same manner every time we're here, I'd bet on it. I hear the clink of silverware and glasses, the low sound of Kevin's voice pitched against my mom's high titter. I wish I could close my bedroom door and read a book for the rest of the night instead of eating dinner with my parents and Kevin. Containing my turmoil has been exhausting. I feel like I've been holding a lid over a boiling pot for three days. I just want to lie down.

"Hi, Dad." I walk over and hug him.

"Very interesting show on channel thirty-six about the brain," he says, as if we were in the middle of a conversation and had been interrupted just a few minutes ago. "For one thing, the human head weighs between ten and twelve pounds. I had no idea." He blinks, smiles at me as if he's giving me a gift. "I'll tell your mother the next time she says I need to lose weight," he whispers conspiratorially. "I'm not ten pounds overweight. It's just my head!"

I don't quite understand my dad, most of the time.

"Come," he says, taking my arm. "To the mess hall!"

"Oh, hello, Leonard," my mom says showily as we walk into the kitchen. "Nice to see you." She hates that my father prefers to spend his free time alone. She's a butterfly, colorfully flitting from lunch date to social engagement to shopping trip with friends, requiring only companionship; he's a strange, myopic, solitary bookworm. They're polar opposites, Barbara and Len Ross, and it amazes me not that they're still married, but that they ever fell in love in the first place. Watching their psychological contortions and battles embarrasses me, feels like spying on them as they tussle in bed. I wish they would keep it to themselves.

"Kevin, my good man," my dad says, ignoring my mom, possibly not noticing her tone. He and Kevin shake hands mock-formally, as they've been doing for nine years.

"Sir!" Kevin says. The table is set properly, the precooked chicken breasts are cooling—they'll be cold when we eat them—while my mom fiddles with a fruit salad made solely of brownish sliced apples and canned mandarin oranges. "How's everything going?" Kevin asks.

"Everything is going swimmingly," my father says. "Just swimmingly." This is the same script we always follow. I could film it, and then next time just send the video.

I ask my mom if there's anything I can do to help her, a calculated strategy Heather and I perfected when we were teenagers to coincide with the moment when she's just finished and doesn't need help.

"Are there napkins on the table? Glasses?" There are. "Then everybody, just sit down," she commands. We do.

My mom pays no attention to my dad or to Kevin, whose sin is that he really likes my dad, and turns to me. "Did I tell you about Stephanie Wagner's baby shower?" She nibbles on an apple slice, wipes her mouth daintily. "Well," she begins, already deliciously outraged, before I have the chance to respond. "Mrs. Wagner, who really had nothing to do with the planning of this shower—it was given by Mrs. Sheffield and Mrs. Gold—decided that she wanted to help. But you know what that means for Mrs. Wagner. She just wanted to get her fingers into the pie." These are women I've known my whole life, but in the lingua franca of these suburban ladies, referring to them by their first names would be sacrilegious. My mother continues with a story having something to do with place settings, where one of the main characters is the Jordan almonds. Somebody is adamantly insisting on, or flat-out rejecting, these party nuts. I don't know. I stopped listening somewhere around the words "baby shower." And my mother, perceptive though she is, is just a sucker for a captive audience, so I nod and nod, and occasionally gasp, which keeps her happy.

My dad and Kevin are chatting amiably about the central nervous system. My dad seems to be explaining something complicated to Kevin about the myelin sheath, and is using mandarin oranges to illustrate his point, moving them around on his plate.

The conversation remains segregated throughout the meal. I catch Kevin glancing over at me a few times, but I can't read his expression. During dinner, my mother regales me with her ideas for redecorating the kitchen (it's all about granite countertops), and I offer my opinions, a bit wantonly: I give myself over to it and suddenly, for the moment, I really do care, passionately, whether she ends up with light wood for the cabinets or dark. ("Blond wood, Mom, would bring so much natural *light* into the room!") My father asks Kevin about his work, Kevin questions my dad about his latest intellectual interest. A few minutes later, my dad asks Kevin's opinion on a problem they've been having with the leaky garage roof, although Kevin has as much experience with leaky roofs as I do (it's *flat;* it *leaks*!). I watch as Kevin chews solemnly, nodding to my father, reflecting on this situation. I take a bite of baked potato that tastes like cotton and wash it down with a long gulp of water. There is so much good in Kevin. How did I ever find a man so unflinching in his devotion to me, whose steady commitment extends all the way to my squabbling parents and their flat, waterlogged garage roof? If Kevin and I broke up, if I left the kind man sitting next to my father, I would never have this again. I would have meals with my parents, of course, but without Kevin, I believe I would never again sit at this dinner table in the same easy comfort of our similar domesticities, the four of us accomplices in the shared, unspoken knowledge that Kevin and I are replicating my parents, that we are justifying their choices, that we are their legacy.

It's somewhere between the baked potatoes and the store-bought lemon chiffon cake that I realize the obvious: I don't have a choice to make. I've already made it. Kevin is my choice. True, I picked him long before I knew David, but so what? When we got married, we said to each other: nobody else, no matter what. I promised. I'm not in high school. I don't need to be so torn up about this. And if being with Kevin feels at the moment more like a life sentence than a lifetime of happiness, well, that's just my burden. I love him, and I'm duty-bound to him. Babies and houses are my future, I suppose. Why should I be any different from everybody else? This is the way grown-ups negotiate their marriages, I finally understand. They bear up under the weight of them.

Kevin and my dad are talking about Freud now, the logical extension, I guess, of their in-depth dinnertime analysis of the brain. My mom is watching them, not participating. She doesn't look peeved, though, just distant, more like she's watching a circus, a freak show she couldn't possibly join, but one she holds tickets to and doesn't seem to mind viewing.

Kevin says, "Freud was the first person to recognize the effect paranoia has on our daily lives."

"A man walks into a psychiatrist's office," my dad responds, waving his fork for emphasis, "and says, 'Doctor, people keep ignoring me.' The doctor says, 'Next!'"

We laugh, because we've all heard him tell this joke a million times, and also because in a weird way it's still funny. Now is the chance for somebody to change the subject, to bring everyone back together. I notice the way my mom is looking at my dad, her head tilted, one hand wrapped loosely around her lipstick-smudged water glass. At first I think that it's just run-of-the-mill annoyance that's causing her mouth to curve into a tiny, enigmatic smile. But I see that it's something else. Her stubborn irritation with him is certainly real, but right now it's background noise, just the daily murmur and thrum of the crowd. Ringing through it like a clear bell, at least for the moment, is fondness. Definite fondness. Or something like it.

DICK IS IN MY OFFICE AGAIN WHEN I WALK THROUGH THE DOOR on Monday morning. On the way over, I prepared myself to sit down and immediately send the e-mail I've been writing in my head all weekend, but I see Dick and I'm grateful for the postponement.

"Hi!" I say, taking off my coat. The fluorescent light above my head is flickering slightly, which means I'll have a throbbing headache by the end of the day. I'll call the maintenance people, who will tell me they'll fix it but won't. Dick is sitting in a rolling chair in the middle of the room next to a huge stack of manuscripts. Are those *slippers* he's wearing?

"What is your opinion of ethics?" he asks loudly, looking up from a piece of paper in his lap. I freeze, my coat shrugged halfway off my shoulders. Ethics? Why is he asking me about ethics? What has he heard? Jesus, does he know? Did he see me with David at the lake?

"What?" It comes out of my mouth as a squeak.

"Ethics, ethics." He plants his suspiciously corduroy-shod feet flatly on the carpeting and rolls his chair around to face me. "It's the age of Dolly the sheep. Stem cell research. George W. Bush. We're behind the curve. I think the journal needs a few essays on bioethics. Some op-ed pieces." He emphasizes the syllables "op" and "ed" so that they sound vaguely Swedish.

Bioethics. I exhale, peel off my gloves, stuff them into my pockets. "I think that's a fantastic idea."

Dick is thumbing through a list of our referees, the scientists and doctors who review article submissions for us. "Ah, ah . . ." He concentrates; his eyebrows converge. "Emily," he says, finally remembering my name. I've been noticing that his expressions have begun to resemble Ronald Reagan's at the end of his presidency, and this worries me. "May I ask you to organize a rather large number of manuscripts for me today?" He sweeps his hand over the stack at his feet like he's performing a magic trick. Poof. Dick has the tendency to foist an unwieldy administrative task on me when the mood strikes him, not minding or noticing that I have a certain system, a certain organized number of jobs to do at any given time, measured out to keep the office running smoothly. Fussy librarian is not really the kind of person I consider myself to be, but I can't stand the break in my routine. So I guess I am. "I seem to have let things run a bit amok," he continues. "I'd like you to divide these articles into groups. Rejected and pending. I'd also like you to fashion a folder for each of them and clear out the extraneous paperwork. Would you be so kind?"

I see my day at *Male Reproduction* unfolding before me: a mountain of typed labels, scattered papers, and folders heaped under the gently strobing fluorescent light. I smile, nod, sigh. He means well. He means well. "Sure, Dick."

I spend the next eight hours categorizing my boss's files, unable to get to my computer and write to David. Heather once told me that the highest level of productivity a company can expect from its employees is fifty percent. At this rate, I'm now due a full day of paid vacation (which I will probably take the next time Dick goes out of town, in the form of one of my patented work slowdowns, involving but not limited to calling Meg, sending personal e-mails, and relentlessly snacking on Junior Mints).

Dick decides to work in my office. As I sit cross-legged on the floor surrounded by the detritus of the journal, he rolls up to my desk and proceeds to make dozens of calls to scientists, asking them to write about bioethics. "Genome mapping," I hear him say. "Genetic counseling." From my uncomfortable perch in the middle of the room, I make up my own topics to amuse myself. "Three gnomes napping." "Frenetic bouncing." I debate sharing my excellent ideas for the name of the section, "Send in the Clones," or maybe "Sperm und Drang." I decide to keep quiet. In between serious conversations with scientists, Dick chats genially to me about his family, his NIH grant application, his favorite kind of pie *(rhubarb!)*, so that I can never enter the zone where I might at least be able to enjoy concentrating on a menial job and getting it done. My day inches along. I spend a full hour typing "Submission" onto folder labels. I spend another forty-five minutes typing "Reject" onto another set of labels. Under these circumstances, how can a girl not feel slightly nudged by the universe? As soon as Dick leaves, I will write the e-mail.

Finally, at five thirty, just when I'd normally be packing up and happily contemplating dinner, Dick calls it a day, tells me I'm swell, pulls on his green-felt beret, and leaves, first attempting to use the supply-closet door before making his way to the actual exit. I worry, sometimes, that the next time I come in to work I'll find him still obliviously wandering the corridors of Pfein Hall.

I wonder if there's a reason that most of the men in my life are such emotionally incomprehensible beings who live so much more distinctly in their heads than in the material world. Dick, who may, in fact, be deteriorating, painting the brushstrokes of his life, long lost to its subtle details, its fine lines and specific shadings. My sweet father, his interior life a mystery, his off-kilter conversations mostly obscure factual references and strange jokes so confusing that they manage to round the bend and arrive on the other side of funny. And Kevin, stiff and controlled and certain that if he just pretends for long enough that I don't have feelings, eventually I won't.

My head is pounding now, since my eyes have, as predicted, failed to keep the pace of the flickering fluorescent light. The sky is dark and it suddenly feels much later than it is. My fingers, finally poised on the keyboard, look cinematic and slightly fake, just a shade wrong, too white, too thin, too large, like when you know that the hands playing the piano in the movie don't actually belong to the actor.

Dear David,

I'm sorry you haven't heard from me in a while. I owe you an explanation for running off the way I did. I had an amazing time with you the other day. I've been having an amazing time getting to know you, which is why this is so hard to write. I don't know how I managed to screw up so badly, but I need to tell you that I'm married.

This is probably not what you were expecting. I can't begin to tell you how sorry I am for not mentioning it sooner. I should never have let our friendship progress the way it did without telling you.

I don't know; I might have imagined that something was developing between us. I'm second-guessing every-thing right now. Either way, I should have said something. I think I let things go too far. I'm so sorry if I gave you the wrong idea. I just enjoyed our time together—too much.

I hope you can forgive me.

—Emily

P.S. If you have no idea what I'm talking about, please just delete this e-mail and pretend I never sent it.

I hit "send." With my hand—mine again—I turn off my computer and head home.

Two weeks tick by. I feel dull and dense, like my body mass has changed. I feel as if I've moved to an outlying suburb of my life. Soddenville. Over to the left is a new golf course, Listless Vista. On the right is a housing development, Low-Level Despair Estates.

I'm awake for hours in the middle of the night, and then I sleep till ten in the morning. I spend one entire day inventing time-consuming chores for myself that require no actual expenditure of energy: I call the toll-free number listed on a can of sparkling water to report that every can in the case we just bought is flat. This water does not sparkle! I dig around and find the phone number of the organization that removes your name from credit card company solicitation lists. I call the accounting department at my dentist's office to question a bill that I suspect is probably right but might not be. I walk ten blocks to the grocery store to buy macadamia nuts. I consider making up a complaint about the *Milwaukee Journal Sentinel*'s shameful coverage of something or other and writing an irate letter to the editor.

I had wheels. And now they're gone. And although I can still walk, although my wheels were not required for basic maneuvers, I was just getting to know them, starting to enjoy them. I was just beginning to feel wild and free and speedy.

I wonder what David is thinking. He must hate me. I guess I'll never hear from him again. It shouldn't bother me; after all, I wrote the e-mail. I put a stop to the whole dodgy mess. Still, at the oddest moments, while I'm driving somewhere, or in the middle of dinner, or during a stupefying telephone conversation with a scientist, I'll start imagining him, thinking about his face as he read my message, imagining his reaction. I picture him pushing his chair back from his computer, raking his hand through his hair. I see him slumping onto his sofa in, what? confusion? anger? sadness? complete apathy? As long as it's my fantasy, I usually imagine that he's devastated, that he longs for me, that he forgives me and wants me. Sometimes, while I'm at it, I continue imagining him. He's combing his hair. He's eating a sandwich. I can't help it. I tried to purge him from my mind. I did the best I could. It hasn't worked yet. But I'm sure it will eventually.

Kevin doesn't seem to notice any of it—not my lethargy, not my distractedness, not my sudden propensity for strange and useless household tasks. Or if he does, he's too wrapped up in the daily muddle of his own life to ask me about it. Worst of all, I don't even feel less guilty. I still feel as if I cheated on Kevin. One emotional entanglement has reconfigured us. The tectonic plates of our relationship have shifted. Will this get better, too, eventually?

On Tuesday, Meg calls and asks me if I'm free "all day Thursday." As it happens, I am. I get excited because I think she's going to suggest a day trip to Chicago, or a long hike in the state park. Then she tells me that we're scheduled to head a classroom full of writhing five-year-olds. Thirty of them. For the entire day.

"Do you know the apples and bananas song?" she asks. " 'Twinkle, Twinkle, Little Star' in Spanish?" She's serious.

"Uh, *no,* Meg," I answer, in a subtle tone that I hope will indicate: *Meg, why on earth would I know those songs?*

"I'll try to print out the lyrics to a few of the kindergarten standards before Thursday," she says, all business. "Can you be at the school by seven forty-five?"

The playground in front of Day Avenue Primary School is a surprisingly calm place at a quarter to eight. Eerily calm. It rained last night, and this morning everything shines. The sidewalks sparkle, the bright playground equipment gleams, and even the few fat, bobbing pigeons on the wet grass are shimmery and iridescent.

Well, this won't be so bad. I see myself crouched next to a sweet five-year-old who is sitting at her miniature desk, feet swinging, intently trying to write her name. I'm gently guiding her, encouraging her as she forms adorably large, crooked letters: *E-M-M-A*. (Meg says all the girls are Emma and Olivia and all the boys are Max, like characters from a novel cowritten by Jane Austen and Isaac Bashevis Singer.) Good job, honey! Oh, heavens, you needn't thank me. That's what I'm here for. I will be Miss Emily, the kind, beautiful teacher's assistant, and when they go home, they'll rave about me to their ragged, overworked mommies. Miss Emily taught me to count to ten in French! Miss Emily told me she liked my dress! Maybe they'll remember me forever. Between scrubbing the bathroom floor and driving the kids to soccer practice, their mommies will resent me.

Gingerly, I ease my too-wide self down onto a canvas swing and wait for Meg.

Just then, the four horsemen of the apocalypse descend: four yellow buses pull up. What emerges from their gaping maws can only be the end of the world. Masses, hordes of screeching, yelping demons pour out of the buses, pushing and shoving each other and running maniacally. They just whirl around, careening off each other, pointy little teeth bared, expressions of pure hedonistic joy on their faces. Wild animals! Hell monsters! It looks like some of them are headed for the playground equipment. I feel myself cower, shrink a little on my swing.

Meg comes up beside me, puts her hand on my shoulder. "Don't worry," she says cheerfully. "They're not all ours."

I stand. I hadn't seen her approaching. "When did you get here?"

"I've been here since seven. I wanted to prepare the room and get my head together. Let's go inside now. We have fifteen minutes before the playground monitor will corral the kids and send them in." I notice a harassed-looking middle-aged lady off to the side. She has a beehive hairdo and is wearing a dress the color of toast. There's a whistle around her neck. She scans the crowd, making sure the prematurely huge ten-year-olds don't crush the few minuscule four-year-olds before eight in the morning.

I follow Meg in the main door, and she guides me down the

echoey hallway to the kindergarten wing. Our sneakers make loud slapping sounds on the industrial tiled floors. I've been here before, visiting Meg, but the identical-looking corridors are always a maze to me. Bright, splotchy paintings on construction paper decorate the walls above the little blue and red lockers. Posters exhorting kids to READ and to SAY NO TO DRUGS cover the remaining wall space. The image of a five-year-old politely refusing a tiny joint pops into my head, and I promptly chase it away. This is not the kind of thing that occurs to Miss Emily!

Meg greets a few of her fellow teachers as we pass. They're a chalk-dusted, sensibly dressed bunch of women. They look harried, but several of them stop to hug her, welcome her back, whisper that they hope she's doing okay, that they've been thinking about her. It's obvious that these women form a close group and that they adore Meg. Who wouldn't? For a second, I'm jealous. Meg introduces me quickly to her colleagues. "My best friend and teacher's aide for the day!" she says. I squash my jealousy like a bug.

We enter Mrs. Rosen's room, a landscape of orange all-purpose carpeting, bright pillows, and multicolored miniature plastic chairs lined up against a long U-shaped table. Meg is whistling a repetitive ditty that seems to consist of just six notes.

"It's nice to see you in good spirits," I offer tentatively.

"I feel great!" Meg says. "This was such a good idea. Em," she adds, "you know how much I appreciate this."

"Shut up!" I say.

She punches me lightly in the arm; I punch her back. We pretend to be guys. "You shut up."

"What's on today's agenda?" I ask. "Mergers? Acquisitions? Hostile takeovers?"

"The lesson plan involves show-and-tell and a recap of the days of the week, followed by a three-martini lunch and an investigation by the SEC." She motions me over to the closet at the back of the room and opens the door. "Art supplies," she says, with a Vanna White swoop of her arm. "Oh, and they'll be working in their journals today, too."

"They keep journals?" I ask. "Can they write?"

"Not really. They draw pictures and scratch out a few words."

"What else?"

"Follow my lead," she says. "Activities last about twenty minutes each. Welcome to short-attention-span theater. A lot of what we do is wander around and give them encouragement, help them clean up. It'll be obvious."

The first students of the day charge into the room, two little girls with pink backpacks and identical haircuts—stick-straight short hair and bangs. Bangs! Maybe I should get bangs. They spot Meg and run up to her, stop just short of crashing into her legs. They haven't learned the concept of personal space yet. "Hi, Miss Schaeffer!" Meg was their art teacher last year, when they were four, and I can see that they love the shock of seeing her now. I remember what it felt like the time my mom and I ran into my third-grade teacher at the grocery store (Did she buy frozen entrées like we did? An exotic kind of soda?), or even when I saw my high school Spanish teacher at the mall, holding hands with a handsome man—the sudden surprise of realizing that they had lives, possibly even complicated lives.

"Hi, Phoebe! Hi, Jessica!" She crouches down to their height and grabs them both in a hug. I can't believe she remembers their names.

"Why aren't you our art teacher anymore?" Jessicaphoebe asks.

"I'm substituting this year," Meg says. "Mrs. Rosen isn't here today, so I get to spend the whole day with you!" Meg is so good at this. If it were me, I probably would have overdisclosed to the little urchins. *Well, children, the thing is, I couldn't get pregnant because of all the stress last year, so I took some time off and got knocked up, but then I miscarried, which was really sad, so now I'm just easing my way back into things. Any advice?* I don't really know how to deal with kids. Meg is in her element. It occurs to me that I don't really have an element. I would like to tell this to Meg, and then we would make a few jokes about chromium and magnesium—no, that's *my* element. Well, I'll take zinc then; you always get chromium—but she's busy.

"And guess what?" Meg continues, motioning me over. "You get to have *two* substitute teachers today!" She seems to be operating under the principle that if you pretend something is a treat for a five-year-old, it becomes one. Guess what? *You get to have a rubella vaccination today!* "This is Miss Ross," she says. I'm not a "Miss," but I'm not a "Mrs.," either, and neither is Meg; we both kept our last names, something we fervently promised to do when we were still in college. Not to mention, Emily Lee sounds like something Porky Pig would say. But "Ms." sounds accidental, like it lost one of its consonants at the dry cleaner's. Jessica and Phoebe look at me suspiciously. I stretch what I hope is a benevolent smile across my face.

More little kids arrive, one or two accompanied by their parents, most in distinct little groups. I watch as one girl tries to join a giggling threesome of girls who seem to be having a conversation about shoes. "Hi!" she says eagerly. "Hi!" but they ignore her. Is it because she wears glasses? Just as I'm about to move in and rescue her, she heads over to another couple of kids who immediately include her in their game of Throw the Jacket on the Floor. They're tiny people, but they already have friends. They've formed cliques! They edge each other out, play power games. Observe the North American five-year-old in its native habitat. Watch its sophisticated interactions, its relentless quest for social survival. What a cruel and hearty beast!

"Hang up your jackets and come sit in the circle!" Meg trills. She claps her hands three times.

It occurs to me that I could leave Kevin. Not necessarily so that I could pursue David, because I've obviously already screwed that up. But maybe David's appearance in my life was a sign, a warning—a sexy, muscular, dark-eyed warning—that my marriage is not going to go the distance. I feel a flutter and a queasy thump in my stomach, simultaneously. Kevin and I are so comfortable together in our ruts and grooves, even in our perennial disagreements, I've just always considered lusty, irresistible excitement to be the plot of other people's stories. But maybe I'm going to end up making it mine. Divorce Kevin. Kevin and I are divorced. I'm a divorcée. A gay divorcée. Hello, I've been divorced for several years now. Suddenly I picture myself as a blowsy forty-year-old with a pack-a-day habit. I wear blue eye shadow and while away my long, lonely nights on a barstool. *Get me another gin and tonic! I don't care if you think I'm drunk, goddammit!*

"Miss Ross! Miss Ross!" Meg has, apparently, been calling me, but I'm not used to responding to that name. She rolls her eyes at me from across the room. "Would you like to join our good morning circle?"

I lope across the room, feeling like I'm Alice and I've just taken the one pill that makes me large, and I plunk myself down, cross-legged, between two miniature people. The curly-headed little boy on my left scrunches closer to me, leans against my arm. I'm immediately smitten.

Meg casts a spell over the twenty-five little kids. She leads them in a few songs, and then through show-and-tell, which is (I don't recall this from my kindergarten days) a competitive guessing game. The show-and-teller gives out three clues, and the rest of the students have to guess the object, which is hidden from view. One girl brought in a Barbie doll. ("It has hair. It is fun to play with. My sister has three." Nobody figures it out.) And another brought in a ball of purple yarn. ("My cat likes to chase it. My mom made a sweater with it. It is soft." One kid yells out, "Cheese!" but several others get it right.)

Kindergarten has very little subtext. I find that it's easy to give myself over to this experience, so immediate, so precisely What It Is. It lives up to a person's expectations: you come, you play, you learn, you go home and eat SpaghettiOs for lunch. I watch Meg at the helm, and I think, *This is her antidote.* I think that my friend is healed, or at least healing. And I'm relieved.

We review the days of the week, which they've obviously been practicing. My little curly-haired neighbor is called to the front for a lesson.

"What day of the week is it today, Ari?" Meg asks him.

He stands, contemplating. He's wearing corduroy pants, I notice, and suede loafers, which makes me want to laugh. I wonder if he has a tiny briefcase and tie in his closet at home. He scratches his head, looks up at Meg for some help.

"Th- Th- Th-," Meg prompts, leaning down toward him, and Ari breaks into a huge grin.

"FRIDAY!" he yells. Meg tells him how close he is, what a wonderful guess he's made.

The morning passes in this strange, surreal way. These three-and-a-half hours are so jam-packed, it's like we're living a full day that's been physically shrunken to fit their size. Meg reads them two stories. Under her tutelage, they make origami houses and slap colored sticky tape to them for decoration. They break for a snack of granola bars and an unidentifiable orange-ish drink. They scribble in their journals and draw pictures of things that are important to them: one boy draws his dog; one girl draws a loaf of bread. They sing an elaborate song about an old gray cat that creeps, sleeps, and chases mice, method acting all parts. They have playtime. They go outside for recess (which seems redundant to me; what do they need a break from?). Between events, they jump around and pick at each other, grooming, tickling, patting each other, or tugging at one another's hair. Unless Meg has her hand raised in the universal kindergarten signal for "Listen here, kid-dies," the decibel level always ranges somewhere from carnival to aviary. Meg and I lumber about, pulling children off other children, listening to sentences like "I had pizza last night!" and "I have a brother" and "I'm going to be a veterinarian!" and responding with all-purpose, high-pitched murmurs of approval.

And then the morning is over. As quickly as the tornado blew into the room, it's gone. The twenty-five little monsters know their routine. The first bell rings, and they immediately begin to put away the blocks, paints, crayons, and books that litter the floor; they pack up their belongings in a relatively orderly manner and, as the second bell tolls, head for the waiting kindergarten bus or their parents in SUVs.

Meg and I converge at the doorway as we see off the last of them. They wave and wave at us, torn between the excitement of leaving and the nostalgia of staying, and my friend Ari turns around at the last minute and wraps his arms around my waist in a fast and surprisingly strong hug. "Bye, Lady!" he shouts, and takes off running down the hall.

Meg blows a strand of hair out of her eyes and wipes her hands on her jeans, then examines her palms and fingers for remnants of glue and chalk. "Let's go outside," she says. "We'll watch them as they leave and listen to the quiet before the next shift arrives." This being kindergarten, we get to repeat our performance in an hour. She links her arm through mine and leads me out, singing the chain gang song.

Outside, a few other teachers are huddled together in the bright sunshine. One woman in a jean jacket is brazenly smoking at the edge of the grass courtyard. School is still in session, since only the four- and five-year-olds are divided into morning and afternoon groups with this hour in between. Some leftover kids are running around or playing on the playground equipment as their mothers look on. The bus pulls away. One or two fathers walk away from the school with their charges, who look extra-short next to the men. I'm exhausted and exhilarated. It feels good to do work that's physical; it feels more real than the work I usually do.

Meg and I lean against the side of the building. She shades her eyes with her hand and surveys the area. I'm suddenly starving, and I'm about to suggest we go back in and grab our lunches when she nudges me. "Isn't that your friend?" She tilts her chin toward a youngish-looking man who's crouched next to a little girl, tying her shoe. They're about twenty feet from us, on the sidewalk in front of the school. I squint, try to make him out. Just at that moment he turns toward me, and I see that it's David. He spots me at the exact same second, so there's no way for me to run away, which is what I would like to do. Anyway, I'm immobilized. I feel like all the blood has been suctioned from my body; I'm dry and brittle and I might turn to dust and just blow away. At the same time, David looks aghast. I haven't told Meg about recent events, not about our walk or the almost-kiss or the e-mail. In the split second that I identify David's particular posture, recognizable even as he's crouching, the contours of his face, the way his dark hair hangs, in the instant that this combination of attributes once again and in spite of everything makes my stomach lurch, I worry that Meg will wave or call him over. I nudge her back, harder than I'd intended, and mutter under my breath, "Don't say anything." Then, my heart thumping and with no alternative, I lift my hand and wave to him.

For a few seconds, he doesn't respond. He just stares at me with the same awful expression on his face. Then he sets his mouth back into place, stands up, still looking at me, takes the hand of the little girl, waves back with his other hand, and turns and walks away.

Meg doesn't say anything for a while. We both watch him as he leaves, the little girl half-skipping to keep up with his long gait. From this distance, I can hear a few notes of her high, singsongy voice. He looks down at her and says something in response. I sense, rather than see, Meg look at me and then look back again at David as he and the girl grow smaller in the distance and finally turn left down a side street and disappear from view. I swallow hard. "Well, that was weird," she says softly.

"Yeah," I say.

"And, ow," she adds, rubbing her side where I elbowed her.

"Sorry about that." I wonder briefly what David was doing with a small child. Then I remember that he mentioned a niece to me on our first date. Our first date.

"So," Meg says, "are you going to tell me what that was all about?"

I don't know what to say. Supporting myself against the brick wall, I sink down to the ground and look up at Meg. I feel a creeping dampness from the wet grass, and immediately hoist myself back up again. "Did I just get my jeans wet?" I ask, turning around to show her.

"No, you're fine. Em?"

I think about David's face next to mine on the bench by the lake, the way his eyes grew darker, softer, as he was about to kiss me. I think about his face just now, horrified at seeing me, his mouth grim, resolute. Meg will definitely not understand this, and I deeply, passionately don't want to tell her. I just don't want to have to defend myself. And anyway, I can't. "I don't want to talk about it right now," I admit. "I do want to tell you, but later. Okay?"

"Sure, I guess," she says, noncommittal. Is she miffed? This is not usually how we operate, holding back, not talking about what's on our minds. With the glaring sun directly above us, we stand for a few more minutes in silence. The breeze picks up, and I shiver, pull my light sweater more tightly around me. Finally, Meg says, "Come on, let's go eat and get ready for the next crew," and we make our way silently across the grass and back into the school.

That night, an e-mail from David comes in:

Arrr$%^@rggh&#*(%@#@!

I'm sorry that I was awkward this morning. I wasn't expecting to see you.

I'd be an idiot if I hadn't realized that something was up the day we didn't kiss. To tell you the truth, Emily, I wasn't going to write back to you at all. Then I decided I'd send you a scathing note, so that you'd feel as awful and surprised as I felt when I got your e-mail. . . .

I was working on that reply (and it was going fairly

well) until it occurred to me that I could rise above it and just tell you honestly what a crummy feeling this is, and ask you what you were up to, because I thought that you and I were pretty connected. I was starting to feel kind of great about you.

   So that's the one I finally landed on. I'm stung, but I'll get over it.

—David

P.S. We should probably put that "relationship expert" assignment on hold for a while (unless you want to write it as straight irony). Check back with me in a few months, if you like. In the meantime, feel free to pitch any other ideas to my editor, Matt Fowler.

Later, much later, I lie awake in our bed and I watch Kevin sleep, his chest rising and falling, his breathing regular and deep. It's this rhythm that usually calms me when I can't sleep, the solid, peaceful hulk of his warm body next to mine; I lay my head on his chest when I'm restless and I'm lulled by his beating heart.

   Tonight, of course, it's my own recalcitrant ticker that keeps me up. I was exhausted when I got home, and I tried to tell Kevin about my day of kindergarten while we sat in front of the TV eating our hastily thrown-together cheese omelets. But the story, so specific in its details while I was living it, became muddled in the telling. My non-interaction with David lay over my thoughts, muffling everything else. I couldn't remember all the things I'd wanted to relay to Kevin, the smells of paint and Play-Doh that suffused the room, the crazy energy of thirty five-year-olds whirling around like tops, the way they listened with their whole bodies to Meg when she read to them. I tried to talk about the things we'd done, the activities and the lessons, but Kevin was distracted, kept turning his eyes back to the TV, which we had put on "mute." I knew he wasn't really listening, and I wasn't even annoyed; I just gave up. We unmuted the TV, watched reruns, and then, after dinner, we both retreated into our own offices for the rest of the night. I sat staring at my computer for two hours, thinking about David. And then I got his e-mail.

I read it over and over again. I analyzed every paragraph, every sentence. I reacted to it physically: his slightly sour tone made my stomach ache; but his basic goodwill and gentleness, the honesty and humor that still shone through the whole message planted a slow, burning regret in my chest. I wanted to write back to him. I wanted to apologize or explain, but every time I tried to compose a few words, I drew a big fat blank. That's the thing about telling a man you've almost kissed that you happen to be married: there's not a whole lot left to explain. In the room of my brain reserved for sanity and clarity, and one that is not always open for business, I knew that anything I wrote would just be the start of something, possibly something mature and friendly, or maybe something illicit and irresistible . . . but whatever I started, it would be wrong. I wanted contact with him. I hit "compose new message," typed in David's address. Desire played tug of war with my conscience, and my conscience won. I couldn't think of any words to write to David. Finally, at ten thirty, I turned off my computer and went to bed.

Now, four hours later, I sneak out from under the covers and tiptoe across the room. At the door, I listen to make sure Kevin is still asleep. As if he'd wake up and surmise my intentions, the intentions I don't even quite know, and cry out, "Where do you think you're going, harlot!?" My dramatic sensibilities have obviously been informed by too many episodes of *Days of Our Lives,* circa 1989. There's a closeness in here, the faint musk of our breathing bodies, despite the window open a crack to let in the air. I slip out of our room and sneak down the hall into my study, flick on the computer, and watch as the ghostly blue glow emerges on the screen and casts a translucent pall over the room.

It's two-thirty in the morning, the universal hour of bad judgment.

"Dear David," I write,

> I'm glad that you wrote back. I deserved it, the things you said. And maybe you don't want to hear from me again, but I felt compelled to get in touch one more time.
>
> I already told you how sorry I am for being such an idiot. I also want you to know that I'd never done anything like this before. I'm not like that. It's embarrassing to admit it, but now that I have nothing to lose, I'll just go ahead: hanging out with you was like being shown a new color, one I hadn't known existed before. I looked around and the world was brighter, more vivid, and I just wanted that feeling to last.
>
> My husband is a great person. We've been together for nine years. I think lately that we've veered away from each other, and I'm not sure we're ever going to come back together. That's the truth.
>
> Well, it's 2:30 in the morning, so I'd better go. I really will understand if I don't hear from you again. If you do want to write back, maybe we can try to be friends. I know I'd really like that.
>
> I'm going to go back to bed now . . . thinking of you.
> —Emily

I send the e-mail. What have I done?

KEVIN CALLS MEG "NUTMEG," AND MEG CALLS KEVIN "Testicle Writer," or sometimes just "Testy." My husband and my best friend enjoy a lively, jokey, independent friendship that I pretend to appreciate, but in fact it rankles me. Even before I met David, I sometimes felt vaguely threatened by the happy collision of my two worlds, the receptacles of my two distinct and distinctly private selves meeting and laughing and forming an exclusive bond. Now, I recognize the heightened stakes of it: what if I reveal to Meg everything about David, and then Kevin asks Meg if something is going on with me, and she feels compelled to confess to him? Separately, Kevin and Meg always tell me how much they like each other, and they invariably add to their declarations of mutual affection something like, "I'm so glad that I love your husband/best friend so much; it makes things so easy."

On Saturday night, just before we're supposed to leave to meet Meg and Steve for drinks, Kevin pulls me down onto the couch next to him. He smells like too much DK Trois cologne, which Heather gave me as a gift. I thought it smelled like cat pee, but Kevin liked the stench of it, so I gave it to him, which wasn't very smart, because now I have to smell it all the time. He brushes a strand of my hair away from my face, takes my hand, and looks me in the eye. Although Kevin is never insincere, these moves feel slightly stylized, and it occurs to me that he's about to say something momentous, something he's been rehearsing.

"I've been thinking," he starts, then laughs self-consciously and looks away from me. He drops my hand and clasps his primly in his lap. I stare, intrigued, as his knuckles whiten before my eyes. "I want to say," he starts, then pauses. "I want to say, there are these things between us lately, and we've been fighting about them, and that's okay." He nods, encouraging himself. "I mean, if we have to argue to figure out where we're going, well, then that's what we have to do." He's staring across the room as he talks now, as if someone is crouched by the window holding up cue cards.

"Kevin, I—"

"Please don't interrupt!" he says. His voice has a sudden, surprising snappishness to it, and his shoulders tense visibly. "I need to say this. I want you to know, Emily, that I'm very clear about what I want for our future. I know you've been having some . . . doubts, or insecurities, or whatever you want to call them. And I can't say that this hasn't surprised me. But I will wait for you." He turns his whole body toward me as he says this, and he casts a benevolent smile down upon me. "I will wait as long as it takes for you to catch up to where I am, to be ready to begin this chapter of our lives together." He unclasps his hands and places them on my shoulders. "Just don't let it take too long."

I feel my mouth drop open. His hands are like heavy warm rodents on my shoulders. "W-wait for me to catch up to you?" I'm starting to take this in. Kevin just keeps beaming at me. There's a tiny, whitish blob of dry spit on the corner of his mouth. "To catch up to you?" I squeak.

"Of course," he says.

The distance between what Kevin thinks he's telling me and what I'm hearing is from here to Glen Valley, first choice inner-ring suburb of Milwaukee; it's from here to the moon. He exudes self-satisfied munificence and expects gratitude. I want to throttle him. I blink a few times and rub my eyes. "But Kevin, how do you know you're out in front?" I finally manage. "What if I just don't want the things you want? What if I'm the one who's in the lead? Should I wait for you to catch up to me?"

Kevin shakes his head, his smile stiffening. "Emily, now you're just being selfish." He tightens his grip on my shoulders. "Wendy says that most thirty-year-old women would thank their lucky stars for a man who wants to buy a house and start a family!"

"Most thirty-year-old women?" I sputter. I feel like a mynah bird. I'm capable only of stunned repetition. "Most thirty-year-old women? *Wendy?*"

"Yeah, Doug's wife." During better moments, we refer to Doug's wife, Wendy Wetzel, as "Prendy Pretzel."

"You've been talking to Wendy about me?"

"No! Well, yes. And Doug. They're my friends, and this has been weighing on me. I'm sure you talk to Meg about this."

No, as a matter of fact, I've been dating instead. I shove Kevin's deadweight hands off my shoulders. "I'm not ready to have a child with you," I say. "And I'm not ready to buy a house with you, either. I might be, someday, but I'm not now, and if you can't respect that, or at the very least just accept it, then. . . ." I drift off, unsure of what I want to say next, down what dark marital alley this is leading.

"Well, I *am* ready." Kevin's voice is cold and controlled. "And I *will* wait. I've made an appointment with Dr. Lu for a physical next week. I'm going to ask him to test my sperm count, just to make sure everyone's swimming. I thought you should know that." He gets up from the couch abruptly. I shake my head to try to clear out the swarm of bees that has buzzed into my brain. Kevin has already made his way to the front door, his keys jangling. "Are you coming?" he calls, as if the last few minutes haven't happened. "We're late!"

.   .   .

When we finally get to the bar, Meg and Kevin act like cousins who haven't seen each other since last summer's family reunion.

"Ike!" Meg yells, and throws her arms around Kevin.

"Tina!" Kevin yells back, the tension of the last hour vacating his stiff posture. Meanwhile, Steve and I give each other awkward pecks on the cheek and sit down at the small table, while Meg and Kevin are still hugging and cooing at each other. I haven't seen Steve since the day at the hospital. He's wearing the same rumpled shirt and pants, I notice; no novelty tie, thankfully.

We meet at Sullivan's Pub every so often, the four of us, even though nobody, it seems to me, particularly likes the strange dynamic of the double date. Meg and Steve have brought a deck of cards. We like to play hearts; the activity of the card game fills up the conversational lulls and prevents Meg and me from veering off down our own, exclusive conversation highway, which, I admit, we have a tendency to do.

We get down to business after the greetings are made and the drinks ordered: Steve shuffles with a few showy flutters and flaps, then deals, telling us a story about a little girl, a new patient of his who had never been to the dentist before and brought along her stuffed shark, Bitey, for comfort. She was so scared of Steve and of the whole situation, the metallic hissing contraptions and the antiseptic surroundings unsuccessfully disguised with bright colors and bubblegum-flavored toothpaste and pictures of kitties, that Steve had to do an entire pretend dental exam on Bitey before the little girl would open her own mouth for inspection.

"Pretend dental," Meg says matter-of-factly, "is a form of meditation."

"You're thinking of transcendental, sweetie," Steve says, not getting her joke until a half beat later. *"Oh!"* he says, embarrassed. In response, Meg ruffles his hair and smooths his shirt collar with a surfeit of gooey affection.

"Sorry, Steve, but who can blame the kid?" I say, running my thumb up along the side of my glass, tracing a line in the condensation. "I myself haven't been to the dentist in over a year. Maybe I could borrow Bitey for my next visit." Steve nods. "Kevin," I add, "has a doctor's appointment next week. It's important to get regular checkups, isn't it?" I don't know why this comes out of my mouth, but it does.

Kevin looks at me like I've just stabbed him in the arm with a fork. I drop my gaze from his and catch Meg and Steve exchanging a confused look. "It is," Kevin says quietly, regaining his composure. "You don't want anything to be amiss." Bastard.

Nobody says anything for a few moments, and the din of Sullivan's takes on a certain musical structure. Behind us and to the left, a table of girls, probably just barely of legal drinking age, gets louder and more raucous, the melody of their high, bubbly laughter like the mating songs of frogs. To our right, a wealthy-looking man and woman clink their wine glasses. A strain of conversation floats over from somewhere, a husky female voice saying, "You couldn't pay me to fuck him!" followed by bawdy laughter.

I glance for the first time at the cards in my hand. It takes me a second to remember what game we're playing, and then I begin absently organizing the cards into suits. I'm not good at hearts. I have no strategy, and, worse, no desire to create one. I like to think I'm lucky, and that this elusive quality will compensate for my inability to think ahead. I would not be a good military commander. Cigarette smoke curls over our table.

"Did I ever tell you guys," Meg says awkwardly, then clears her throat, "speaking of doctors' appointments, about the time a couple of years ago when I had the idea to get all my medical appointments out of the way in one day?" While I was listening to the sounds of the bar, Meg, it seems, was scouring her brain for a way to pick the mutilated conversation back up off the ground. Steve lays down the first card.

"I had my eye doctor appointment in the morning," she continues, "and they dilated my pupils, and then I had a gynecologist appointment two hours later." She slaps down a card. Kevin follows. Then me. Steve pulls the four cards toward him, keeping control of the hand.

"I had to fill out this questionnaire, but I couldn't read any-thing, because of my eyes. So the receptionist had to read all these really personal questions out loud to me, in front of everybody in the waiting room, and I had to answer them. 'When was your last period?' 'How many sexual partners have you had in the past year?' 'Do you use condoms to protect against STDs?' Everybody in the waiting room knew me quite well after that."

Chuckle, chuckle, chuckle. Slap, slap, slap, slap. Meg takes the cards.

We play in silence for a while. Two cards lie on the table in front of me, and I realize I have no diamonds to set down. "Hey, everybody," I say, pulling out my jack of hearts. "I'm breaking hearts!" I like to be the one who says it. Kevin quickly lays down another heart.

"Oh, crap," Meg says, laughing, reluctantly taking the pile as Steve gives her a sympathetic smile. "Can we have a do-over? Does that turn count?"

"What about sperm count?" I ask. Meg and Steve both groan. Kevin shoots me another look.

We concentrate on the game for a while, the four of us finally settling into a pleasant rhythm, punctuated by the occasional com-ment, a refill of drinks, an observation about someone or some-thing at a nearby table. I try not to ignore Kevin. I try to act like we're okay. But I can't bring myself to use the normal currency of our communication. I can't touch his knee the way I would usually after he says something funny, can't look at him for very long before I feel like turning away. I restrain myself from making mean comments and find that I am barely speaking to him at all.

The well-dressed, wine-glass-clinking couple at the table to our right gets up to leave. The woman's hair has that deep brown sheen that you sometimes see on the coat of a really well cared-for dog. Three men in their twenties, who had been standing off to the side, barrel over to the empty table; one of them knocks into my chair. Another sets his beer mug down with a loud thunk, as if he were claiming the table for his country, and shouts, "Score!"

Kevin leans forward and does his best jock imitation, just loudly enough so that only we three can hear it: *"Score!"*

Meg tells us about a special on birds that she saw on public television. The lyrebird, she informs us, perfectly imitates everything it hears, including other birds and animals, but also car alarms and chainsaws. I think that I knew that once but forgot it. It seems like one of those things.

Steve says, "I heard a story on public radio the other day. . . ." His face brightens, and he smiles, and I notice that there's a small piece of food stuck between his two front teeth. The skin of a peanut? You'd think a dentist would be more sensitive to food between his teeth. "Aren't we clever, my wife and I? Public television, public radio?" He reaches over and squeezes Meg's hand, the brown morsel gleaming wetly as he smiles. "Anyway, a woman in Oklahoma is divorcing her husband and she's using her parrot as a witness in court. Apparently she found out her husband had been having an affair when the bird started saying, 'Be patient, honey, I'm going to divorce her. Be patient, honey, I'm going to divorce her.' "

And that's the moment when I can't take it anymore. I feel suddenly like the air has been vacuum-sucked out of my lungs; the sounds of the bar close in on me, pour into my ears with a painful, underwater pressure; the crowd of bodies feels like it's bearing down on me, pressing against my chest, my back, my limbs.

"I'll be right back," I say, standing up. "I have to use the ladies'."

"I'll come with you," Meg says, and she's up and next to me before I can stop her.

We make our way through the throng, Meg in front of me. We sidle between people, twisting and turning like dancers to the far back of the building. I concentrate on breathing, on not panicking. As we approach the bathroom, I pull Meg off her course and direct her toward the exit. "I need some air!" I have to shout it so that she can hear me. We finally push our way out and emerge into the cool, dark night.

I take a few deep breaths. The patio, jam-packed during the warm months but deserted now, curves along the side of the building. Meg and I sit in uncomfortable metal chairs at a wrought-iron table.

"Thanks," I say. "I felt like I couldn't breathe." I brace myself for her coming inquiry. She will have noticed something, the tension between Kevin and me, my strange, cold behavior.

"This is good," she agrees. Then, "God, I can't *stand* it."

"What?" I stare over her shoulder, beyond her, at the few headlights beaming through the dark side street. The night is sharp and chilly, and the light wind blows right through to my skin, wakes me up.

"Steve. He can't bear to see me sad, so he suffocates me instead." Meg leans her head back and her hair drapes behind her. When I was little, I used to pretend to have long straight blond hair: I'd put a yellow turtleneck on, stretching its neck across my forehead, and toss the shirt backward, over my own frizzed-out mop of brown hair, over my shoulders, flipping it and prancing in front of the mirror. Meg's soft veil of hair is the picture of the effect I was aiming for. She stretches her arms out to the sides, raises them above her head, brings them back down, her bracelets jangling. She straightens up, looks at me. "If he would just let me be miserable, I could get over it. I mean, I'm *getting* over it. But he's treating me like I'm a hothouse flower, and it's driving me nuts. Haven't you noticed?"

"No," I say, considering it. "Steve's always so devoted to you. To tell you the truth, it hasn't seemed unusual."

"Mmph," she snorts. "His devotion is a way of not understanding me! It's the easy way out!"

"Huh?"

"He reacts against my grief by being *solicitous*," she says, lingering, snakelike, on the *s*. "Whenever I'm down, he tries to jiggle me out of it, instead of dealing with me! He couldn't even stand it when I lost that last hand of hearts!"

"Like that would send you into a hormonal meltdown," I say.

"Exactly! And he'd be left with a puddle of me at his feet!"

"So, what's to be done? It's only because he loves you."

"That's why I feel like such a jerk," she concedes.

I've almost forgotten about my own problems. "Can you talk to him about it?" I ask.

"Sure," she says, sighing. "I guess. Only, this makes me wonder about the future of our marriage. What will it be like when something really awful happens, when my parents die or something . . ." She sighs again, and her gaze drifts. She seems to be letting go of the topic, relegating it to the emotional back burner, where you set the perennial, unsolvable problems on simmer. We're both quiet, enjoying being outside, close enough to our husbands, to the action inside the bar, but far enough away to feel like we've escaped for a while. "What about you?" she asks, coming back to herself. "What's going on with you and Kevin? Seems tense."

"You wouldn't believe," I say. Which part of this melodrama am I going to divulge? The last few weeks of my life are a collage of details, and I don't know which piece of it to offer up to her. "Tonight he told me that he's willing to wait for me to be ready to move to the suburbs and start a family, but that I shouldn't take too long."

"Jesus Christ," Meg says, her hand covering her mouth.

"And that, apparently, most women my age would be grateful to have such a family-minded man as Kevin."

Meg makes a sympathetic gurgling noise in her throat.

"And at his doctor's appointment next week," I say slowly, for dramatic effect, "he's going to get his sperm count tested. *Just to be sure.*"

"Oh, my God," Meg says, not moving her hand from in front of her mouth. It comes out muffled.

We stare at each other for a second. Then we both start to laugh. And it finally feels like the one proper response to all of this, to Kevin and his eager sperm; to David; to the fact that I almost kissed another man; to the way I seem to have messed everything up with my cheating heart and my reluctant uterus. "Oh," I say, trying to catch my breath, "Oh!"

Meg is snorting, the way she does, wiping her eyes. Then, just as we're starting to calm down, she says with a wheeze, *"Just to be sure!"* which sends us sliding back down into whoops of laughter.

I notice, in the midst of our hysterics, that a crew of guys, all wearing their baseball caps backward, has just exited the bar, a swell of noise and smoke emerging with them and hushing as the door closes behind them. They huddle near the wall, swaying a bit, like tipsy grizzly bears, looking over at us. After a few moments, Meg and I have finally slowed down enough that I can breathe again. My stomach muscles hurt, and I feel, without a doubt, better. I look over and see that the guys are focused on the spectacle we are surely making.

"Girls! Hey, girls!" one of them, in a Milwaukee Brewers cap, calls out. "What's so funny?"

Meg and I look at each other, in grave danger of falling into the well again. Her mouth twitches a little. I shake my head at her.

She rests the palms of her hands flat on the table. *"Sperm count!"* she shouts, and we're gone again. I can tell that they're intrigued, drunkenly interested in two women alone in the middle of a fit of out-of-control laughter, apparently struck down by the concept of semen. They probably think we'd be an easy score, thrilled as we are by a function of their anatomy. Plus, I've noticed, men tend to find it disconcerting when two women share a joke. They like the idea that we can let loose and have a good time, but they secretly suspect we're laughing at them. Which I suppose we usually are.

They approach en masse, five of them, bulky. "You ladies seem to be having an awfully good time," Yankees Cap says.

"Mind if we join you?" Plain Dirty Blue Cap asks, already pulling out the chair between us.

Meg stretches her arm in front of her, holds her hand up to stop them. "Sorry, boys, not tonight."

"Come on," Plain Dirty Blue Cap slurs, turning from Meg to me and back again. "Let us in on the joke."

"We're really happy," I say, "because we've both just completed the last round of hormone treatment for our gender reassignment procedures."

Meg says, "It's been a long haul, but we're finally free to live on the outside as the women we've always been on the *inside*." She tilts her head up at the hulk of bodies and smiles her best, irresistible flirting-Meg smile. The five boys back away as one. They don't believe us, or they wouldn't if they weren't drunk, but they're just sober enough to know when they're not wanted.

"Not bad," Meg says admiringly, after they've gone.

"Thanks," I say, suddenly remembering that Kevin and Steve are inside, waiting for us. I scrape my chair back from the table and stand up. These last few minutes have already begun to feel like a fever dream. Once again, I've avoided telling Meg about David, about the substance of my feelings. "Shall we reenter reality?"

Meg stands up, smooths her hair, wipes her hands down the sides of her shirt. "Such as it is," she says.

When we get home, I check my e-mail quickly while Kevin is in the bathroom. In my dark office, I can see my reflection in the computer screen as the machine whirrs to life. His name is in my in-box; with surreal clarity, my face is superimposed onto its letters. The subject heading is "Why not?"

> Okay,
> I'm game. Let's give it a try, the friendship thing.
> I have to do some research at the Museum on Friday.
> Do you want to meet me there? 2:00?
> —David

He's not giving me much; he might even sound a bit cold, unconvinced of the merits of a friendship with me. But it's enough. I want to write back, "Yes! Of course! Anything to see you again! Yes!" But, with composure I'm sure I will be proud of later, I just write:

Sure. See you then.
—Emily

Kevin calls out from the bathroom, our earlier tension mostly suppressed, "Any interesting e-mails?"

"Not a thing," I yell back, and shut down my computer. The sudden absence of the machine's low hum is the only evidence that, a moment ago, it made any noise at all.

THE MILWAUKEE PUBLIC MUSEUM IS NOT THE KIND OF PLACE that pulsates with activity, not the sort of establishment that is often full of people exclaiming over new exhibits, accidentally bumping into each other in the throes of lively learning. Downtown Milwaukee on the whole is a pretty vacant affair. Workers in business attire exit office buildings every so often, blinking like moles in the sunlight, but then, mostly, they're only walking to their cars. Today the museum is practically deserted. When I arrived ten minutes ago, four or five groups of children were boarding school buses outside. Now, the entrance plaza echoes like a tunnel.

I sit down at a plastic table near the coffee shop, my left thumbnail immediately fiddling with the skin around my right one. The atrium is bright and sunny. White light reflects off white tables and chairs, off polished, unscuffed floors. An elderly couple walk slowly past, leaning against each other. They look companionable, as if they've been making their way through life in exactly this way, together, supporting each other, for fifty years. Then I get a good look at them, and I see that the man has an angry scowl etched into his face, and the woman looks wispy and scared, her eyebrows unnaturally dark and high on her face.

What's it going to look like, this brand-new friendship? I want something. I just don't know what. I don't even know if it has anything to do with David Keller. I'm desperately open to the world, to anything new, to a taste, a sound, a sight—anything to file under *A* for "Alive" in the Emily Ross dictionary.

I feel a sudden, surprising pressure on the top of my head, and for a second I believe that the shaky old couple, who have disappeared behind me, must have mistaken my head for a tabletop or a ledge, that one of them is using me to keep from falling over. I turn, startled but cautious (since I don't want to be responsible for anyone's broken hip) to the sight of a man's upper torso in a dark blue shirt; I look up and see David Keller's broad shoulders, his unshaven face, his guarded smile. I notice that he's wearing glasses, which I haven't seen on him before; small round silver frames. Like a reflex, like my leg shooting out in front of me to the response of a doctor's tiny hammer, an elevator of lust rises and falls in my stomach.

"You are absolved," he says softly. He keeps his hand on my head for another second, then removes it. "I absolve you."

"Oh!" I say. "Okay! Sure!" I stand up, clumsily, and a flicker passes between us. Do we hug? Kiss each other on both cheeks, *mwah*? Do nothing? David shoves his hands into his pockets: decision made. We do nothing.

"So," I say. Once again, I'm unprepared, but I want to make amends, to admit something true. What I say next, I think with a certain self-conscious portentousness, will chart the course of what's to come. *I'm so sorry.* "I'm such a jerk," I say, and it sounds as inadequate as it feels. A stupid little involuntary smile inches up my face.

"It's okay," he says. "You screwed up. It's not the end of the world."

And there it is. He means it. I know he does. He's a good person, and he forgives me, probably not least because what we had wasn't very much, and it doesn't cause him pain; if it did at first give him a twinge, it doesn't anymore. He's over it. He's over me. These thoughts flash through my head as we stand there, facing each other, and what comes to rest, finally, inside me, is disappointment.

I cross my arms over my chest. We're still the only two people in the museum's entryway, but I notice, behind David, some people milling about the first-floor exhibit, others walking in and out of the gift shop. "I'm really glad you feel that way. I'm glad you still want to be my friend."

"Well, we'll see about that," he says. His voice is teasing, gentle, his smile doesn't fade, but his eyes are shadowy, impenetrable.

I look down at my shoes, worn-out blue Keds. They make me look like I'm about twelve years old, it suddenly strikes me. I bought them two springs ago, right after an ill-fated shopping trip with Meg. I'd been on a quest for a swimsuit and had ended up not only without one, but depressed and a little bit shocked about the state of my pale, winter-thickened body. I bought the shoes as a pick-me-up and understood for the first time the appeal of the purchase of footwear, something Meg had been trying to explain to me for years: you can gain ten pounds, but shoes always fit. I'm thinking about that April day and having my usual reaction to stress: my mind wants to flee the scene of the crime, to travel to strange and inaccessible places. *Come back. Say something.* I look at David. "Why are you here?" I ask. Oops. Not quite right. "I mean, what were you doing here?"

"I'm helping one of our reporters with some research," he says, "for an article on town planning in Milwaukee. I had an appointment with one of the curators." He is very serious, more formal than he's seemed to me before, less approachable. Well, naturally.

I suddenly feel like I should be home, working on something vastly important. Oh, yes, me, too; I myself am writing an article about challenges to the Constitution. *A think piece.*

"Oh," I say instead, looking back down at my shoes. This is going nowhere. My throat feels tight. I'm about to say that I've just remembered another appointment, something I have to do, somewhere I must be immediately, when he reaches over and touches my arm.

"Emily," he says with a little shrug. "I want to hang out with you." I meet his eyes again. He's smiling. This time the kindness in his voice has traveled up to his eyes, lightening them. "Should we explore?" he asks. I nod. We make our way over to the big map of the museum and stand, gazing at it. First floor, Peoples of the World, Our Living Oceans, and my favorite, the Streets of Old Milwaukee. Upstairs, the Butterfly Wing, Native American Pow-wow, and Aztec Market. The Milwaukee Public Museum has a charming, small-town, amateurish quality about it, which includes its excess of lifelike mannequins. Virtually all of the exhibits feature model people going about their papier-mâché business, as if history would be inscrutable without fake Guatemalan villagers selling plastic acorn squash. Which, come to think of it, it might be. At the Powwow, Native American mannequins revolve around on a giant lazy Susan, accompanied by tape-recorded drumming. On the Streets of Old Milwaukee, you wander around, peeking into shop windows where a mustachioed mannequin barber shaves his mannequin customer, a glass-eyed butcher hacks away at a bright orange sausage. If you've been here once, you've been here a thousand times. And I've been here a thousand times.

David leans in toward the map, squinting. "Peoples of the World," he says.

"Is that where you want to go?" I ask.

"Not necessarily. I just thought it said 'Beagles of the Wild.' Until I looked more closely."

"Beagles of the Wild," I say. "I've heard of them. Famously undomesticated breed. Known for stealing children and then licking them to within an inch of their lives."

"Not as savage as the wild golden retriever," he says, shaking his head.

"Really?"

"Oh, the puppies are the worst. They wield their cuteness as a weapon and can throttle you with their waggy tails."

"Their waggy tails?" I say, laughing.

David gives a grave, exaggerated nod. "How about the Streets of Old Milwaukee?"

"Good." We head toward the exhibit, down the quiet hallways, past Peoples of the World, past the Buffalo Hunt, a diorama of nineteenth-century Native Americans on horses, their spears held aloft, chasing frightened taxidermy buffalo. The exhibit is particularly surreal to me; I've been coming to this museum since I was a small child, and the scene has never changed: the stuffed buffalo are in a perennial state of terror, the hunters' expressions fierce but vaguely sad, too, as if they know they will never make their kill. On the edge of the exhibit, there is a small stand covered in real buffalo hide, which you can touch; the patch of fur has been rubbed almost bald, like a beloved teddy bear. It gives me the shivers now, this opportunity to touch the soft skin of something long dead.

David keeps his distance from me. I think of our walk by the lake, just a few weeks ago, but somehow seasons ago, eons ago. I think of the way we leaned toward each other then, the physical space between us a gap to be bridged. We were like two magnets drawn together, but I've altered the force field, and now we're pulled apart, repelled. I *feel* repellent, unbeautiful in the face of this change. I'm suddenly aware of every flaw: my frizzy hair, my short-waistedness, my ungroomed eyebrows. Being desired, like a makeover, had made me pretty. Its absence uglifies me.

We wander around the corner to the tunnel-like entrance of the Streets of Old Milwaukee. "I remember coming here as a kid," I say, absently trying to smooth my hair. "I was a little bit scared of this exhibit."

"It is dark," David agrees. "And there's some resemblance to a haunted house."

My memory of this place is fixed and sensory. The cobblestone streets, the working water pump, Olinger's Sausage Company and the knife-swinging mannequin butcher, it all washes over me like a strong scent. David strolls over to the butcher shop, with its grotesque hanging plastic animal carcasses. I peer into the candy shop two doors down, the jars of bright sweets gleaming. The cobblestones are bumpy beneath my feet.

"That was my niece, by the way," David says. It takes me a second to figure out what he's talking about, and then I remember, the little girl he was walking with outside Meg's school. The girl with the untied shoes.

I turn to face him and nod. "I wondered. Not that it was any of my business," I say.

"Yeah." I don't know if he's confirming that the little girl is his niece, or agreeing with me: yeah, none of my business.

"I was helping my friend," I say. "She's just getting back into teaching after a break, and she needed a hand. She teaches kindergarten," I add.

"Rachel's in first grade." I wait, peer intently back into the candy shop as if discovering something: oh, look, a fascinating nineteenth-century lollipop! David walks over to me and faces the glass, looks inside. I hear him exhale. He's next to me, close, but I don't look at him. "So," he says.

"So." Prices are handwritten in frilly script on the outsides of the jars. *Mints, one cent. Fudge, two cents.* We're alone on the Streets of Old Milwaukee. "There's no excuse for what I did," I say softly. I'm talking to the shiny glass window. My breath makes a cloud of fog on it, dissipating and reappearing. David doesn't answer. I finally turn to him. "I know you're over it, and I'm grateful for that, but I want you to know . . ." I trail off.

"I do," he says. "And I still like you."

Still likes me? Still likes me how? Stop it.

"I guess my marriage is sort of troubled at the moment." I feel sunken, admitting this. Flattened down like there's a weight pressing on my head.

"Troubled doesn't mean doomed," he says.

"No."

David clears his throat. "How about the butterflies?"

Huh? I smile as if I know what he's talking about. An obscure Zen reference to struggling marriages?

"How about we go see the Butterfly Wing?"

"Oh, sure." As we head toward the elevator, some of the space between us closes. I begin to relax into the day, into the actual, surprising friendship we just might make work. I feel grateful and happy. Being with David is starting to feel comfortable, practically like hanging out with Meg, I think. And I almost manage to convince myself of it.

A child's screech echoes from down one of the hallways, followed by a short silence and then tragic sobs. "When you're thinking about kids," I say to David, without really considering what I'm about to tell him, "about having them, or not having them, they're suddenly everywhere." The wailing gets louder as we walk, then slowly diminishes, the toddler Doppler effect.

David looks at me, surprised. "Really?" he says. "Is that something you're thinking about?"

"Oh," I say, my stomach suddenly tightening. He must think I'm a freakish collection of neurotic symptoms, first dating him, then confessing that I'm married, finally admitting to thoughts of childbearing. Lovely. There should be a wing for me in this museum, a mannequin Emily lounging in a replica of my apartment: Twenty-first-Century Psychological Mess. This species of American female was known for muddling her love life beyond repair. Fortunately, she did not reproduce. "Not really," I say. Backpedal! Backpedal! "I mean, no." Then I remember: we're trying to be friends. "It's one of the sore spots of my marriage," I admit.

"That must be rough," David says. I note that he makes no effort to offer advice or try to fix this problem, the way every other guy I've ever been friends with has done when confronted with some murky emotional detail, as if it's a busted carburetor. We're standing at the elevators now, waiting. "I went out with a woman for four years," he says, "and we ended it over that very issue." He looks at me, waiting for a clue that I want to hear the rest. I nod. "She wanted kids, and I wasn't ready."

"Maybe she just wasn't the right person," I say.

"Probably not."

The Butterfly Wing is the most crowded spot in the building. A small collection of people huddles around, waiting to enter the room full of live exotic butterflies. This may be an actual line. David and I take our place at the back of the group. To get in, you have to walk through one door, let it close behind you, then wait in a short hallway for a green light and a buzzer to allow you to go through the next door. This is so no butterflies escape. It makes me feel like I'm in butterfly prison.

The room itself is a sauna, a good twenty degrees warmer than the rest of the building, and so humid I begin sweating immediately. Steam pours in through the vents. I peel off my sweater and tie it around my waist.

One night last fall, Kevin and I attended a party at the home of our friends Rob and Karina. We spent most of the evening talking to Monica, a friend of theirs, an American who'd just returned home after a decade in Paris and was now a high school French teacher. Monica was funny and adorable, delicate and perfectly coiffed, of course, and she exuded a fish-out-of-water quality that made Kevin and me both want to take care of her. Monica and I sat on the couch, plates of hors d'oeuvres perched on our knees, and Kevin pulled a wooden kitchen chair in front of us. The three of us talked for hours, ignoring party etiquette, forgoing polite mingling in favor of this real connection we were making. Kevin's head swiveled back and forth between Monica and me. We got along so well, the three of us, I was certain a friendship match had been made. I imagined us meeting for Saturday morning coffees, strolling along the lakefront, going to obscure independent movies together and having stimulating arguments after. At midnight, as Kevin and I were walking the four blocks back to our apartment, he tipsily slung his arm around me and said, "If I'd met her before

I met you, I'd have wanted to date her." He was effusive and clueless, and he leaned into me, probably waiting for me to agree, to confirm my own affection for, even attraction to, Monica. We had both fallen a little bit in love with her.

That, of course, was not the point. I didn't talk to Kevin for the rest of the night and half of the next day. And the one time Monica called, a few days later, to ask us out for a drink, I told her we had other plans and that we'd call her again soon. We haven't seen her since.

Only, now, this is exactly what I understand about David, this simple fact. He fits into a closed room inside of me. The Butterfly Wing of my heart. After much ineptitude on my part, it's finally clear that nothing will happen between us, and that I'm obliged to slog through with Kevin. But if I'd met him before I met Kevin . . .

David is standing in the corner, intently reading about various species of butterflies, and I perch myself on a cement rock nearby, looking around at the flying creatures. In such profusion, these butterflies are strangely frightening. They don't just flutter around whimsically, they zip and zoom, like the flying insects they are; occasionally they seem to be aiming for my face.

This corner of the room is secluded, sheltered by hanging tropical plants and trees. Four young boys in brown Cub Scout uniforms, accompanied by two women who don't look old enough to be den mothers but must be, pass by. David comes over and sits down next to me; the fake rock is realistically slopey and uneven, so, as he sits on an incline, we're the same height. He points to an electric blue butterfly with black polka dots. "I think that's an Indian something-or-other," he says.

"Really? An Indian something-or-other. I don't believe I've ever heard of that kind."

"Well, I can tell you for sure those are monarchs," he says, pointing with his chin to a cluster of five of the only obvious kinds of butterflies here. I turn to him, roll my eyes. A drab brownish butterfly zooms past us. It looks like a moth interloper in this exotic world. It pauses midflight, then dive-bombs toward a mass of foliage. A large placard a foot away tells us that if we sit very still, butterflies may alight on us.

"I'm sitting here," I say, "and I'm hoping nothing lands on me."

"They're kind of like colorful bats," he agrees.

We sit in silence for a few minutes, watching them. I shoo one away from my nose with a shudder. Is this place benign or dangerous? David stares at a yellow butterfly poised motionless on a branch beside us, then turns to me, just looks at me and smiles. There's a trace of sweat on his upper lip.

Propelled by a combination of longing and recklessness, I lean toward him. Beautiful insects fly close to our faces. My eyes are open. I kiss him. After a second, he closes his eyes and kisses me back.

Here is how Kevin asked me to marry him: I had been editing a manuscript all day and was taking a break. I was sitting in the rocking chair, biting my cuticles, rocking back and forth, flicking through the TV channels, edgy. Kevin walked in from the kitchen, nibbling on a bagel.

I looked up and glared at him. "Could you please use a napkin for that?" I snipped. "I'm the one who ends up cleaning the crumbs off the floor. You don't even notice."

"You're in a good mood," he said, cupping his hand under the bagel.

"I hate my job. I hate editing. I hate testicles and semen and premature ejaculation and prostates! And the apartment's a mess! I had to throw out a ton of rotten vegetables this morning. They were expensive! Why don't we ever eat vegetables? Why don't you ever vacuum? I hate everything." It was a beautiful warm spring Saturday, and Meg had invited me to go to the park with her, to lie on a blanket and read trashy novels and eat potato chips. I had had to decline, in order to edit a lengthy, stultifying, practically unintelligible manuscript on erectile dysfunction in aging rabbits.

"You're a barrel of laughs," he said sulkily. "I do vacuum. And I cleaned the bathroom last week." He plopped down on the couch. I was about to say something even snottier about using a goddamn napkin, when he looked at me.

I stared back. "What?" I asked.

"Why don't we get married?" He leaned across the coffee table and took my left hand. He slid the gnawed bagel onto my ring finger. Crumbs scattered onto the table.

"Right," I said. "Yeah, *sure*." But my heart was pounding and I didn't take the bagel off my finger. Kevin and I had agreed a long time ago that we didn't need to get married. "We're great together the way we are," we would insist when some friend or family member would needle us. "Why mess with success? We don't need a religious ceremony to be happy."

"Marriage improves a relationship," people would tell us, usually newlywed people. "It deepens your commitment in ways you can't know about until you do it."

"They think they know better just because they're married," we would tell each other smugly. "They don't know us." But deep down, I always sort of suspected that they were right.

"I'm serious," he said now, adjusting the bagel. He wasn't letting go of my hand, the palm of which had begun to sweat profusely.

"Are you just saying this to make me feel better?" I asked.

"Well, do you?"

We got married six months later, in my parents' backyard, in front of twenty of our closest friends. We spent our honeymoon in Oregon, most of it at his parents' house—most of it, in fact, *with* his parents. We had been planning on going that summer anyway, and had already bought our tickets.

"Sweetheart," my mother said to me last night on the phone. I had been distractedly stirring a pot of pasta and trying to figure out what to put on top of the noodles when she called. All we had in the refrigerator was a jar of apricot jam, a container of milk, and an onion, and I was just trying to decide whether those three ingredients might make a roux.

"Mom," I answered. "We have nothing to eat here," I said. "I haven't eaten in weeks. I probably have rickets." I propped the phone on my shoulder.

"I was reading an article in *North Shore Lifestyle* about a Russian immigrant who had been a physicist in Russia," she said, cheerfully ignoring me. "And when he came here, he had to work in a *junkyard*. And now he owns the jewelry store next to your apartment building. Isn't that interesting? I always thought it was owned by a woman. Also . . ." She pauses, takes a breath. Most of my conversations with my mother have a certain ADHD quality to them. "Your brand of tampon is on sale at Osco, I noticed. Oh, come to think of it, maybe it's Heather's brand. Would you like to have lunch with me tomorrow, darling? I imagine you'll be very hungry."

My mother and I only meet at one place, her favorite faux-urban café, the Uptown Market. It's a little bistro on the edge of the North Shore suburbs, near the lake. Whenever I walk into the bustling restaurant, I imagine for a second that I might be somewhere else, somewhere funky and full of itself, where people drink trendy imported beer in the middle of the afternoon, but then I adjust to my surroundings and it becomes clear that the clientele is mostly young mothers with streaked blond hair, real estate agents, and the random businessman looking hungry and bewildered in the midst of it all. I spot my mother immediately: she's the only person here wearing a sequined denim dress. With her big gold earrings and chunky necklace, she sparkles in the sunny restaurant like a human disco ball.

Since Friday, all I've thought about is the kiss with David: the shudder that passes through me at regular intervals is sometimes a tingle of remembering it, sometimes a heave of nausea and self-hatred. Getting the mail, bicycling to work, shopping for groceries, that kiss has metamorphosed into a thin blanket and draped itself over me, a comfort and a burden simultaneously. There's no coming back from a decision to kiss someone who is not your husband. I may never see David Keller again; Kevin may never find out that I've slipped from him. But I'm somewhere else, somewhere outside my marriage, in a place where guilt and elation somehow coexist. It's where I live now.

My mom and I tend to spend our lunches together in companionable silence. After she's done excavating her warehouse of gossip, Barbara will cheerfully regale me with random details for as long as possible: a strappy new pair of shoes she's just bought; her latest idea for remodeling the den in shades of ecru; my dad's most recent sartorial abomination ("Last night he wore your old knit hat to bed, the one with the purple pom-poms. He says he can't afford to lose eighty percent of his body heat through his head"); some fact about my sister Heather's life that I undoubtedly already knew. When she's done, I'll provide her with a few safe tidbits about my own life: a new restaurant Kevin and I tried last weekend, the movie we rented, what Dick told me the other day about frog sperm. This will peter out after a few minutes, after which we'll both just eat our food and smile at each other. Occasionally, when one of us is moved to, we'll start another short but pleasant conversation until that topic, too, is clearly finished, like the obvious end of a pop song, and we'll turn back to our food.

It's never awkward; it's not even exactly boring. It's simply the relationship we've cultivated, my mother and I, and we are both completely aware of its contours: she loves me unconditionally and pays for lunch. I bask in that particular glow. We tell each other about how we've been passing our days. But I've never revealed my heart to her. The depths of my fears and desires I've always reserved for Meg and Kevin, the two people who understand and love me as Emily, not as a now-grown but still immature child. Only now, my ugly heart is private, and it's bursting in my chest.

For her part, my mother has never tried to usher me along the twists and turns of her private psychological trail. And the raging sixteen-year-old inside me doesn't want her to.

We're sitting at a tiny round table in the middle of the restaurant, the only one that was empty when we arrived. I'm blowing on a steaming-hot bowl of vegetarian chili, and my mother is mixing her Caesar salad with two forks.

"I hate it when they don't properly toss the salad!" she says adamantly.

"I hate that, too!" I say. She nods, pleased that I share her strong opinion, until she looks up at me.

"Didn't anyone ever teach you that it's not polite to mock your mother?" she asks. I shake my head sadly. She puts down the fork in her left hand, and skewers a piece of chicken with the fork in her right. "Em," she says, "I need to ask you something?" Her voice rises tentatively. My assertive mother doesn't even ask questions in a questioning tone of voice. When she ends a sentence as if she were a teenage girl in math class, I know something's up.

"Yeah," I say, against my better judgment. It comes out surly.

"It's probably none of my business." She chews slowly on a leaf of lettuce.

I resist the urge to say, "Then don't ask me." Instead I act like the thirty-year-old I am supposed to be. "It's okay," I say. "What is it?"

"You and Heather are the joys of my life," she says, nodding for emphasis. Oh my God, is she dying? "And I am not getting any younger."

I gulp my overpriced ginger ale; it barely makes it past the lump in my throat. "Are you sick?" I squeak.

"No, no, no, sweetheart, I'm fine," she says, too loudly. Her voice recalibrates to a whisper: "I just want grandchildren." She smiles at me, moist-eyed and a little bit embarrassed.

I'm holding my glass between my mouth and the table, unable to put it down, unable to lift it up. A wisp of steam from my chili wafts up between us.

"I want to know if you're planning on having a baby anytime soon," she continues. She's clearly rehearsed this. "I want you to have the joy of your life. And I don't want you to wait so long that it's too late."

I open my mouth to say something, although I have no idea what that will be, but she holds up her fork to stop me. "I'm not done," she says, gaining confidence. "I know that this is your business, yours and Kevin's. AND YOU KNOW THAT I DO NOT INTERFERE. But I'm worried. I. Am. Worried. Do you remember Carolyn Alt?"

Another daughter of one of my mother's friends, Carolyn is five years older than I am and lives in Berkeley. She studies bonobo chimps. I barely knew her growing up, since five years was an entire generation back then. Is this another famous Barbara Ross non sequitur? No such luck.

"Carolyn Alt has been trying to have a baby for four years," my mother says, still munching on her salad between her invasive exploratory surgical procedures into my private life. "But she cannot. She and her husband have just been through their fourth round of in vitro, and they can't afford to try anymore. They've used up their life savings. Also, Paul Mancuso and his wife, Renata, I don't know if you remember them; Paul was two years ahead of you and come to think of it, they didn't even live in our district; I think he went to Deerwood High School. He and Renata met in Los Angeles and got married last year and do you know, two months later Renata was told she had to have a hysterectomy—"

I sense that this is my cue—"hysterectomy," the magic word!—and if I don't stop her now, I'll still be sitting here in the Uptown Market in twelve years, listening to horror stories of infertility, too old to bother, too washed-up to care. "Mom." I shake my head at her. "Mom, I do appreciate this." I don't. But even in shock, I know some things about strategy. "I do. But you have to . . ." I want to say something about letting me live my life. "You have to . . ." I want to say something about trusting that I will make the right decisions, that she raised me to make the right decisions, that life is more complicated today than it was when she and my dad got married. "You . . ."

And then, just like that, my resolve is gone. It doesn't weaken or wilt or slowly abandon me. It's just gone. In its absence, I slump in my chair. I've lost my appetite. I swallow the dried spit that's collected in the back of my throat, and I look into my mother's brown eyes, my eyes, and I say, softly, "Kevin and I aren't doing too well." Then I lower my head, run my finger up and down the raised geometric pattern of the tablecloth. I concentrate on just breathing, prepared for the worst.

My mother is oddly unmoved by my announcement. She's still fiddling with her half-eaten salad. She doesn't say anything. For three long minutes, we're both just sitting there, fiddling. While my life burns.

"A person doesn't always end up in the situation she thought she would find herself in," she says finally. Her voice is thin and quiet; it travels to me under the din of the restaurant. She puts down her silverware with a clink and lays both hands out in front of her, palms flat, a certain inevitability, a *that's-that* quality to the gesture. "A young girl marries and expects perfection, despite what she sees around her. But, my darling, that is not how life works. And sometimes we are forced to make the best of what we have."

I can feel my adrenaline rising. My face gets hot. I take deep breaths through my nose; I feel like a bull, ready to charge. What does she know? Who does she think she is, my mother who is trapped in her car wreck of a marriage, paralyzed under tons of emotional steel and broken glass. Does she think she can offer me a dose of sound psychological advice? She can't even connect with my father in a meaningful way, and yet she can't leave. I see them! I'm their daughter, my DNA a concoction of equal parts Len and Barbara. I know!

But today she is bent on having her say, regardless of my pink face, my trembling fingers. "I believe that the passion one feels at the beginning of a relationship"—oh, please, don't let my mother have just said the word "passion"—"changes, later on, into the passion one feels for one's children." She's locked her gaze with mine and refuses to look away, probably so that I won't interrupt. "Do you know who you married?"

"Huh?"

"Sweetheart, do you know who you married? You married a kind, gentle, intelligent man who doesn't seem to place much value on the fine art of communication. Darling, you married your father. Perhaps you could have done better. But believe me, you could have done worse." She sighs.

Of course I married my father. Does she think this is a revelation to me? Only, here's the difference, Babs: Kevin may resemble Dad, but I am not you. I'm not paralyzed, a suburban insect frozen in the amber of her own newly decorated living room. Nope, that's not me.

I just can't do it, can't accept my mother's offer. I know what she wants from me; she wants me to reach for her from across the divide and admit that, yes, we both live here: we are proud pioneer women who must make our own happiness from within the harsh plains of our own imperfect marriages. But I won't do it. "If Kevin is Dad," I say lightly, "then we *definitely* shouldn't be having children." I wipe my mouth with my napkin. "Do you want dessert or something?" Before she can answer, I push my chair away from the table and make my way to the pastry counter, in search of something sweet.

"HEY, BABE-A-LICIOUS AND MR. LICIOUS!" HEATHER SOUNDS like she's shouting into a megaphone on our answering machine. "Tell the maid to fluff up my pillows and make sure there's plenty of whiskey in the liquor cabinet. I'm a-comin' home for Thanksgiving!"

Ever since my mother and I had lunch together and she served up her all-you-can-eat buffet of cautionary tales—age-related infertility, emergency hysterectomies, and other tales of childless woe—I've been thinking: what exactly will I leave behind? Will the genetic buck really stop here, with me? In deciding not to have children, I must surely be breaking some serious biological rules. I wonder if I even have the right not to reproduce. Here I am, the living by-product of generations of jealously guarded DNA, thick ancestral lines of beloved children brought up with tenderness and care so that they would survive to adulthood in order to have more babies . . . and I, Emily Ross, have the gall to say, "That's the end of that"? Because of me, the big quilt of our family, the shimmery, gossamer threads of history interwoven with the bright yarn of the Ross family, that's just going to unravel, blow away in gorgeous, impermanent wisps, until there's no more solid flesh, until there's nothing left of us but air? Because I say so?

Well, there's Heather, of course. I suppose I could count on her to reproduce. But I've never been able to count on much with Heather. We're two years apart, but there are a thousand miles between us.

As soon as she graduated from high school (while I was about to start my junior year in Madison as a serious, studious English-literature major), Heather fled to Minneapolis. Ostensibly, this was so that she could attend the University of Minnesota, but she only lasted three semesters. She's smarter than I am, but she's a dilettante; her most consistent lifelong pursuit has always been boys. As soon as she dropped out of college, she moved in with her first in a long series of what Kevin and I call the TIBs, the Totally Inappropriate Boyfriends. "Heather has a new TIB," I'll tell him, or, "That TIB didn't last long." Her first live-in TIB, when she was just nineteen, was Bill, a twenty-eight-year-old slacker/punk who, I'm pretty sure, hit her. She never confessed, but when she came home for a weekend visit in October, she had a nasty bruise on her cheek from, she said, walking into a wall. My parents drove to Minneapolis a week later and helped her move out. Bill the slacker/punk was definitely the worst of the TIBs; after him, they've mostly been harmless, usually nice guys, and Heather's always the one who calls it quits. She told her mechanic boyfriend that she couldn't be with someone who didn't have a more intellectual job, and then she hooked up with a lawyer. Six months later, she broke it off with him because, she said, "he walked around with his big lawyer head up his big lawyer ass."

I love Heather, and we go through periods of relative closeness, by which I mean we talk on the phone once a week. But then one of us does something: I make an (accidentally) condescending remark about her (incredibly) irresponsible choices, or she calls me stodgy, boring, criminally analytical, and then one of us storms off, figuratively, in a huff. That's the problem with sisters, or at least with Heather and me: we think we have every right to judge each other's life. Even as we're doing it, we both know we're just trying to make our own choices feel like better ones, and it back-fires every time. After a few months we always come back together. (Although once it took us an entire year, after a particularly nasty screaming match. It began as an argument about whose turn it was to drive to Chicago to pick up Aunt Mimi for our dad's sixtieth birthday party, but it diverged and hit its ugly nadir when Heather admitted that every time Kevin started talking she fantasized that she was somewhere else, and I told her that I was fantasizing right at that moment that she was a normal adult with an actual job and a boyfriend she'd been dating for more than two weeks.) Our relationship is four parts thick sibling love, and one part volatile, fundamental, often deliberate lack of understanding.

People say that Heather and I look alike, but this is what I think: I've seen photographic experiments where the right and left sides of a person's face are halved and then digitally recombined, so that there are two pictures of the same person, one a combination of the two right sides of the face, the other a combination of the two left sides. One photograph is always subtly but significantly more attractive than the other, because, it seems, our faces are asymmetrical and actually quite disparate. This is Heather and me. Heather is the pretty right side, with her straight nose and her brilliant smile. Even her hair, although as dark and curly as mine, is somehow smooth and orderly, falling in Botticelli ringlets to just below her shoulders. I, of course, am the left side—on a good day, I look interesting. Heather gets by on her looks in a way I never could, even if I wanted to. And who knows? Maybe I would want to.

Heather's current boyfriend is the least Totally Inappropriate of all the TIBs. He's a TAB. Sam is her age, twenty-eight. He formed his own Internet start-up company when he was just out of college. It was supposed to be a virtual community for political liberals, a place for all varieties of left-leaning Web surfers to come together and brainstorm about changing the world. The problem was, he called it "e-ville." E-ville. Poor Sam. It's all in the execution. Instead of the peacenik Web surfers he'd hoped for, e-ville attracted all manner of devil-worshipping loonies and Goth ne'er-do-wells. The company went bust three years before the rest of the Internet economy collapsed. Which, in the end, was a good thing for Sam: he found a new job before his geeky, ambitious competition hit the pavement. Now he's the computer guy at a big Minneapolis nonprofit environmental agency. I've never met him, but he sounds great, and he loves Heather. They moved in together in June. She'll probably sabotage it within the next six months. She tends to cheat on the really nice guys.

Come to think of it, maybe our genetic code *should* just quietly sputter to a halt, like the used, rusty 1985 green Ford Escort we shared in high school: useful enough for short trips, but not so reliable in the long run.

"Heather is definitely coming home for Thanksgiving," I tell Kevin as we wander around the empty rooms of an ugly house in an ugly subdivision ten long miles from our apartment. If it's Sunday, this must be a split-level. Suffused with guilt, I readily agreed to accompany Kevin on today's housing safari. Last Friday, while I was kissing another man, Kevin was busily arranging appointments with Tom Lindermeyer, friendly real estate agent with Glenbrook Homes.

"Heather?" Kevin asks, unconcerned. "That's nice." He knows Heather's visit means both that she will stay with us for a night or two, leaving a trail of wet towels and dirty dishes in her wake, and that my sister and I will probably have a big fight. But he likes Heather; he likes her spunkiness, and he doesn't know that she finds him boring. He's smitten by my sister, in a brother-in-law sort of way, and he's untroubled by our troubled relationship.

I flick the light switch in the kitchen on and off a few times, illuminating the green Formica countertops and dimming them; I watch, mesmerized, as they go from an unappetizing shade of lime to an equally revolting avocado, lime to avocado, light to dark, until Kevin pulls my hand away. Then I begin fiddling with the faucet, pretending to be interested in the water pressure. There must be an art to buying a house, but I've certainly never learned it. "Home equity" has always sounded to me like the idea that everyone should have a house. Vague ideas about property taxes and water heaters rattle around in my mind, bumping into each other like the big, colliding retro polka dots on the curtains that hang in the kitchen windows, but I have no idea what sorts of questions a person is supposed to ask when she is considering shackling herself to four walls and a roof for the next thirty years. Maybe, "Where's the escape hatch?"

"How old is the roof?" Kevin asks Tom Lindermeyer, who has been shadowing us like an eager puppy as we've traipsed around the eerily deserted rooms, a few remnants of another family's life, like the psychedelic curtains, still lingering in this empty house.

"Well," he says brightly, "that's a very good question. It's been here since the current owners moved in. So it's at least six years old. Could be just six, could be older! I can find out for you!" Tom Lindermeyer says everything like he's announcing a bargain over the loudspeaker at a discount store. "Attention, K-Mart shoppers! Plastic wrap is on sale for ninety-nine cents a roll in aisle seven! The floors underneath this brown all-weather carpeting are oak!"

"Oak, huh?" Kevin says, his interest piqued. He's a sucker for a nice wood floor.

I don't know what I'm doing here. It's my life's refrain. I don't know what I'm doing here, walking purposefully through somebody else's abandoned house and contemplating a thirty-year mortgage, half-listening to the cheerful yipping of the real estate agent. And I don't know what I'm doing *here,* with Kevin, my scrabbling, oblivious husband, when in my mind I'm still kissing David Keller.

His lips were as soft as I expected them to be, and just a little bit salty. David was surprised at first, and for a second those lips were slack, and I almost pulled away, mortified at my miscalculation, but after that momentary pause—if I ever wanted to tell myself that he kissed me first, to try to justify any of this, I would only have to remember that pause, that indelible, unarguable pause that declared, "You, Emily Ross, started this"—after that blink of an eye, David reacted; he kissed me, and I knew that he wanted to as much as I did, and we inched our bodies closer on the fake rocks, and we kept kissing. He put his arms around me, and I touched his face, his rough jaw; my fingers lightly grazed his neck. I breathed him in, and we kept kissing. I thought, *Oh,* and then he moved his tongue a little bit inside my mouth and then I thought, *I understand how it's supposed to be,* and we kissed some more, and then we stopped. David moved his head away from mine and put his hands on either side of my face and looked at me for a moment, and he said, "Oh, boy."

I said, "Oh, boy," back. My heart was thumping so hard I could hear the blood pounding behind my eardrums.

David got up then and took my hand, gently pulled me up beside him. "I should go," he said softly, and I didn't say anything back this time. We just walked hand in hand through the Butterfly Wing and out the dark hallway to the museum's exit. He kissed me right outside the door in the bright, surprising sunlight. It was as quick as a handshake, but he put his hand on my face again and said, "Bye, Emily," and then we went our separate ways.

"Is anybody in there?" Kevin asks. He's sidled up next to me and interrupted my reverie, and I feel my face grow hot. Luckily, it's dark in the foyer, where I hadn't even realized I'd wandered. Kevin slips a hand into the back pocket of my jeans and gives my butt a little squeeze, a gesture that takes me by surprise. Reserved and somewhat formal, Kevin doesn't usually act in public like we are two people who have sex in private. I still feel warm, but now some of the warmth is transferred over to my husband, which is both confusing and appropriate.

"I was daydreaming," I say. And then I lie, "Just trying to imagine what it would be like to live here," which, as I say it, is no longer a lie. There's a master bedroom upstairs and one other room painted Pepto-Bismol pink, which I imagine belonged to a six-

year-old girl named Danielle who probably aspired to be a balle-
rina or a mermaid. I superimpose a vision onto her, startling in its
vividness, its utter psychological distance from everything else I've
been feeling for the last few months: we live here, Kevin and I and
our own six-year-old girl. Her name is Norah and she's a tomboy;
she insisted we repaint the bedroom bright green and has filled it
with books about botany, and an ant farm, and her pet gerbil,
Leopold. Kevin is a little bit scared of Leopold, and we laugh about
that, and we laugh about our grubby, fearless girl and her affection
for worms and leaves and rodents.

"Me, too," Kevin says. "The kitchen is nice. But the whole
place isn't much bigger than our apartment, is it? And I don't trust
Tom Lindermeyer's answer about the roof," he adds in a whisper. I'm snapped back from reverie number two, in which we are
a happy family in our cozy house. I'm no longer kissing David
Keller; I'm no longer brushing my daughter's tangled, unruly hair.
I'm just here, in the dark foyer of somebody else's house, unbeliev-
ably scared, watching the walls close in around me.

LAST NIGHT, WHILE KEVIN WAS AT THE LIBRARY, I sent another e-mail to David Keller, asking if he'd like to see me. Asking if it would be all right if I went over to his place one night this week.

If I were on trial, now would be the moment that I would throw myself upon the mercy of the court. I knew exactly what I was doing last night, in my dark study, a stubby blue candle flickering beside me, the window open a crack so that the flame bobbed and quivered and tossed gaudy shadows around the room, and I was thrilled and horrified to be doing it. I have never invited myself over to a man's apartment: not when I was single, and certainly not since I've been with Kevin. I had to think, before I hit "send," I had to think, *This is it*. I knew what I was doing: I was quite possibly sentencing my marriage to death.

I love Kevin. Is it possible to do something so awful and so obviously wrong and so *deliberate,* and at the same time to feel heartbroken for the victim of your own crime? I think so: that's how I felt.

Another layer of my not-so-pretty self falls away: I felt sympathy for Kevin, pity, and piercing guilt, but that was nothing close to the way I felt for myself. Sparks of energy ran over my skin like squirrels across a telephone wire. I had invited myself over to David Keller's apartment to seduce him, to sleep with him, to consummate whatever strange, amazing, banal, glorious relationship we've found ourselves in.

So many voices echoed in my head before I finally sent the e-mail. It was a Greek chorus in there. I heard my mother: "Darling, the passion we feel for our spouse *changes* into the passion we feel for our children." Kevin: "We need to make an appointment with a mortgage broker. Do you have time on Wednesday? Bring last year's W-2." Meg: "I'll regret what I did with *Pay*-ter Yo-*han*-sen for *the rest of my life*!" Louise Aslanian, my former adviser: "Life is the petri dish for Art." Heather: "Go for it, sistah!" My father: "Did you realize that Marie Curie was Polish? I was not aware of this. Obviously, I was under the impression that she was French." And David. I heard David Keller among the clamor, and he was whispering, and his soft, one-syllable word hummed at a frequency below all the others, quieter, more persistent. And that one word was "yes."

But when the cacophony of competing voices and whispers finally quieted, what I heard in the end wasn't even a voice. It was my own heart: its familiar thump-thump, the rhythm of its stubborn desire. I listened to the steady beating of my heart and found it to be heightened, louder just then than it had been in years. That was what I heard. It was the sound that convinced me.

FOR SOME TIME NOW, I'VE BEEN WORKING ON A BOOK of poetry. It's a series of love poems to fish called *Sole Mates*. I'm trying to carve out a niche for myself as a writer of love poems to nonhumans. If amphibians had disposable income and marketing clout, I might be on to something. As it is, it keeps me amused. Next on the agenda will be a volume of romantic verse dedicated to a more varied cross section of marine life, tentatively titled *Sealed with a Kiss*. I've outlined the whole cycle. From marine animals, I'll most likely move on to the vegetable kingdom with *Tomato, My Tomato,* or possibly, if my poetic vision shifts toward the star-crossed, *Lettuce Be in Love*.

So I'm in the middle of "My God, What a Cod," when Meg walks into White's. In fact, I should be finishing up an editing assignment. I'm supposed to be proofreading *Hooray for Plate Tectonics!*, a fifth-grade science textbook for the children's-book publishers I freelance for (I did *Three Cheers for Photosynthesis!* last week), but I'm having more fun sorting out rhyme schemes and tweaking "When You're Feeling Crappie." I'm in the middle of struggling with the last verse of "Cod"—

So swim to me—quick!—you clever cod
I'll feast my eyes on your intriguing lips
I long to caress your scaly bod
Your fate: much more than fish and chips

(notes: does "scaly" have unromantic connotation? is last line too Borscht Belt?)

—and I don't notice Meg until she throws her arms around me from behind. I manage to surreptitiously shove my neon pink notebook under *Hooray for Plate Tectonics!* as she plants a kiss on the top of my head and sits down next to me. She looks sparkly; her cheeks are flushed.

"What's the good word?" I say. I hear myself spout this Len Rossism; as I grow older, it's just one of the many ways I find myself unwittingly channeling my parents. One day soon I'll be strolling around in the summertime in Bermuda shorts with black socks and dress shoes, greeting strangers with a hearty salute.

"The good word," Meg says, barely able to contain herself, "is 'pregnant.' The two good words are 'I'm pregnant.'"

"Meg!" I say, and I throw my arms around her and hug her tightly, and then I think, maybe you shouldn't hug a pregnant person too tightly, so I loosen my grip and say, "I'm so happy for you," and I mean it.

"I just found out this morning," she says. "I did the test first thing, before Steve woke up, and I started yelling from the bathroom, 'Steve, come quick! Two lines! Two lines!' and Steve thought I was having a nightmare about two lions, and he came running in, and he slipped on the bathroom rug and cracked his front tooth on the edge of the sink. Can you believe it?" Meg is out of breath, rushing her words together. She looks horrified and then laughs, and then looks horrified again. "He's at the dentist now." She clasps her hands together, as if she's praying. "He gets a discount from other dentists. Did you know that?" My best friend seems different to me. I recognize this as a cliché, but it's true. Her light brown eyes shine like bright amber, and her lovely skin is even clearer than usual. "Besides Steve, you're the only one who knows," she adds.

"How pregnant are you?" I ask. For some reason, Barbara Ross likes to say, "There's no such thing as a little bit pregnant!"

"About three minutes," Meg says. "Two weeks from conception, actually, which means I'm four weeks. They count a pregnancy as forty weeks, starting from your last period, instead of the actual thirty-eight weeks from conception. I guess the medical establishment thinks women aren't smart enough to know when they conceived. I know exactly when I got knocked up," she continues. "Down to the moment." She winks then, lewdly.

I want to ask her if she's worried, if her last miscarriage hovers over her, casting a shadow on her happiness. But she just seems delighted, unclouded. Any emotion untempered by pessimism worries me. For once, though, I manage to keep my mouth shut. "I'm so happy for you," I say again.

"Me, too," she says, and grabs my hand, squeezes it. "Auntie Emily. Can I tell you something?"

Auntie Emily? I picture myself as a thin spinster, my gray hair pulled back tightly in a bun. I clearly have no need to color my hair. My high white lacy shirt collar is tight and itchy around my neck. Men ignore me. Children fear me. I subsist on Lean Cuisines and Ritz crackers and live in a dark, furnished studio apartment with rust-colored carpeting. If only I hadn't ruined my marriage, the one good thing I managed to achieve in this life . . .

Meg continues, unaware of my fantasy. "I know this is going to sound crazy, but I think it's a girl. I had a dream two nights ago. I dreamed that a twelve-year-old girl with long brown hair and pretty lips came up to me and said, 'Hi, Mom, it's me. I'm fine.' I didn't even know I was pregnant yet! What do you think of that?" Meg's cheeks flush, but whether it's from mild embarrassment or just the heightened emotion of the moment, I can't tell.

"I think . . ." I don't exactly know what I think. All my fears of

abandonment by my best friend come flooding back to me, in spite
of my efforts to suppress them. They're mixed with unadulterated
worry for Meg, for the zygote she has already imagined as a
twelve-year-old. I take a deep breath and let my love for Meg rise
up in my chest, let all my hopes for her happiness wash over me; I
exhale. Life is delicate and fragile, and every breath is sort of a miracle, really, if you're inclined to think in those terms. Every rising
and falling of the chest is like faith, spontaneous trust in the next
breath, belief that it will not be your last, nor will the next one,
nor the one after that. You just keep breathing. It's almost divine, if
that's the way your thoughts run. Meg is pregnant, right now, and
maybe, if she's very lucky, she'll end up with a new person out of
it. I say, "I think *Yay!*" And I hug my friend tightly again.

We're midhug when I hear the screech. "Meg and Emily!
Ohmygosh, just like in college! Ohmygosh, You Guys Are TOO
CUTE! AREN'T THEY TOO CUTE?" The high-pitched hooting
is coming closer to us with every word, like a teakettle whistling,
or maybe, I see as I look up, more like peckish jackals scooting up
to nibble on an antelope's carcass. Meg and I disengage from our
hug and brace ourselves against the descent of Becky and Angie,
the two girls who lived across from us in Devlin Hall during our
freshman year of college. They were best friends, like Meg and
me, which seemed at first glance like enough of a commonality, so
we all hung out together for about fourteen seconds during freshman orientation week. Almost immediately, and simultaneously,
we realized that a friendship match had not been made, which bothered no one. We stayed friendly, and Becky and Angie remained an
important part of our lives, because from then on, they provided
excellent fodder. We defined ourselves by their reflection; we were
everything they were not. Sometimes, late at night, as we were drifting off to sleep, Meg or I would whisper, "Becky, do you have any
more hairspray? I'm all out, and my bangs are less than two feet
high," or "Angie, did you use the last of my Calvin Klein Obses-
sion? I can't go to the Kappa Kappa Kappa Kappa Kappa party
without spraying at least a quart of my signature scent!" And more

than once just the quickest imitation of one of Becky's or Angie's prodigious verbal tics disrupted a spat between Meg and me and sent us into gales of laughter. In a way, we owe them our enduring friendship. Of course they don't know that. I heard a few years ago that they had both moved back to Milwaukee.

"Hi-eeeee," Meg says, doing a perfect imitation, even after all these years. But the smile on her face is genuine; surprisingly, it is kind of nice to see them.

"*YouGUYS!*" Becky says. "Still together, just like us!" A cloud of sweet, expensive perfume hovers over them. "Of course, we're not Becky and Angie anymore," she continues, tilting her head dramatically and brandishing her left ring finger; Angie picks up the cue and does the same. "We're Becky and Tyler and Angie and Glenn! What about *youguys*? Are *youguys* married?"

"Not to each other!" Angie clarifies, and then she giggles, and it's the first time I've actually heard the sound "*tee hee!*" come out of a person's mouth.

I hold up my left hand and wiggle it, and Meg does the same. I'm wearing my wedding ring, for a change. But no diamond engagement ring shines for their approval on my finger. When we decided to get married, Kevin, ever practical, suggested that we take the two months' salary he would spend on a diamond and put it into a retirement fund instead. "An IRA is a better symbol of my love for you than a ring," he said then. "We're not like that. You don't even wear jewelry!" He was right. I didn't tell him then that in spite of my carefully honed cynicism on the subject, I *wanted* one of those silly diamonds. I notice Becky's and Angie's manicured nails, and my bitten, ragged ones. I quickly put my hands back in my lap.

"We are both totally married!" Meg says. "And I'm pregnant!"

I understand that this announcement probably just explodes from Meg's mouth unbidden, driven out of her lips by the force of her excitement. Still, what's she doing telling these two mynah birds? I look at her, furrow my eyebrows as discreetly as I can. She looks at me, then back at Becky and Angie, smiling.

They both scream so loudly that the entire coffee shop turns and looks at us. *"No way!"* Angie cheeps.

"That is so super!" Becky chirps.

They mean it, of course; the happy news of marriages and pregnancies is clearly their métier.

"I just had a baby boy six months ago," Angie says. She's rooting around in her oversized handbag, presumably for a photo.

"And I had a girl last December!" Quicker on the draw, Becky whips out her wallet and unfurls a series of photographs of a fat-cheeked little girl in varying stages of hair and tooth growth.

"She's beautiful," Meg says, and I nod. She is.

"Hannah," Becky says. "Thirty hours of labor and an emergency C-section!"

"And this is Glenn junior." Angie passes us a photograph of what may be the ugliest child I've ever seen, a wan, bald-headed, morose-looking creature who resembles a baby eagle more than a human. "He's my little charmer. Pushed him out in nineteen minutes and got a stage-three tear. Ripped almost all the way from front to back! Anyone want a piece of gum?"

Meg is still smiling, but her eyes register horror. I just shake my head and flash what I hope is my own smile, but it feels more like a grimace.

"So, when are you *due*?" Angie asks, as if Meg were a library book. Her sleek black hair and her tiny, pointy nose call to mind a friendly, curious rodent. Maybe a ferret. This image is much meaner than I feel; I banish it.

"July," Meg whispers.

"And what about you, Emily?" Becky asks. "Is there the pitter-patter of little feet in your house?" I shake my head. Who says these things, anyway? "Any plans for little ones?" she goes on, clueless, her big white teeth gleaming.

"Some day . . ." I say in what I hope is a mysterious and aloof tone, my voice drifting off. Actually, my husband is mercilessly haranguing me about this *very topic,* but I'm *super busy* these days, because I've decided to have an affair. "Probably not for a while." I look over at Meg again, hoping she'll have worked out a polite way of extricating us from this situation. But Meg is staring intensely at the duo, blinded, perhaps, by their tasteful tennis bracelets, and I get no sense that she's planning our escape. Maybe she's too busy imagining some version of her future.

"Where do *youguys* live?" Angie asks. She and Becky nod politely as we tell them: Kevin and I in our rented apartment, Meg and Steve in their bungalow in a less-than-desirable neighborhood. "Mmmhmmm," she says cheerfully, clearly unimpressed. "Becky and I are neighbors in Morgan Heights," she announces, leaning a little bit onto her tiptoes with the news. Morgan Heights is the wealthiest suburb in the metro area. She and Becky immediately launch into a catalogue of names from our shared past and where they all live—lots of people from Madison have apparently ended up in Milwaukee—and, to spice up the discussion, Angie offers a corresponding list of what they all paid for their homes. Angie, it seems, is a real estate agent. "I *was*," she emphasizes, "before Glenn junior came along."

Becky and Angie have seamlessly morphed from 1990s sorority queens into expensively dressed suburban matrons, slim and toned and encased in brightly colored cashmere coats. They both wear up-to-the-minute shoes, I notice, too—a sort of sneaker/pump hybrid that I heard Melissa-Katherine Parker-Samuels discussing on *Entertainment Today*. Did Becky and Angie plan for their lives to turn out this way? Did Angie meet Glenn and draw up a flowchart of his personality traits so that she was absolutely certain she'd end up in a huge house with a cleaning service twice a week? Did Becky stand in front of the mirror one day, carefully applying mascara and thinking, I'll go to business school to meet a man, and I'll get my MBA *and* my MRS? Or did it all just fall into their laps? Because I barely have the foresight to plan dinner. And it has always seemed to me that the smallest, most random choice in your life can lead you where you never thought you'd be.

"*Youguys*," Becky says. "We should totally have lunch some time." She says it so warmly, so sincerely, that I'm about to agree.

Just then, Angie catches a glimpse of *Hooray for Plate Tectonics!* on the table. "Neat!" she exclaims, reaching for it. Underneath *Hooray* is my pink notebook, on the front of which I've scribbled the title, *Sole Mates,* along with several earlier contenders, including *Marlin, My Darlin'; Loves and Fishes;* and *Salmon to Watch Over Me.* I've also drawn pictures of fish shaped like hearts, hearts shaped like fish, fish swimming in a pond of hearts, and fish kissing. Meg takes one look at the notebook and giggles; Becky and Angie glance at it and then at each other, and before I can stop her, Angie drops *Hooray for Plate Tectonics!* back on the table and grabs my notebook instead.

"That's just nothing," I say, my face hot. "I'm working on an editing project. That's just something I'm playing around with." I half–stand up and snatch it out of Angie's hands. "It's nothing." I stare at Becky, then Angie; I dare them to laugh at me. Meg I ignore, since she already is laughing at me.

I hastily drop the notebook back onto the table, where, as if it has free will and is out to spite me, it promptly flips open to a short verse I wrote a couple of months ago, while I was eating a tuna melt. For some reason, lost to me now, I scrawled this particular poem in large, purple block letters.

> Fish, my love for you sticks
> but are we meant to be?
> How I wonder, ponder, flounder
> But I fear our love is doomed,
> for I am scared of water,
> chicken of the sea

Becky and Angie stand there for a while, their heads cocked toward each other, staring at the poem, puzzled. Becky purses her lips as if she's about to ask a question but can't quite form the words. Angie's perfect eyebrows arch, then furrow. I try to reach for the notebook, but for a weird moment, I'm paralyzed. Meg claps her hand over her mouth, snorting with glee. The tips of my fingers feel itchy and prickly. I look from the notebook to Becky and Angie. Becky reaches up and smoothes a stray wisp of her subtly highlighted blond hair behind her ear. After a long pause, she says, not unkindly, "You were always so creative, Emily." She and Angie stand there for another endless minute. Nobody says anything. Meg's hand is still clamped over her mouth. Another snort escapes her.

"But there's no money in *that*," Angie finally adds, nodding in agreement with herself.

"Mmmhmmm," Becky concurs. They both look like they feel very sorry for me. I'm starting to feel very sorry for me. *Sole Mates*. Love poems to nonhumans. What was I thinking? I feel like that dream everyone has, where I'm walking down the hallway of my high school naked. I feel like all the choices I've ever made, right down to the carrot-bran muffin in front of me, have been wrong. Wrong, wrong, wrong, wrong, wrong. The muffin disgusts me. What was I thinking, ordering a carrot-bran muffin?

After they finally leave, half-decaf no-foam skim lattes in hand, Meg turns to me. "I'm going to mock you later," she says, giving my arm a little squeeze. "But right now I need to panic!" Meg won't really mock me later. She'll chide, maybe heckle. But in a nice, best-friend-who-believes-in-me kind of way. She reaches for my muffin and takes a huge bite. "Was there any frontal lobe activity in those two!?" She tears off another big chunk of muffin for when she's finished chewing this one. Meg is a nervous eater. "Am I going to turn into that?"

"Sweetie," I say. "It's going to take much more than a baby to lobotomize you." I push the muffin across to her. "Do you remember what they were like in college?" I say. "Just like that, only with bigger hair and baggier sweaters." I can calm Meg. I know that vapid, complacent motherhood is not her destiny. I can feed her reassuring bits of pastry and tell her honestly that she won't turn into anything she doesn't want to be. Her way is clear. Meg is solid. It's my own amorphous self I'm worried about right now.

"They were nice, though, weren't they?" Meg says. "I mean,

it's probably really complicated, once you have a kid. It might be easy to slip into that lifestyle." She looks around the coffee shop, then back at me. "You want the best for your child, and the next thing you know you've bought a house where it's safe and quiet and *all white,* and you're driving your six-month-old to his private baby algebra tutor in your Ford Explorer, to hell with the planet!"

"Meg," I say, patting her arm, "that's not how it's going to be. You'll make the right choices for this baby. You won't give in to the pressure to buy an SUV and vote Republican, because you don't give in to that kind of pressure now. You never have. You'll be a fantastic mother." Coffee-tinged acid rises up in my throat. Something has to give.

DAVID KELLER'S APARTMENT IS NOT WHAT I EXPECTED. But then, neither am I.

I came over straight from White's. I still can't believe I'm here. After forty-five minutes of comforting Meg, I told her that I had to go to work, which in fact was true. She left, full of muffin and reassured about her life. Then, coolly, I packed up my books and notebooks and slid them into my green backpack. I dabbed at my mouth with my napkin and carefully tidied up the table, wiping the crumbs into my palm. I was all movement. I was automated. I searched through my backpack for my cell phone, which I had, as usual, left at home. Undeterred, I thanked the surly girl behind the counter and walked steadily to the pay phone in the back of the store. I called David Keller. I knew his phone number by heart, knew the exact pattern my fingers would make on the keypad, even though I'd never actually dialed his number before. It was two-thirty. As the phone rang, I thought, *If he's not home, it's a sign. If he's not home, then this is not my destiny, and he is not the answer to my problems. If he's not home* . . . But of course he was home. I said, "Do you want to see me?" He said he did.

Saying, "I'm on my way," that was the moment my robotic calm turned into a shaky anxiousness. My heart started beating fast at that moment and it hasn't slowed. Next I called work. The phone felt strange and cold against my ear. I thought about how many germs public phones must harbor. I knew a girl in junior high, Katie Wu, whose mom used to carry alcohol wipes with her. She would scrub down public phones before she'd allow Katie to use them. Dick answered. It took him a moment to remember what to say. "Ahhh," he said, "Ahhh . . . *Male Reproduction*."

I told him I wasn't feeling well. "Stomach flu," I said, and I felt guilty, but less guilty than if I'd said I had a cold, because, really, my stomach was feeling awfully weird.

"I'm so sorry, my dear," Dick said. My scalp began to tingle. Dick told me to rest and to take care.

Then I called Kevin at work, praying his voice mail would pick up. It did. "Hey, it's two thirty," I said. "I'm heading to work now, but I forgot to tell you, Dick has an errand for me to do today, so I won't talk to you this afternoon, but I'll see you tonight." I did this so that Kevin wouldn't call me at work. My voice sounded perfectly normal to me as I left this message.

As I walked down the street to my car, I became aware of how often I was blinking. I started to feel as if I were blinking too frequently, and that people might notice and keep their children away from me. I felt as if I were very rapidly going crazy, just a heartbeat away from talking to parking meters. But I got into my car. I turned on the heat and the radio, and I took some deep breaths; everything was familiar, and I started to feel like myself again: a very not-normal sort of myself.

I drove through the city, obeyed the traffic signals, arrived, parallel parked as if I were going to buy shampoo. I pressed David Keller's apartment buzzer, and then I spent an interminable moment in the common hallway during which I carefully examined my reflection in the plate glass and noticed a hair growing out of my chin. David buzzed me through the front door before I could do anything about that, and I made my way up the flight of stairs and down the corridor to his apartment, number six.

And there he is. He's standing in the open doorway, dressed in a green T-shirt and jeans, smiling awkwardly. He looks as nervous as I feel. His hands are in his back pockets, elbows jutting out at strange angles, a pose that manages to look both practiced and ridiculous. He's barefoot. As I maneuver around him and walk through the door, he doesn't make a move to touch me, and I keep a good ten inches of space between us. All I can think about are bodies, his body, my body, the imminent collision of the two. All I can think about is heat. I can't look at his face; I can't make eye contact.

The front door leads directly into the living room, and for a minute I just stand there, taking it in: the apartment of my downfall, the den of my adultery. It smells a little bleachy. He takes my jacket, drapes it over a chair. I know as I look around that I will never forget a single detail of this place, not a lamp, not one sofa cushion. My hands are so slick with sweat I have to rub them surreptitiously up and down my jeans to dry them; my stomach is a carrot-bran knot. I can taste tinny nervousness in my mouth. I feel about as sexy as a garden slug.

The living room looks generic, devoid of personality. It's perfectly respectable, perfectly neat and tidy, but it looks like an apartment law offices might rent out to their summer interns. There are two black leather chairs and a black leather sofa placed artlessly around the central object, the large flat-screen television. Tastefully framed black-and-white photographs decorate the walls. The carpeting is off-white and very clean. There's a coffee table next to the couch; it's made out of chrome and glass. I think back to our first conversation, mine and David's, about the astrology behind personal home decorating styles. He told me he inherited his decorating inclinations from old roommates. I wonder who his former roommates were. Actuaries? Computer programmers? This is not what I pictured David Keller's home to look like. I imagined, in a vague, daydreamy way, that it would be as sexy as he is.

"So," he says. He moves a few steps closer to me, his hands still in his pockets. We're still maintaining a distance between us that would be recommended by the Centers for Disease Control and Prevention if one of us had smallpox.

"Um," I say. Clearly, today's events will not include scintillating conversation.

"I'm happy you called," he says. He shifts his weight from one foot to the other.

"Me, too," I say. I'm rooted to the floor. I look around the room, my eyes resting on the black halogen floor lamp. This could take all day.

But just then, just as I'm wondering how long I can stand here without moving before my legs finally grow numb and I collapse in a stiff, twitching heap on the floor, David Keller begins walking over to me. He's looking right at me, and he's smiling; he's moving toward me, this man, soon to be my *lover,* this strange, warm body in a green T-shirt, and my hands are shaking, and now he's close enough, finally, that I can smell him underneath the scent of soap, close enough that I can hear him breathe. He touches my shoulders, moves his hands slowly down to my wrists, steadies me. I lean into him, and he looks down at me, and I gasp suddenly, because it seems that I haven't been breathing for the past few seconds. He holds my hands for a moment and then he places them on his face, like we're playing statue. His skin underneath my fingertips is rough and not Kevin's; this is not Kevin's skin, not his face, and I am breaking apart, and then David kisses me, he kisses me back together, back into myself, and then he leads me into his bedroom.

For a long time we just stand there, at the foot of his bed, kissing. And for one brief instant, that frozen, crystallized fragment of time before the long dive into the water, I think, *Could this be enough? Could it stop here?*

But then. We're on his bed, he's undressing me, he is still not Kevin, not-Kevin, he's throwing his own clothes onto the floor and he's next to me, he's on top of me, every angle of him new and amazing, every touch specifically his, all the things I already know about him and everything I've yet to learn and every single thing I will never know reaching up through his body and landing on mine. His fingers are like fine, fine sandpaper against my skin, skin I never knew had so many nerve endings. Here we are, being carried off, swept away, pulled under, *it's all true.* He looks at me, whispers, *Are you sure?* and I am.

An earthquake is an awesome force of nature! What causes the earth to move under our feet? The answer is *energy.* Sometimes pieces of the earth's crust may break off when they are under enormous *stress.* This produces vibrations, or *seismic waves.* These waves radiate outward from the source of the earthquake, causing the earth to shake and quake, move and vibrate, tremble, shudder, and quiver.

An earthquake is nobody's *fault.* But many earthquakes occur along fault lines! What's a *fault?* A *fault* is a break in the earth's crust. There are three kinds of faults: normal, thrust, and strike-slip. Normal faults occur because of tension, thrusts happen as a result of compression, and strike-slips happen in response to either of those stresses: pulling or squeezing, tension or compression.

Even if there was recently an earthquake along a fault line, more are likely to follow.

Earthquakes can cause serious damage, sometimes in unpredictable ways.

"Emily," David says, watching me from the bed as I'm getting ready to leave, "I don't think I'm going to be able to get enough of you." And my whole body goes liquid, all my bones melt for a second and then harden again. I have my back to him; I'm buttoning my jeans, covering the body that, astoundingly, just a few minutes ago, was beneath him, next to him, on top of him. And I have to pause, midbutton, because my fingers have stopped taking orders from my brain; for a second, I don't even belong to myself. I know that what he said is true. We aren't going to be able to get enough of each other.

By sleeping with David, I've probably sealed the deal on utter chaos. I'm sure I have. I'm not some soap opera diva; I haven't forgotten Kevin, haven't repressed the part of this incredible event that is nothing but treachery. Still, I can't help but feel clear and strong and hopeful, and happier than I've felt in a long time. Possibly ever. Maybe that makes me a horrible person. Probably it does. But I turn, half dressed, smiling, and I see myself the way he sees me: I'm something amazing.

David was a new song on the radio, one that gets into your head, under your skin, and you don't even realize that your body is moving to the beat. He was a ripe mango, when all you've ever had before were mealy apples and watery, seedy, off-season oranges. He was electricity, when you've been squinting in the dark. A person can't help but compare. Honestly, was it the best sex I've ever had? Well, how much sex have I had? Not that much. But, yes.

"Don't worry," I say. "I'll be back." I say this in my best Arnold Schwarzenegger imitation, which I instantly regret, since a guttural Austrian accent is something of a mood killer. Although not for Maria Shriver, I guess. But David just keeps gazing at me from the bed, surrounded by rumpled dark blue sheets and scattered pillows. I'm momentarily taken aback by the tableau of it, the sordid vision of the naked man in repose, his face still flushed, the absence of me there next to him practically a palpable presence. It's a snapshot of sex, and the caption underneath reads, "Girl Deliberately Loses Track of Self, Commits Adultery." My chest tightens; I recognize this feeling as remorse, an even bigger mood killer than an Austrian accent. So I repress it, a skill I hadn't developed until recently.

The afternoon light has already faded, and even if my imaginary errand for Dick had caused me to work late, it's still time for me to go home.

Dressed now, I wait a minute for David to get out of bed and see me to the door, but for some reason he doesn't make a move to get up. And it doesn't seem quite right for me to go over to him and kiss him good-bye, somehow; it seems too affectionate, too familiar. I'm the tiniest bit disappointed that he's not walking me out, but he's probably just tired, or processing what has just occurred, and who can blame him for that? So I wave like a movie star, and then I turn and leave.

I barely manage to get the key in the door of the car. My hands have started to shake. Inside the car, my breathing suddenly seems fast and shallow, and my stomach starts to hurt. Maybe I really do have the flu. My skin has gone clammy and I've begun to sweat; I can't quite swallow. I feel like I'm on the verge of a panic attack. I pull down the visor and look at myself in the mirror: my hair is messier than usual; my face is a startling shade of gray. My lips are still swollen from kissing David. I crank up the heat, rake my fingers through my hair. I can't seem to catch my breath.

It's not as if I didn't think this through. But I guess I didn't think through: how a person feels when she's suddenly alone in her very warm car on the street in front of her lover's apartment after she's just had sex with him for the first time; how a person feels when for once she's done something, instead of always letting life do things to her, when she's acted on her cheating heart's desire, when she's finally, irrevocably Done It; how a person feels when she's only thirty and quite possibly having a heart attack. I grip the steering wheel and stare at my knuckles, at the blue veins on the backs of my hands. I have to concentrate on breathing.

My marriage is over. Or it's not: it will survive and be the kind of marriage I never thought I'd have, one with a huge lie like a crater at the center of it. Or I'll tell Kevin I slept with someone else and his heart will be smashed into tiny pieces, and he'll be the one to decide if our marriage survives or it doesn't. I roll down the window, but that doesn't let in enough air, so I throw open the door, lean out over the curb on Stowell Avenue, and swallow huge gulps of fresh air like I'm trying not to drown.

When I pull up in front of our apartment building, the familiar redbrick exterior smacks me in the face with the feeling it evokes, unbidden, of comfort and refuge. Cheaters don't deserve refuge; adulteresses aren't allowed comfort. I can't go inside. So I detour across the street to Meyer's Market, a fancy specialty grocery store. I'll buy a few things for dinner. I'll cook Kevin a nice dinner. If I cook for Kevin for the next month, will my debt to him be erased? How about if I do all his laundry, too, for the next forty years? I'm not that stupid. But I am that scared.

I slowly stroll up and down the aisles of Meyer's. The store is lush with overpriced produce and tempting displays of nine-dollar boxes of cookies. Jazz drifts softly through the aisles. Because it's right across the street, Kevin and I shop here almost every day, but since it's so expensive, we're never extravagant. We buy grapefruit, cheese, bread, yogurt, occasionally something from the deli for dinner if neither of us feels like cooking. But now, I take my time, pull jars and boxes from the shelves and examine them. If I like what I see, I place it carefully in my cart. I probably look like I'm savoring this shopping excursion. I doubt a casual observer would notice my trembling hands. I'm sure I don't look like a criminal who can't bear to take the perp walk back up to her apartment.

The store at 5:00 p.m. is crowded with women and young children. Strollers colonize the narrow aisles. An exasperated mother stands near the refrigerator section, her hands on her hips, and scolds, "Gwyneth Kate Metzger, if you don't get over here right now, I Am Leaving Without You," while Gwyneth Kate Metzger ignores the empty threat, gleefully rearranging cartons of soy milk. The line at the bakery counter is full of toddlers clamoring for cupcakes.

I don't mind the delay. I'm an anthropologist, observing these women—female humans, just like me—and their children. It swirls around me, warm and messy and colorful, this life I could have had. But I slammed the door on it. And now I'm alone in an expensive grocery store at the end of the day, shopping for food for the husband I've just cheated on. The music suddenly gets louder. Two women at the end of the canned goods aisle laugh. A small child in pink overalls bumps into my leg, looks up at me, smiles, then careens away.

It's only at the checkout counter, forty-five minutes later, that I realize what I'm about to take home: two cans of water chestnuts, a one-pound deli container of roasted red peppers, a box of bland-looking Scottish cookies in the shape of women drinking tea, a wet hunk of fresh mozzarella, two organic tomatoes, one jar of extra-spicy pineapple salsa, a can of chickpeas, and twelve dollars' worth of kalamata olives. It's too late to stash my shopping cart in a corner and turn tail and run. So I hand over my credit card and smile. The checkout girl scans my items and, I'm pretty sure, raises her eyebrow at me like I'm either insane or bulimic. *I'm a professional chef,* I think. *Prove that I'm not.*

Kevin is home when I get there. He looks the same: his fine blond hair is sticking up in strange places, as usual; his gray pants are too long. His pale, hairless chest is visible through the unbuttoned top of his shirt. I thought he might look different. A rush of affection for Kevin flows through me with such surprising force that for a second, I can't move. He smiles and waggles his fingers at me from the living room couch, where he's watching the news. There is a sudden, metallic taste in my mouth: if self-loathing had a flavor, this would be it. I take my shoes off, hang my coat up, take my time changing into sweatpants and a sweatshirt. I sniff the clothes I wore today for traces of an unfamiliar scent, then stuff them in the bottom of the hamper. Even though it's almost completely dark outside, Kevin hasn't turned on any lights or closed the blinds. I can see our neighbors in the apartment building next door. The

STILL LIFE WITH HUSBAND

couple on the east side of the second floor are eating dinner and watching TV. The single man in the apartment next to theirs is lifting weights, wearing a muscle shirt. Even from here, I can tell that he's red-faced and sweaty, most likely grunting from overexertion. He probably swigs protein drinks and eats raw eggs. I suddenly hate him. The single woman in the apartment below the beefy weightlifter's doesn't seem to be home yet. Her apartment is dark. I spy on this woman in particular as she's going about her business, moving around her apartment. She looks like she's my age. She goes to work in the mornings and comes home most evenings at around six, once in a while much later. I don't think she has a boyfriend. I never see anyone but her in the apartment. I wonder if she's lonely. She looks, at least from my window, serene.

"Em!" Kevin calls. "Come here, will you?" He's in the kitchen now. I hadn't even noticed that he'd gotten up from the couch.

I close the blinds slowly. "Coming!" I yell. Maybe the weightlifter only pumps iron to suppress his despair, and the single woman who looks so peaceful weeps silently into her cornflakes every morning. Maybe they're soul mates, but they've never seen each other, never bumped into each other at the mailboxes, never realized that destiny is just a flight of stairs away. I could set them up. I could make a big sign: HEY, WEIGHTLIFTER GUY AND SINGLE WOMAN! YOUR LONELY DAYS ARE OVER! I walk from window to window, carefully smoothing the blinds to block the light from the street below. I suddenly realize that I should have jumped into the shower as soon as I walked in the door, should have scrubbed my body from head to toe. I can still feel David's hands on me. What if I exude his raw, wrong scent? What if, like a dog, Kevin picks it up? I sense that I'm not thinking rationally. But for the millionth time today, my heart hammers in my chest.

"What is it?" I say to Kevin as I walk into the kitchen. He's standing with his back to the counter, leaning against it, my absurd culinary purchases arrayed next to the empty Meyer's grocery bag. He's tossing the can of water chestnuts up and catching it. His face registers confusion. If he has somehow psychically uncovered my deceit, it hits me that I will deny it. It flashes through my brain like fireworks: *Deny! Deny! Deny! No, no, no!* I suppose that in moments of crisis a person's true self shines forth. My true self is a coward. I'm already adopting a defensive posture. I cross my arms over my chest. "What's up?" I say again, more coldly than I mean to.

"What's the deal with the groceries?" he asks quietly. Slap—the can of water chestnuts lands in his palm. "Twelve dollars' worth of olives? Tea biscuits and spicy pineapple salsa?" Slap.

"I—" Shit. Shit, shit, shit, shit. It suddenly dawns on me where this is going.

"Is there something you want to tell me?" he asks in the same even tone. Sweet, transparent Kevin. Clueless Kevin. There's a trace of excitement on his face, and I can see that he's trying valiantly to mask it. I'm sunk with shame.

"No, oh, God, no. Kev. I honestly don't know what I was thinking, buying all this crap, but I'm not pregnant. There is no physical way I could be pregnant." Unless I became pregnant approximately three hours ago. "No way at all!" I repeat, my voice surprising me with its decibel level. I need Kevin to know this. "I was really tired at Meyer's, and I kind of spaced out. I guess I was preoccupied." This, at least, is not a lie. "So I ended up with all this crazy stuff." I try to laugh, but it comes out a sort of whinny. "I mean, it's a good thing we both like olives, huh?"

Kevin doesn't laugh with me. He presses his thin lips together into hard white lines. His shoulders hunch. In the dim light of the kitchen, his blond hair is almost translucent, like a baby's. He looks like a disappointed Muppet. The image of David Keller's face appears for a second, superimposes itself on my husband's. I turn toward the groceries, away from him, so that he can't see my face. *Kevin, say something,* I think. I turn back to him as he places the can of water chestnuts down gently on the counter, picks up the box of Scottish cookies, and returns to the living room couch.

· · ·

Later that night, Kevin emerges from his office, blinking. He retreated there after dinner, mumbling something about instructions for a food processor. Kevin takes work home sometimes, but I know that he finished this project days ago. (He told me how he struggled, as he always does, with the cautionary phrases: Beware of sharp blade? Blade is sharp and dangerous? Keep fingers away from blade? Don't touch the blade, idiot?) But I didn't argue with him. Instead I took my time doing the dishes, and then I spent the rest of the evening aimlessly channel surfing, replaying the day's events over and over in my head. Again and again, I recalled the rhythm of David's breathing, the weight of his body, and I had to close my eyes. I wonder if he's thinking about me.

"What, um . . ." Kevin looks around, disoriented, scratches his head. He always does this, takes a few minutes to shift from his computer to his life, from his brain to me. I've always found it endearing, and right now it makes him seem even more innocent and vulnerable than it usually does, as fragile as a baby bird. I hate myself. I press the mute button on the remote control but keep the TV on. I look at him and wait. "What kind of errand were you doing today?" he asks, finally.

"I told you, I zoned out in the store. I'm really sorry I came home with that ridiculous bag of groceries."

"No, Emily," he says with a sigh. "I don't care about that. I mean, what kind of errand were you doing for Dick today?"

In a better mood, Kevin likes to refer to both my boss and the actual journal as "Dick." I had forgotten the lie I concocted about that errand. I rub my eyes, trying to think fast, covering for myself by acting tired and confused, pretending I'm still oddly spacey. "Oh, right." What kind of errand was I doing? What kind of errand was I doing? I let the remote control fall from my hand to buy myself another moment, then I bend and retrieve it. My mouth is dry. What the hell kind of errand was I doing? "Dick wanted me to drop off a manuscript with one of the reviewers across town," I say, straightening in the chair. This is something I have had to do on occasion; local scientists at the Medical College or Marquette or the infertility clinic on the west side of town often review papers for *Male Reproduction*. It's more than plausible! I'm relieved, so I keep going. "Then he had me wait while the reviewer read it and made his comments." I flash what I hope is a little smile. "I had to wait in this guy's office for an hour!" I scratch my wrist with the remote control. "He had a fish tank," I add, inexplicably.

"Oh," Kevin says. "Because I called you at work before I got your message, and Dick said you'd called in sick." He takes off his glasses, looks at them, and puts them back on. "I was worried. I almost came home."

My first thought is, *You heard I was sick and you* almost *came home? Shouldn't you have just* come home? Then I realize, of course, that I wasn't sick. "Well, you know, Dick isn't playing with a full deck these days," I say. "He obviously got confused. I think one of the secretaries was sick today. I'm glad you didn't leave work for me."

"Yeah," Kevin says. He stares at me for what feels like a long time, then turns and heads back into his office, where he'll likely stay until after I'm in bed. If I didn't know my husband to be both blinkered and supremely trusting, I'd say he looked unconvinced.

poor little eel
lonely and blue
looking for love
simple and true.
searching the deep
for affection uncheap,
she placed her bid
on a fine friendly squid
and could finally rest
in his comfortable nest;
lonely no longer,
the grateful young conger
swam gladly amid
her fine friendly squid.
so why, one would wonder
was she destined to wander?
as if on a whim
determined to swim
away from his pleasing, eight-armed embrace
back into the ocean's competitive race.
was it adventuresome, eely abandon
that caused her to search for a different companion?
she found nothing more than a fisherman's net
poor eel, swimming blindly
in a sea of regret

I'm conducting an affair. I'm standing in front of the high school orchestra that is my life, waving my hands madly, trying to get the oboes to stay on key, the trombones to come in on cue, the cymbal players to quit horsing around. Everything is out of control. But if I close my eyes, it's music I hear.

It's Saturday afternoon, and Kevin is at an all-day Hasting seminar on warranties. "We have to stay up to speed on federal regulations," he said to me this morning, dabbing at a tiny dribble of milk from his cereal that was running down his chin. "There'll be an attorney there. And lunch!"

"Have fun," I said. I walked Kevin to the door in my ratty pink slippers and old bathrobe and handed him a bottle of water and his glasses. He kissed me on the cheek. I watched him as he walked happily down the hallway. "Don't work too hard!" I called out, his footsteps echoing down the stairs. That was three hours ago.

Now, David pulls up in front of my apartment building, sees me, and waves. In the week since we've slept together, this will be our first public outing. I feel bold and reckless. I spring up from the bench where I've been waiting for him and blow him an extravagant kiss. I'm wearing sunglasses. My hair is held back in a bright blue scarf. I could be anyone.

Just before I came outside, I scribbled "Out for a walk" on a scrap of paper and left it in the middle of the kitchen table, on the off chance Kevin would come back early. "Home soon," I wrote, and the word "home" looked strange and skewed to me, bumpy and distorted, all its connotations of warmth and honesty spiraling away in light of what I was doing. But I didn't feel guilty. I felt thrilled.

I slide into David's little white car and brace myself for a wet greeting. Brian the dog, too big for the tiny backseat, wags his tail so hard it thumps against the rear windshield. He licks my hand lovingly, although I've never met him before. David's friend Roger broke his leg recently, so today we're taking Roger's greyhound to a dog park. David drapes one arm around me and squeezes my shoulder. There is never a time when I don't want this man.

"Hi, boys," I say. Brian shoves his snout into my neck and sniffs me. I pat him on his head, which is disturbingly slim. David turns to me and smiles, and I think my heart actually stops for a second.

"He likes you," David says.

"Oh!" I say, suddenly embarrassed.

David turns back to the steering wheel, still smiling. "Smart dog."

I click my seatbelt. "Smart, huh? Isn't this the dog who once ate a dirty diaper?"

"Well, true," David agrees, merging into the traffic of our busy street. "So maybe 'smart' is too strong. But he's clearly a good judge of character." Brian is nuzzling my face now, breathing his foul dog breath directly up my nose.

"Cats are more discerning," I say, scratching behind the dog's soft, floppy ear. "I respect that. Dogs are sluts. Aren't you a slut? Aren't you? Hmm?" Brian licks my cheek.

"I had goldfish growing up," David says. "Now there's a discriminating pet. You can't buy their love."

"Goldfish?" I say, as the dog tries to climb from the backseat onto my lap. "Just goldfish? That's tragic. Were you raised in an orphanage?"

"Did I forget to tell you that my last name is actually Copperfield?" With his right arm, David gently eases Brian's front legs off me.

"Poor little foundling."

He glances at me, then reaches over and tucks a loose curl behind my ear. I consider suggesting that we find a motel. There is an easy closeness between us that somehow coexists with the sharpness of desire, and I have the sense for a moment, as we speed toward the park, that I am flying. I have never felt this way about anyone.

The exurban hinterland of New Germany (pronounced, inexplicably, with a hard *G*) is twenty minutes outside the city. When we turn down the back road toward the dog park, Brian starts barking and turning around in awkward circles, his nose twitching furiously.

"Why is this dog named Brian?" I ask.

"It's Roger's older brother's name." David veers into the gravel lot and pulls into a space. "He thought it would be funny."

"It is, in a weird way." David holds the dog by the collar as I unhitch the fence into the park, then he lets go. Brian barks again and then takes off, faster than I had expected. For the first time, it clicks with me that greyhounds are racing dogs. I've never been to a dog park. Do most dogs stick close to their owners, like shy toddlers? Are there rules about this kind of thing? "Should we go after him?" I ask.

David reaches for my hand. "He's getting away! Quick, do you think you can catch him?" In a flash, the canine lightning bolt is thirty yards from us and gaining. David leans into me, his shoulder against mine. "It's a dog park. They run free."

The day is bright and breezy, almost cold. We meander across the hard dirt ground toward a picnic table. We're in a small clearing; there are wild, branch-covered paths and reedy bogs all around—dog paradise. The park is crowded with hearty-looking pet owners, young couples, families with small children, single guys circling the perimeter. A symphony of variously pitched barking rings out. Two middle-aged women stroll nearby, discussing recipes for homemade liver treats. "Sneezer loves the liver brownies," one says, "with beef hearts and just a touch of cumin. He prefers beef liver to chicken, but Olaf's not as picky!"

David sits down on the bench and pulls me onto his lap. "Mmm, liver brownies," he murmurs into my neck. "Beef hearts."

"Oh, baby, don't stop," I whisper, and we kiss, just gently, the continuation of a joke. But then, David's hands are working my scarf loose from my hair, and my hands are moving under his shirt, my fingernails on his back. We make out for a while, frenzied as fifteen-year-olds, and I wonder, fleetingly, if my chin will be chapped from his stubble, and how I will explain that away. I can feel the hard muscles and the heat of his legs against mine. His back is smooth. My hands travel downward and come to rest just above the waist of his jeans, and we kiss and kiss. Just as things are veering toward inappropriate for a public place, we stop, pull away.

"Whew," David says, out of breath, handing me my scarf. I push my hair back from my face.

"Young love," someone says. I glance around, terrified. I was sure we were safe here, certain I wouldn't know anyone at the dog park, as far away from my life as a Christian rock concert, a rodeo. For a second, I'm almost paralyzed. But it's just one of the liver brownies ladies, eyes fixed on us, amused. I hadn't realized they had planted themselves at a nearby picnic table. David turns to them, unembarrassed, and smiles. I slide inelegantly off his lap.

"Where's your friend?" the other lady, the one with a pouf of teased hair, asks pleasantly.

"Our friend?" David says.

"Your canine companion," the brownie baker says, laughing. "Did you forget who you came here with?"

"Brian!" I say, startled. "Where is he?"

"Brian!" David calls, standing. "Brian?"

Just then, Brian comes bursting out of the underbrush like a bullet, a slightly overweight yellow lab trailing behind him.

"Oh, look!" Teased Hair says, clapping her hands together. "My Anastasia's found a friend!"

"How wonderful," Liver Brownie exclaims, and then, to us, confessionally, "Anastasia can be a bit shy."

"And insecure," Teased Hair says. "She has some body image issues."

David looks at me, his eyes wide. I nod at the ladies. Well, why not? Anastasia and Brian romp and play, taking turns chewing on a stick and barking at each other. The ladies are laughing and delighted, and I feel tugged into this happy story, this innocent dog park friendship: the shy girl meets the dumb jock and, against all odds, they grow close. "Good boy, Brian!" He's so sociable!

And nonjudgmental! He has hidden depths. I'm suddenly as proud as a parent.

Just then, as if on cue, Brian climbs on top of poor, unsuspecting Anastasia, who lets out a surprised, high-pitched yelp. Teased Hair yelps identically. "Ope!" she cries. "Ope! Oh, no! No, no, no! Bad dog! Bad *dogs*!" She claps her hands together again, this time in distress. Her friend looks at us accusingly.

"Um, Brian?" David calls. "Hey, guy! Um, hey?" But he's starting to laugh, and the "hey" gets caught in his throat. "Hey?" he tries again, as Brian and Anastasia continue their lewd business.

"Anastasia Althea!" Teased Hair scolds with surprising force, but even she seems to realize that this is a losing battle.

David has, by now, sat back down next to me, his face buried in his hands, his whole body shaking with laughter. "Oh, God," he murmurs from behind his hands. "I can't look!"

"Oh," I tell him quietly, "you really should." The dogs are humping, the liver ladies are glowering at us—helplessly, disapprovingly, our oversexed behavior of a few moments ago clearly now being cast in a new and sleazy light.

Brian and Anastasia finish. Brian stands next to her, sniffs the ground, nonchalant. Anastasia barks. David, peering out from behind his fingers, whispers, "Too bad we don't have any cigarettes."

"Too easy," I say. "This is like shooting fish in a barrel."

The liver ladies stand and glare at us some more. "Anastasia Althea," Teased Hair yells, *"Come!"* An odd choking noise comes out of David's throat and he turns quickly away from them; he's laughing so hard, tears are rolling down his face. The ladies clip Anastasia's leash to her collar a bit roughly, it seems to me, and they drag her away, possibly to some kind of dog convent; Brian bounds over to us happily and flops down at our feet. I imagine Anastasia mouthing, *"Call me!"*

It hardly seems possible to feel this loose and free and happy; hardly possible, under the circumstances, to be laughing at anything. It is duplicitous, unforgivable, practically sinister to be creating shared memories and inside jokes with a man who is not my husband, and the Emily I thought I was would feel, at the very least, troubled by this—if not consumed by guilt, then at least distracted by a vague tightness in the chest. But here we are, at the dog park, David and I, next to each other, tired from kissing and laughing, and I'm free from the anxiety that should be holding me down; I am untethered. I drop my head onto David's shoulder and rest it there. For what feels like a very long time, neither of us moves.

EVERY NIGHT I SIT AT MY COMPUTER, AND DAVID AND I WRITE to each other, some nights for hours at a time. I told Kevin I've been proofreading manuscripts for *Male Reproduction*. October has been a productive month at the journal, I told him. Autumn is a notoriously busy season for the study of flaccid monkey penises, I told him. I keep a stack of papers next to my computer, in case he walks in. If he can hear the sound of my typing, if it makes him wonder, he never asks.

It didn't take long for the guilt to descend. How can I be doing this to Kevin, to the man I have loved for nine years? My intestines are squeezing together, an accordion of regret. How can the Emily who sits at the kitchen table on a Sunday morning and reads the paper and says, "We need more milk, Kev," be the same Emily who, later that day, slides into a red satin bra and says, "I'm going for a walk?" The guilt seeps through me: when we're eating dinner, when I'm putting away dishes, when I'm in the shower. It seems naïve now: I look back with fondness on the person who had no idea what this would be like, who didn't realize that unfaithfulness moves overhead like a storm front. I never expected the humid swell of remorse to hang over me all the time.

But if that were the only thing, then I would end it, wouldn't I? If it were only regret, I would stop sleeping with the man who is not my husband. But part of me doesn't care. Uglier than the act of betrayal itself is the part of me that shucks off the guilt—that tiny husk of decency, the ability to feel guilty—and laughs in its face. I'm caught in the moment with David, emboldened by my very boldness. Some nights, it's all I can do not to grab my coat, tell Kevin I'm off to have sex with another man, and dash out the door. In the narrow beam of light that illuminates my relationship with David, nothing lurks in the shadows, not even my husband, and I am happy. In bed, as the afternoon rolls past us, our bodies still radiating each other's heat, sometimes I try to explain this to David, this rush. He only gets quiet and warns me to be careful.

When we e-mail, we don't talk about anything in particular. Sometimes, but less often than I would have thought before I had an affair, our e-mails are graphic. "Remember what you did to me yesterday? Remember the popsicle?" I try, but I can't take it seriously, our version of cybersex, our pornographic haikus. "Yes, that popsicle was good." And I get easily confused. What we did yesterday: Was it hot? Was it cold? Should I ask? More often than not, I steer the conversation back to familiar terrain. "Speaking of popsicles, it's supposed to be unseasonably warm next week!" I've never been comfortable talking about sex, although I've always enjoyed conversation during it. Once, in the middle of making love, I asked Kevin how his day had been. He stopped, pushed away from me, and sighed. "Emily," he said, "I was kind of in the moment there."

Instead David and I tell each other about our daily lives. I try to make mine sound lively and unpredictable by distilling a series of long, boring moments into charming anecdotes. I don't tell him about the forty-seven manuscripts I logged and labeled. I tell him about the graduate student who stopped me in the hallway on Monday, grabbed my wrist, and said, "You look exactly like Cher! Before her plastic surgery!" I don't tell him about the two-hour collating project I undertook to help Dick organize his office. I tell him about Dr. Viktor Yiannous, the brilliant but volatile researcher in the lab next door to the journal who, furious that his experiment had failed, pulled the fire alarm in a fit of pique and set off the science building's sprinkler system.

His e-mails to me are usually longer, a little bit sloppier. He discusses the newsroom in detail, complains about his colleagues, describes his latest article about Milwaukee's mayoral race, about the current scandal rocking the city's sanitation department, about anything, about nothing.

Sometimes I write about my husband. I tell David that Kevin skipped dinner one night recently in order to attend a seminar on mortgages, that he has stopped even pretending to hear my objections to moving away from the city and into a subdivision. I write about how we hung around the apartment last Sunday but only said 172 words to each other the entire day; I counted. But in the messed-up moral cosmology that is an affair, I try to stay somehow ethical when it comes to saying too much about Kevin. I feel—there's no other way to put it—*loyal* to him. So I don't tell David what I need most to confess: that lately the thought of actually spending the rest of my life with my husband knocks the wind out of me so hard I sometimes can't breathe. This, I keep to myself.

When it gets late, and our messages have become shorter and shorter, one of us finally says good-bye.

"I can't wait to see you again," David will write.

"Me, too." I'll write back, and then I'll hit "send," and the truest words of the night will disappear from the screen in an instant.

MY MOTHER IS HAVING A ROOT CANAL. SHE'S BEEN PUTTING IT off for months, so my dad wouldn't let her cancel, despite her protestations. My mother's teeth are prone to cracking under the slightest pressure, like cowardly spies, and to spectacular rotting, despite her excellent oral hygiene; she seems to need a root canal every three or four months. Because of the frequency of her visits to the dentist, or maybe in spite of it, she's made my dad come with her: for molar support, he says. And Kevin is home fast asleep. He didn't come to bed until 3:00 a.m. The squeak of the door woke me up as he tiptoed into our room, and I rolled over and looked at him. He was grayish and out of sorts, and he mumbled, as he climbed stiffly into bed, that he had gotten caught up in a late, late movie, and then he rolled over without another word and sighed deeply. This is why I find myself alone at the airport at nine-thirty on a cold Saturday morning in November. I'm meeting Heather.

Like every other family, we're mostly just a rerun of ourselves. I always feel giddy and excited before Heather comes to visit, then blurry and inarticulate while she's here, then surly and pissed off when she's gone. Right now, I'm at gate 32E, breathing in the airport smell of Starbucks and shoe leather, standing behind a freakishly short family, waiting for Heather to walk off the plane. I'm bouncing a little, standing on my tiptoes, although there's no need to, since no one in the family in front of me could possibly be taller than five-foot-three. Like a limo driver meeting a CEO, I'm carrying a sign for Heather. This one reads ANITA MANN. Others, in our history of airport pickups, have included Pat Hetic, M. T. Headed, and Drew P. Drorrs. Heather and I subsist on a diet of silly inside jokes and old habits. I'm beaming at the uniformed check-in ladies, at the luggage cart drivers, at every overburdened traveler who catches my eye. I can't wait to see my sister.

Ten minutes later, I'm still waiting, poking my head as far around the corner as I can: it looks like everyone has disembarked, but there's no Heather to be found. She must have missed her flight. I can't believe it. The man standing next to me rushed to his girlfriend as she stepped off the plane and swept her into a passionate embrace five minutes ago; they're still going at it a few feet away. A blond woman got off the plane, and a small Asian child nearby raced into her arms, buried her head in the woman's neck. The short family surrounded an improbably tall man who had to bend double to receive their kisses. They're all long gone. Still no Heather. I look around, wonder if she's playing a joke on me, realize that that would be difficult, since I've watched every single passenger walk off the ramp and into the terminal. My cardboard placard is resting at my feet, defeated, a joke fallen flat.

And then there she is, walking slowly down the ramp, the last person off the plane. Heather, my beautiful sister, her hair thick and shiny and pulled back into a heavy ponytail at the nape of her elegant neck, her camel-colored coat buttoned all the way up, her long legs loping toward me: it's like seeing a gazelle version of myself. Heather, my partner in crime, my companion, my confidante. It hits me in a flash: I'm going to tell her about David Keller. We'll put our curly heads together and I'll whisper my secret to her, and she'll know what to say. Who ever would have thought that I'd be the one with the unpredictable life? Heather sees me and raises her hand in a gleeful wave. "I fell asleep on the plane!" she calls. "I'm so sorry!" My sister has always enjoyed her naps.

She waves some more. I see her, she sees me, but she keeps waving. I wave back. Then she tilts her head to the side and waggles her fingers dramatically, and I finally notice it: the diamond on her finger. In the fluorescent airport lighting, it practically winks at me. It takes a second for the stubborn synapses in my head to make the impossible connection: my sister, the impulsive troublemaker, the renegade Ross, my sister is engaged.

My mouth drops open, and an "Eeeeeeeee!" that Becky and Angie would be proud of escapes from it. "Oh my God, oh my God, oh my God!" I scream, as Heather throws herself into my arms.

"Memma," she says, calling me by the name she used before she could say Emily, an echo of our primitive connection. "Can you believe it?" She kisses my ear. "Can you even believe it?"

I squeeze her. "Tell me Every. Single. Detail. How did it happen? When is the wedding? Why didn't you tell me over the phone?" I squeeze her again. "Did Sam propose? How did he do it? Where did he do it? When did he do it?"

She pulls back from our dancing hug. Love for her washes over me. We study each other for a second. My God, she has good skin. My baby sister is getting married. She smiles, but sheepishly. "Erm . . . yeeaaahhhh," she says, drawing it out into a long syllable, like a deflating balloon. "Yeahhh. Well, see, Mem, it's not exactly . . . it's not . . ." She chews on her lip for a second. "Well, it's not Sam."

Not Sam? She's engaged, but not to Sam? My hard drive is crashing. My brain is full of squiggly lines and indecipherable characters. "Can we sit down somewhere?" she asks, and without waiting for an answer, she hoists her suitcase, takes me by the hand, and pulls me away from the terminal. We head for the coffee shop at the end of the corridor.

In line, we don't talk. My brain is still struggling to reboot.

Heather is intent on the task at hand: ordering herbal tea, dunking the teabag; pouring what seems to be a very specific amount of honey into her cup. I order a black coffee, set it down on the table, and look at it for a while. Finally, Heather says, quietly, "It's all been kind of crazy."

"I bet it has," I say. "What happened?" It's so strange to be here with my little sister, in a crowded airport coffee shop, so strange to be surrounded by the bustle of travelers as we sit in our vacuum of stillness, as I wait for the gory details of Heather's crazy life. I lean toward her, prop my chin on my elbows, as curious as I've ever been in my life. "What on earth happened?"

She blows on her tea. "Before I tell you, can you please promise not to judge me?"

I feel myself snarl at Heather before I can stop my lips from curling. "That is so mean," I say, recoiling. "I don't *judge* you!" I do, of course. "I can't even believe you'd start with that, after we haven't even seen each other in—"

She cuts me off. "Emily, I don't want to fight with you. Can we skip all of this, please? All of this I'm-the-unreliable-one, you're-the-good-girl crap? I just want to tell you about what have been probably the most important and . . ." She waves her left hand again, this time in an attempt to find the right word. ". . . fateful few months of my life. I just want you to be my sister and listen to me."

I sigh. There's so much rivalrous, disputable history in what she just said. I could lead a group of scouts through the twisted underbrush of those accusations. For God's sake, I'm not the good girl! But Heather looks tired again, and I realize that she has a point. " 'Kay."

"Well!" she says, buoyed by my easy capitulation. "I met him . . . and by the way, Mom and Dad don't know. I met him on a business trip to Colorado." Since when does Heather take business trips? What does she even do for a living these days? Last I knew, she was working in a bakery. "We had this crazy fling in Boulder," she continues, "and I can't explain it. It just felt right.

And it happened so fast," she says, her eyes wide, as if, in telling me the story, she's surprised by it herself. "We both just knew it." And I think of David Keller, and I want to clap my hands together and shout, *"I know what you mean!,"* but do I? I'm not exactly registering for fine china with David Keller. Of course, I *am* already married. "So I told Sam," she continues without pausing, without, I think, even breathing, "which totally sucked, I still feel totally awful about that, and I moved out of the apartment, and then I moved in with Rolf."

"What," I say slowly, still trying to process the barrage of information that has just come at me. "What . . . what kind of business trip was it?" It's all I can think to ask.

Heather doesn't miss a beat. "Did I tell you I got promoted at work? The Reeds—they're the couple that owns the bakery, 'member?—made me the morning manager. Of course I was the only person who worked the morning shift, and they didn't give me a raise, so it was meaningless, except for I got to go on this trip. It was the first annual Tiny Business Management Conference, for establishments of two or fewer employees. It was totally lame. Of course, after I met Rolf I didn't end up going to half of the workshops, but they sounded lame. 'Synergizing Your Very Small Staff,' 'Your Employee, Yourself.' Rolf," she continues proudly, "owns the only kosher-style deli in Minneapolis."

"Rolf," I say. The name is a tennis lob on my tongue that stops at my front teeth. Kosher-style deli?

Heather takes a huge swig of tea. "Rolf is sixth-generation Swedish! He has more than one employee, of course, but he was giving the keynote address. He's very successful," she says proudly, glancing, unintentionally I'm sure, at her ring. "So then, anyway, I got fired. Because the Reeds found out I blew off the whole stupid conference. Because Jessie, the girl who works afternoons, was there. She got promoted, too. Anyway, she ratted me out. Which I was totally pissed about, but in the end it was actually for the best, because now I'm working at Rolf's deli, and we're together all the time!"

"Heather, I—" I don't know what to ask her, but there must be more questions.

"Wait, just wait. There's one more thing." She takes a deep breath, licks her lips.

"More?" I ask. I feel my mouth drop open a little bit, and I press my lips back together.

"Rolf is . . . well, he's a little bit older than I am."

"How much older?" I ask evenly.

She licks her lips again, as if she's tasting how old Rolf is. "He's, um, kind of in his late thirties."

"Late thirties," I say, waiting. "How late?"

"He's forty-three."

"Heather! He's fifteen years older than you!" It shoots out of my mouth like a bullet before I can stop myself, and she immediately glares, leans back in her chair, crosses her arms over her chest. "I'm sorry," I say quickly. "It's not that big a deal! I mean, fifteen years, so what? Right?" I do quick, silent calculations: he'll be a doddering, forgetful seventy-year-old when Heather's a trim fifty-five. She'll probably be running marathons and mastering tae-kwon-do, and he'll need one of those little beeping plastic containers to remind him to take his pills. He'll be one-hundred-five when Heather's a spry ninety! "That's no big deal!" I say again.

"And he has a toddler," she mumbles, so fast I'm not sure I've heard her correctly.

"A rottweiler?" I ask, hopefully.

"No," Heather says, finally smiling at me again, this time the toothiest grin, a smile like she's swallowed the whole word. "A toddler. A little boy. Silas. He's . . . he's three. He's a terrific kid. I'm going to be a stepmommy. A stepmommy!"

I close my eyes.

"Rolf has joint custody with Salomé, his ex-partner," Heather continues.

Forty-three. Stepmommy. Salomé. Ex-partner. Oh, God. "Congratulations," I tell her calmly, as neutrally as I can manage. "That's wonderful." I look around, take in the panorama of travelers who are rushing past the coffee shop toward their gates, the people at tables near us who are not Receiving Momentous News, who are simply having coffee.

"It *is* wonderful, and I hope you can see that." Heather fiddles with the top button on her coat, her shiny ring reflecting the light. "I know this must sound crazy to you, but, listen, it's *right*. I know it is. Rolf and I are going to get married and we're going to be a family, with Silas, and I so want you to be happy for me, but even if you can't be, it's still right."

"I am happy for you, Heather; of course I'm happy." I feel like a blender has been turned on inside my stomach. "It's true, it does seem . . . well, it did happen kind of fast, but why wouldn't I be happy for you? You're my sister. Of course I'm happy."

Heather pushes her chair back and moves around the table, toward me. She pulls me up into a hug, nuzzles her face into my neck. "Thanks," she says, and I hug her back.

"Hey," I say finally, pushing her gently away from me. "Meg's pregnant." Heather and Meg have never gotten along. They're just similar enough—both beautiful, gregarious, opinionated—that they can't stand each other. They each insist that they're nothing alike. "You two will finally have something to talk about—you can talk about being mommies." Heather bends to pick up her suitcase, and I grab it before she can. She loops her arm through my free one, and we head toward the exit.

From the shower I hear the phone ringing. Kevin is already gone for the day, and Heather is asleep on the couch. I don't want it to wake her, so I leap out of the bathtub and run, naked and dripping wet, into the living room. Since she arrived three days ago, though, Heather has been zonked on our couch for ten or eleven hours a night, able to sleep through ringing phones, blaring police sirens, and the TV blasting from the apartment next door. I remember this just as I grab the phone. I glance over at Heather; her head is buried underneath the blue striped blanket Aunt Mimi crocheted for me before I left for college. Her feet are dangling over the end of the couch. She can't be comfortable. A puddle of water pools at my feet before I remember that the phone is cordless. I head back toward the bathroom.

"Emily," Dr. Miller says briskly, and I wonder in a flash how exactly I've screwed up this time. Dr. Miller, my other boss, Dick's coeditor, has called me at home before, early in the morning, more often when I first started the job, but once or twice in the past few months. He always claims he's calling because he can't find something I've misfiled, or because I haven't finished something I promised to have for him by the end of the previous day. Usually his phone calls are meant to remind me that I've messed something up, not because he really can't find what he says he's looking for. Once, during my second week on the job, he called at six-thirty in the morning to tell me that seventy-four doesn't come after seventy-five; I had accidentally misnumbered the manuscripts. Dr. Miller is the real prick of *Dick*.

"Hello, Dr. Miller," I say sweetly, rubbing the foggy bathroom mirror with a corner of my towel. I steadfastly refuse ever to let him know that he's flustered me.

"Emily, I have some bad news. I'm sorry to tell you that Dick is dead."

At first I think he means the journal. At first I think he's referring to *Male Reproduction* by Kevin's and my nickname for it. At first I think, *Well, there's me, out of a job.* But then I get it. And although I had expected this for some time, although I had actually imagined this very phone call once or twice in the past year, my knees turn to jelly, and I have to steady myself on the sink, and it's like I'm seeing myself from across the room. I hear a gasp, and it's coming out of my own mouth. "Oh," I say. "How?"

"Emily." Dr. Miller's rough tone is a bit softer. "Dick had been in congestive heart failure for the past year." He clears his throat. "I think that's why he'd been so distracted lately," he says quietly, almost to himself. "He knew he didn't have long. He died at home last night." Dr. Miller's voice breaks on "night," and he's silent.

"Okay," I say, my throat thick. Dick knew he was dying. He died. He's dead. I'm still dripping, and now I'm shivering, too. The bath mat underneath my feet is sopping. I readjust my towel. "When is the funeral?"

"Tomorrow at eleven. At North Shore Presbyterian. Do you know where that is?"

"Yes," I say, even though I don't. I wonder if I should still come to work today. "Is there anything I should do?" There are still papers on the testosterone levels of spawning salmon to reject, vast quantities of files to organize—Dick's haphazard files, specifically. Last Friday, before he left for the day, Dick came into my office, his Sherlock Holmes hat perched jauntily on his head. "Emily," he said, "I thank you for your good work, and I bid you a fond adieu." He patted me on the head and ruffled my hair as if I were his beloved dog, a cherished French poodle. I remember thinking that from anyone else, this gesture would have been intolerable, but from Dick, it just was what it was: an expression of pure, loopy affection. I looked up at him then and smiled, and I did not say "woof," even though I was tempted to. I wonder if the journal will shut down after all. I wonder if I ought to resign in protest. Dick should not have died.

"I'll pass along your condolences to Dick's family," Dr. Miller says crisply, his voice resuming its usual imperious tone. "I'll see you back at work tomorrow," he says, and hangs up.

All I want is to see David. All I want is to lie next to him. Since we started sleeping together, my reactions to things are buffed smooth and shiny: immediately upon hearing a piece of news, good or bad or anywhere in between, I want to climb into David's bed. When Colby Wirth, my editor at *Me,* rejected my pitch on alternatives to traditional relationships ("Monogamy: The Relationship of Fools?"), I called David, picked him up at his office, and sped back to his apartment; we didn't even make it all the way to his bedroom. When my mom told me that my second cousin Ronald lost his job, I felt a familiar liquid urge, and I told Kevin I was going to pick up dinner, which I eventually did. And when

Heather first arrived, four days ago, I brought her home, made lunch, and then I told her I had to do some research at the library and drove straight to David's. The immediate consequence of sadness, it turns out, is no different from that of disappointment, fleeting sympathy, or happiness laced with ambivalence. I finish drying off, sit down on the closed toilet seat, and dial David's cell phone number.

"Hey," I say quietly, when he picks up. The image of Dick in his rakish green hat is still in my head. "My boss died. I'm really sad. Are you busy? Can I see you?" I hear the noise of the newsroom in the background. Only seven people work at *The Weekly* full-time, David has told me, but they yell a lot and generally act like ace reporters from the 1940s, drinking and smoking and swearing. "I'm not writing alder*person*! That's fucking bullshit!" someone shouts.

"I'm sorry, babe," David says. "I'm sorry about your boss. I'm swamped, though."

For the first time since Dr. Miller's phone call, I feel tears well up behind my eyes. David has no idea how much Dick meant to me. But still. "Oh. Okay."

"I'm on deadline for two articles and the calendar," he says.

"Sure. I understand."

He hesitates. The din in the background recedes. "You don't sound so great," he says.

"I'm not."

David pauses again. "I suppose . . . I could . . . Okay, I guess we could meet. . . . No, why don't you pick me up here in an hour?" There's something unrecognizable in his voice.

"I don't want to interrupt your work," I say, barely able to get the words out. How can Dick be dead? How can David not want to see me?

"No, no," he says, "no, no, no," regaining his enthusiasm with each "no." "Of course you're not interrupting. Of course I want to see you." His voice returns, its familiar register and the low crackle of desire. "Meet me here in an hour, okay?"

We hang up, and I slowly get dressed and wander back into the living room. An hour gives me time to hang out with Heather, who is awake now and has moved to a sitting position on the couch. Aunt Mimi's blanket is wrapped around her shoulders; somehow, on Heather, it looks almost stylish.

"Did you sleep well?" I ask, sitting down in the rocking chair across from her. I smooth my hair and try to compose a normal face. The problem is, I have no idea what normal is anymore.

"You bet," she says, still groggy, rubbing her eyes. "What should we do today?" Heather used to pounce on me in the mornings, jumping on my bed, sitting on my chest, threatening to drool on my face unless I got up and played with her. "What's on?" she asks.

As soon as it comes out of my mouth, I understand that once one thing is a secret, everything is. "I'm going to work," I say. I can't tell Heather that Dick has died, because then she'll wonder why I'm going to the office. The accordion of all the other things I can't tell her unfolds. "I've got, uh, stuff to do this morning. I'll be back in the afternoon, though," I say, watching the disappointment skitter across her face and then lift. "We can go for a walk with Mom and get ice cream or something, okay?"

"I've got some reading to do anyway," she says, motioning toward the stack of books she's brought with her. Heather is reading up on nontraditional families the way Meg has been poring over pregnancy books lately—in the midst of their giddiness they both seem desperate for guidance, hopeful that a few select tips on what to eat during your second trimester or how to discipline a toddler when you're not his mother will map the stars for them as they blast off into the solar system. But Dick is dead! And how can you predict anything? Heather studies my face for an uncomfortably long moment. "You okay?" she asks.

"Why?"

"I don't know," she says. "You seem on edge."

"Nope. I'm fine." I'm not fine, and apparently I'm not a very good actress, either. Suddenly an hour seems like an awfully long time to sit here and not tell my sister anything true. "I should get going, though," I say, rising. And before Heather can catch another glimpse of me, before her sympathetic face forces me to spill everything, I grab my coat and click the front door shut.

As soon as I see David, everything is all right. He's waiting for me near the side of the building, his jacket collar pulled up around his ears, his shoulders hunched a little bit against the cold, sunglasses on. The sight of him is a Band-Aid on my heart. I pull in beside a NO PARKING ANYTIME sign and watch him for a minute before he spots me. I know the angles and contours of that body underneath the jacket and gray shirt and faded jeans. I know the taste of it. Just as I'm about to honk, David crosses his arms in front of his chest and looks up at the sky. Even from across the street, I can tell that he's impatient. He must be as eager to see me as I am to see him, I think; he must crave my body the way I do his. The alternative—that he's just feeling impatient—is not quite bearable.

He sees me before I beep and he dashes across the street, folds himself into the front seat, and moves toward me in one graceful motion. The cold air and his leathery scent fill the car. Without a word, he puts his hands on my face and kisses me. His icy fingers and warm mouth create a current that shoots through me. For a second, I consider sliding my clothes off right here in the tow-away zone. He moves his hand up under my hair and tugs it lightly. Just then, a delivery truck drives up and honks at us, so my plans for an uncomfortable romp in the car are thwarted. "Drive fast," David whispers, and I do.

When we get to his apartment building, David practically pulls me up the stairs. We haven't said a word to each other since we turned off Michigan Street, two miles ago. "I just wanted to see you," I said then, slipping around the Buick in front of me. I thought about Dick again and how I hadn't even told Kevin yet. I thought about how Dick used to bring me trinkets from medical conferences: a pad of paper or a pen emblazoned with a pharma-

ceutical company's logo, a mug or a T-shirt, my favorite souvenir a
smiling stuffed carrot sporting the name of a prominent anti-
impotence drug. I felt my throat close up again and I had to concentrate on breathing.

"I know," David said.

Now we're in his apartment, now his bedroom, shedding
clothes as we move toward the bed, the wrinkled blue sheets as
familiar to me now as my own. Somehow, David wants this as
urgently as I do, which seems impossible, since I want to disappear
inside him. We're puzzle pieces; we're magnets; we're fast hands
and hot breath. Sometimes, with Kevin, I can't help but think
about the absurdity of it all, two bodies plonking around together.
With David, no words come into my head, and I feel only friction,
skin on skin, soft against hard, fusion. David cries out just as I'm
pulling his head down toward my neck. When it's over I feel just as
hungry as I did when we started.

"I wish I could stay here with you all day," David whispers a
few moments later, still catching his breath. I'm lying in the crook
of his arm. My body feels rearranged, a not unpleasant, shaken-up
feeling I get every time we have sex. But my brain is still buzzing.

That's nothing, I think. *I wish I could stay here with you forever.*

"But I really have to get back," he adds quickly.

It occurs to me that David's heated urgency thirty minutes ago
might have been more about a newspaper deadline than about having sex with me, but I decide that, in light of today's events, I will
let myself push that thought to the back burner. Besides, the privi-
leges of marriage, where you get to needle your spouse with your
every insecure notion, don't extend to an affair. David still thinks
I'm confident and mysterious, which, I sense, is an important
ingredient in the stew of our relationship. So I just roll onto my
stomach and lean in to kiss him. "I'll get dressed and drive you
back."

"No, it's all right," he says, already pulling his clothes on. "I'll
catch a bus. It stops right on the corner, and there's one every ten
minutes." He's getting public transportation back to work. I'm

still warm from our lovemaking and he's about to jump on a bus. This is tawdry.

I swallow the lump in my throat and flash what I hope resembles an assured smile. "Okey dokey," I say, which is a phrase I don't believe I've ever used before. The boulder in my chest that had begun to break apart starts to re-form. I roll over, feel the strange expanse of this bed without David in it.

"I'm really sorry about your boss," he says again, and it looks as if that sentence, along with the last half hour, will have to be enough.

When I get home, feeling strangely removed from myself, Kevin and Heather are sitting on the couch together. This is a somewhat unusual sight, given Heather's intolerance of my husband's deadly slow conversational pace. Kevin is leaning slightly toward Heather. A somber-looking gray tome with a cookbook title, *The Blended Family,* lies open on her lap. They fall silent when I walk through the door, then turn their faces to me simultaneously; Kevin reddens, and Heather quickly looks down at her book.

"Heather was just telling me, um, how cute Silas is," Kevin says sheepishly. He shifts on the couch cushion, leans away from her.

"I was telling Kevin about the *cutest* thing Silas said to me the other day," Heather confirms, closing her book and turning it over in her hands. "He said, 'You're almost as pretty as my mommy.'" Her fingers tap-dance on the book's spine.

"Right," I say, unzipping my coat. "Cute." Heather and Kevin glance at each other, silently confirming that they're the worst liars on the planet. They were talking about me. I turn back toward the kitchen. "Who wants lunch?"

"Emily," Kevin calls after me. "Can you come back in here?"

"Who's hungry?" I ask cheerily. Are they conspiring against me? "Where's the blender? I'm in the mood for a blended family!"

"Please," Heather says. "Can you just come here?"

When I was seven, Karen Krakowski and I tried to flush two

bologna sandwiches down the toilet in the girls' bathroom. When it overflowed, a sycophantic kindergartner, witness to our crime, turned us in, and we were called into Principal Vanderbilt's office to be reprimanded. I was terrified, but I remember feeling defiant, too. This is how I feel now.

"Yes?" I say, returning to the living room. "At your service." I rest my hands on my hips.

"Kevin and I were just talking," Heather says, studying the back cover of *The Blended Family* as if it holds the secrets of eternal happiness. "We were just saying how you've seemed kind of . . . I don't know . . . weird or something, or . . ." She looks at Kevin helplessly.

"I know things between us have been . . . um . . ." he says, letting the rest of the sentence drift off. "But something else is going on with you." His tone is neutral, inscrutable. He crosses and uncrosses his legs. "You haven't been yourself lately. That much I know. Is there something you want to tell us? Or me?"

I look around at our cozy living room full of books and plants and things that I love, my grandmother's candlesticks on the bureau, an array of colored glass bottles on the coffee table. The sunlight is making shifting patterns on the walls that Kevin and I painted together. I think about my double life, my affair with David, the way I'm deceiving Kevin every single day, how I've lied to him, to my friends, to my family, how I continue to lie to them. I think about Meg and Heather having families, opening up their generous hearts to new little people, huge changes. I think about how Kevin wants to start that phase of our life together, too, how he deserves to. And now the room is spinning, and I have to sit down, but three feet to the rocking chair seems like an impossible distance, from here to Alaska, so I sink to the floor, and I just sit there for a minute. When I imagined myself at thirty, this is not what I saw. I'm in a deep hole that I've dug for myself, and I can't get out. I let my head fall forward into my hands, because, truly, I can't look at Heather or Kevin. "Dick died," I say from behind my hands. It comes out muffled.

"Fish fry?" Heather asks.

"Pigs fly?" Kevin suggests, a half beat later.

"Are you guys serious?" I lift my head. They look serious. They look serious and utterly baffled. My face feels hot and wet. "Dick died. Dick died. Dick died!" It does sound strange, actually, the more I say it.

"Oh, Em." Kevin's voice is full of sympathy. He slides off the couch and reaches for me. He has to crawl past the coffee table.

"Who's Dick?" Heather asks, still trying to catch up. "Wait, who's Dick?!" She's on the floor now, too, trying to push past Kevin to give me a hug, but Kevin's fighting her for hugging rights, they're shoulder to shoulder, both still a foot away from me, and the sight of it is so absurd, my sweet husband and my eager sister in a scuffle on the living room floor, that I start to laugh, which confuses them both again; they look up at me, and now I'm laughing and crying, because Kevin and Heather resemble nothing more than two big pale crabs thrashing about on the carpeting, and Dick is dead, and I'm having an affair, and I think Kevin knows.

ONE NIGHT TOWARD THE END OF OCTOBER, A WEEK OR SO AFTER I'd started sleeping with David, Kevin turned to me in bed. We hadn't made love since before David, and I wasn't sure if I would ever be able to touch my husband again. It was bad enough to be cheating on him. I couldn't fathom actually having sex with Kevin, doing it with two men—making love with one in the afternoon, only to go home and have sex with another in the evening, the memory of the first one, the *feel* of him, still lingering. How was a person supposed to do that? I had no idea. And, less abstractly, would Kevin know? Would there be subtle clues? Would I move slightly differently, respond to certain of his familiar touches in ways that surprised him just a little, ways that felt just a tiny bit peculiar? Would my body have absorbed David without my even knowing it, and would it then, despite my intentions, spill my secret?

So I had been avoiding Kevin, going to bed early and then feigning sleep, complaining of cramps or a headache in the late afternoon so that, if the situation presented itself, I could say, *No, Kev, remember?* I figured Kevin would just think I was still traumatized about our conflicts, and that he would, as usual, leave me to my own emotional devices. For his part, Kevin hadn't exactly been smoldering with passion for me. On the rare nights we were in bed together and both awake, he usually buried his face in a book and acted like I wasn't there.

That night, though, Kevin rolled toward me and rested his hand gently on my cheek. I looked at him, at the lines and curves of his pale face, the shape of his nostrils, the pores on his nose, the arch of his blond eyebrows. His face was a collection of parts, some assembly required. *Insert nose roughly in middle of face. Attach pale eyelashes sparingly to eyelids.* He inched up close to me and kissed me. Immediately, I started thinking about kissing David; just as suddenly, Kevin's lips felt like suction cups I couldn't detach from; his tongue was a squirming fish in my mouth. I pushed him away. "Um, Kevin, I'm just, I'm really kind of exhausted."

Kevin was not swayed. He pulled me close and pressed his hand against the small of my back. "I'll do all the work," he said, low in my ear, still holding me against him, his breath hot on my face. I wanted to shove him away from me, hard, and retreat as close to the edge of the bed as I could without falling off. I wanted to roll out of his grasp and jump up, claiming urgent stomach troubles. I wanted to shout, "Get OFF me!" I thought of how David explored the bend in my elbow with his tongue, the soft skin behind my knee with his fingertips; I thought of the way we held on to each other when we made love, pulling closer and closer until sometimes, in the heat of it, I would look at a body part and think, *Whose leg is that? whose hand?*

Kevin slid his fingers up my back and whispered, "Come on, Emily," and it was Kevin's voice, urgent and pleading, but it was a voice I had never heard before; it was as if he were inside out, as if I was listening to his blood and his bones. *Okay,* I thought, *okay.*

I went limp. I tried to detach from my body. I tried to separate from myself. I thought that the only way to reconcile making love with the man I was cheating on was to rise above my body, to watch two people move together in my bed. But as he touched me, as he whispered to me and kissed me, I was jolted back to a horrible tenderness. His soft voice in my ear recalled our decade together, our hikes through Oregon, Kevin quietly pointing out the native plants he grew up knowing: bearberry, bitterroot, wild ginger; our language of jokes and references, his likes and dislikes as close to my heart as my own; the knowledge of him, of every inch of him. His hands on my body reminded me of all of the times we'd made love, all the places—the first time, in his twin bed, almost silently, his roommate asleep on the other side of a flimsy wall; in a tent next to a still lake in northern Wisconsin; on the kitchen floor, the first night in our apartment; on an air mattress in his parents' dark basement; in our bed, our bed, again and again and again. I felt him then, and I thought, *I am cheating on this man. This is the man I am cheating on.*

When it was over, Kevin whispered, "Love you," and he held me, and I lay there, hunched inside myself, silently, with the useless, unbearable knowledge that I loved him, too.

"SILAS SAID ANOTHER ADORABLE THING THE OTHER DAY," Heather gushes, swatting a bug away from her peanut butter sandwich. It's the morning of Dick's funeral, and Heather and Meg and I are sitting at a picnic table in Lake Park. It feels strange and incongruous to be here, as if my sad, confused autumn self has tumbled down a black hole and emerged into carefree summertime. I was awake for hours last night, tossing and turning, hotly kicking the blankets off and then, ten minutes later, just as desperately rooting around in the dark to cover myself up again. Kevin barely moved all night, breathing evenly, his back to me, and I never knew if he was awake or asleep. When it was finally morning, I fully expected to greet a day that would reflect the sadness of Dick's funeral, a day to mirror my turbulent soul: I opened the shades anticipating great dark clouds billowing across a slate gray November sky. But today is glorious and warm, Indian summer, and the heavy, sweet smell of wet fallen leaves is the only reminder that it's late November, not late August.

Heather tears off a hunk of her sandwich. "He said, 'Hevver,' because he can't quite pronounce my name, but that's not the adorable part. He said, 'Hevver, do you know what rhymes with sugar? *Booger!*'" She looks first at me, then at Meg, proud, grinning. "Don't you think that's adorable?"

"Adorable," I repeat, incredulous and no longer hungry.

"Sweet!" Meg echoes pleasantly, digging into her own sandwich, obviously not conjuring up the same disgusting image that's in my head.

I take a big gulp from my water bottle, squint up at the blue sky. This cheery wife- and stepmother-to-be is my cynical, hard-edged little sister. This is my sister who, just last summer, stared back at a little boy on the sidewalk who was gaping at her, the way toddlers do, and muttered, "Take a picture, kid; it lasts longer." This is the girl who at *fifteen* tried to convince my parents to let her get her tubes tied.

"I mean," she says now, grabbing her napkin as it's about to blow away, "I just think it's so unusual for a three-year-old to be able to come up with a rhyme like that!"

"*So* unusual," Meg agrees, without sarcasm. She rifles through her bag and pulls out one of the pregnancy bibles she now carries with her at all times. Most of Meg's pregnancy books look like they're geared toward mothers-to-be with questionable IQs, or maybe pregnant teenage cheerleaders; they have bright covers, zippy illustrations, and titles like *You Grow, Girl!* She flips through the pages of *No Thanks, I Gestate.* "Gosh, I hope peanut butter is okay!" she says to no one.

Kevin went to work this morning and is planning to meet me at Dick's funeral this afternoon, so I suggested to Heather and Meg an impromptu picnic in the park. I needed a way to pass the time today that didn't involve David. Although he was my first choice, he e-mailed me this morning to say that he wouldn't be able to get together until the middle of the week at the earliest. It felt like a preemptive strike. "I've got a crazy deadline again," he wrote. "Should we plan on seeing each other Wednesday or Thursday? Friday might even be best." I was so close to writing back to him: "Why can't you see me? What have I done wrong? Are we through? Do you want to end this?" I actually had to sit on my hands to prevent them from putting on such an embarrassing display. So I sat there, staring at David's message, my throat dry and my hands numb, and I thought, *What now?* And then I heard my father's voice in my head. "When life gives you lemons," Len is fond of saying, "take them back to the supermarket. What do you need lemons for?" I called Meg, and by the time Heather woke up, I had already packed the picnic basket.

"Emily," Heather says. She flips her hair back with a toss of her head, like a pony. "Isn't it wild? You're going to be a step-aunt!" which immediately makes me think of something small and squished on the sidewalk.

Meg laughs and squeezes Heather's arm. They've been talking about babies and toddlers for the past twenty minutes. I sigh, then stuff a carrot stick in my mouth to cover it up.

"Rolf and his ex-partner practiced attachment parenting with Silas," Heather tells us with a serious nod, "which I think has made him *extremely* self-confident." I imagine a self-confident three-year-old, a tiny Napoleon. Aren't toddlers too self-confident to begin with? Isn't that the problem?

"I completely agree!" Meg practically shouts. "Steve and I are going to co-sleep, and I fully intend for one of us to be holding the baby at all times!" She crunches happily on a pretzel.

"That's *so great*," Heather says, intense as a recent convert, adamant as a cult member.

"I just hate it when I see moms carrying their babies around in car seats," Meg continues. "They seem so lonely in there, the poor little things. I've already bought myself a sling."

"I didn't know you were broken!" I say, my mouth full of carrot, and they both ignore me. This is exactly what I wanted: for Meg and Heather to connect. In twelve years, this is the first time they've engaged in anything more substantive than a five-minute chat. I'm glad for them. I just thought I'd be able to get a word in. This was the morning I was going to tell them about David.

"So, when did you first know you were pregnant?" Heather asks Meg, leaning forward, an eager disciple.

"Well, we were *trying*," Meg says, the undertone of a slightly tawdry confession in her voice. "But after my miscarriage I wasn't convinced it was going to happen, so I was telling myself not to think about it." Meg takes another bite of her sandwich; Heather is rapt while Meg chews, swallows. I look around at the empty picnic tables nearby, stifle a yawn. Two squirrels chase each other up a tree. "I was kind of pretending I didn't care, so that I wouldn't be disappointed. But then, one day, it occurred to me that I hadn't gotten my period. And I'm usually bang on time."

"That's what you and Steve did!" I say loudly. "Bang on time!" Suddenly I've become a fourteen-year-old boy. Once again, I'm ignored.

"Sure enough," Meg continues, rolling her eyes in my general direction, "the test was positive."

"That must have been such an amazing moment," Heather says, and it occurs to me with a jolt that Heather and Rolf are probably planning to give Silas a brother or sister before too long.

"But what about you?" Meg says. "You're already a mother, in a way. What's that like?" And they're off, the two of them, Heather describing in detail Silas's many charms and the complex task of relating to a small child, Meg interjecting with questions about potty training and sleep training and how to train a picky eater, as if she were getting ready to adopt a puppy. Heather is waxing poetic about Silas's love of avocados when it hits me: bang on time. I'm usually bang on time, too, and I can't remember the last time I got my period.

Heather reaches across the picnic table and tugs my hair, the way she used to when we were little, to get my attention. "Are you there?" she says. "Are you with us?"

"Huh?" Apparently I've lost the thread of this discussion, frozen by my own realization. If I'm pregnant, my God, if I'm *pregnant,* then I'm carrying David's baby. *Probably David's. David's?* I suddenly feel nauseous, which makes me feel even more nauseous. David and I have been careful, but once in a while things have gotten dicey. At least, thank God for small favors, Kevin and I haven't even had sex since . . . suddenly I can't remember the last time Kevin and I had sex. I try to do fast calculations as Heather waves her hands in front of my face. "Yoo-hoo!" she trills. My head is starting to float away from my body like a balloon, barely attached to a flimsy string. The last time Kevin and I were together was—before my last period? After? Holy God, I might be pregnant, and *I don't know who the father is.* I look up at the sky and whisper, "No," a prayer, a plea.

"No what?" Heather asks. "Emily, what's going on?"

"Nothing," I say. "I just . . . I don't like avocados."

Heather and Meg shoot each other a look. "Okaaay . . ." Heather says.

"You don't have to," Meg says in a slightly too-high voice, looking at me, perplexed.

I used to be a good person. I always told the truth, and I never cheated on a test, much less a man. I've never stolen anything or even undertipped a waitress, and one time, when the bank teller accidentally handed me an extra twenty dollars, I gave it right back. When I held Kevin's hand in my parents' backyard on a bright spring day five years ago and said my vows to him, my voice quivering and tears rolling down my face, I meant it; I meant every word. But this clinches it: I'm not a good person; I'm not the Emily I thought I was. I look at Meg and Heather, in the happy throes of making something of themselves, of being adults, of moving forward. If I tell them about David, they won't be impressed, or deliciously scandalized; they won't giggle and clap their hands over their mouths and demand details. They'll be appalled by what I've done. They'll be disgusted. And then I realize: they're not the ones I need to tell. I have to clean up this mess and set things right with Kevin, whatever that means. I have to figure out who I want to be with. But first, I need to find out if I'm pregnant.

KEVIN SQUEEZES MY HAND. "DO YOU WANT TO LEAVE?" he whispers. It's a valid question: I haven't stopped crying since we walked through the door of the church. I took one look at Dick's tiny, brave wife, and I started sobbing, a full fifteen minutes before the service even began. Tears just poured out of my eyes, and they haven't stopped. I gush, like a burst pipe, like a sprinkler system in a burning office building. I've been crying so hard that people keep turning to look at me. They probably think I'm family. Even Dick's family looks at me, puzzled. The minister mentions Dick's kindness, and I dab at my eyes with a soggy tissue. He talks about Dick's devotion to his wife and children and grandchildren, and I swipe harder. He illustrates Dick's lovable domestic incompetence by telling a story about the time he tried to surprise his family by cooking dinner and accidentally gave everyone food poisoning, and noises that sound like a lamb being strangled escape from me.

Kevin squeezes my hand again. "Really, we can step outside if you want to." I'm hiccupping now, loudly. The sympathetic look that's been etched onto Kevin's face since I told him Dick had died is only deeper and more compassionate, but it's underlined with the slightest tinge of embarrassment, and I can't blame him. I'm practically hyperventilating. In college, Meg learned in a history class that Victorian women would sometimes be diagnosed with hysteria and forced to undergo the removal of their reproductive organs. For months, when we were laughing really hard at something, or crying during a movie, one of us would whisper to the other, "I need a hysterectomy!" I would say this to Kevin now, if I thought he'd have any idea what I was talking about.

I shake my head at Kevin, try desperately to gain control. Dick's wife is sitting in the front row between their two children, Elizabeth on one side, and Richard, the son I've never met, on the other. They all look so stoic and yet so crushed, with their excellent Presbyterian posture and their pale, pale faces. I feel like a hired mourner, crying my hot, ethnic tears, crying enough for all of them.

Since having been struck by the lightning bolt realization this morning that I might be pregnant, I haven't been alone for a second, much less for the time it would take to go to the drugstore, buy the pregnancy test, and then come home and take it. And that's only half the battle. I wish there were a companion test you could buy, perhaps in the Brazen Hussy aisle at Walgreen's: half price when you purchase one Easy Step Pregnancy Test, a Who's-the-Daddy Indicator Stick. Beeps once for Your Husband, twice for Your Lover! But Meg and Heather came back to the apartment after our picnic, and then they walked me to the church, where Kevin was waiting. So all I've been able to do today is ruminate over the incredible, horrible, self-induced cataclysm that is my life. Every time I close my eyes, I see a different version of the same child, a Mr. Potato Head baby. If David is the father, the baby would be dark and exotic looking, with big brown eyes and strong features. If Kevin is the daddy, the kid would be a more neutral balance: lighter eyes, lighter hair, a smaller nose . . .

There's a hush in the church now, as Dick's son rises to give the eulogy. This is starting to feel like a wedding . . . although of course the groom is dead. And there's no bride. And everyone is really sad. But the ceremony feels familiar. Maybe it's the reverence of it, the seriousness of what is being marked, and the way everyone knows his or her role—the grieving family, the supportive relatives, the darkly dressed, subdued (except for me) mourners. This is only the second funeral I've ever been to, but I suddenly see that these events are not so much about honoring the wedded or the dead, but about ensuring that everyone else knows what to do.

Richard makes his way to the podium, shuffles a few papers around, clears his throat. He looks like Dick, without the paunch. His face is the same; I can see that even from fifteen feet away. His eyes have the same almond shape as Dick's, the same kindly crinkles edging toward the sides of his face. Their foreheads furrow into identical patterns. Dick used to talk about Elizabeth constantly, less about Richard, with whom his relationship was more distant, more formal. But when his son's name did come up, Dick would puff up with pride. "Richard," he would say, "has been given quite a large promotion at his *agency,*" as if he were talking about a Fortune 500 company instead of the tiny environmental nonprofit Richard toiled away at. "Richard," Dick told me the other day, standing, as usual, in the doorway of my office, arms crossed proudly over his barrel chest, "has just received more *accolades* for his very important work on behalf of our rivers and lakes." I have a hunch, studying Richard as he pulls himself together in front of a room full of Dick's friends and family, that he has no idea how proud he made his father, and I'm seized with the urge to stand up, right now, and tell him, because life is obviously way, way too short.

"My dad," Richard says, looking down at his notes and then peering into the crowd, "would have been delighted to see you all here. Dick loved a party." And a new geyser of tears erupts from me.

After the service, as people are beginning to leave for the cemetery, I make my way over to Dick's family. My eyes are finally dry. I'm just as desolate, but I think I've emptied myself of liquid. I was a grape; now I'm a raisin. I feel shrunken and parched. I probably won't have to pee for days. I lean against the wooden armrest of a pew and wait awkwardly at the fringes of the small group surrounding Dick's family. I look around, fiddle with my hair, adjust my dress, shift from one foot to the other in my uncomfortable shoes. I know that I don't really belong anywhere near this intimate circle, but I need to make contact. Finally, spotting a small opening in the crowd, I squeeze in next to Dick's bird-like wife, Jane. Dick once told me that, before their children were born, they had a dog named Spot, just because they couldn't resist. "Neither of us even wanted a dog," Dick said. "Never did care for that mutt." Jane looks at me, her pretty, powdered face a network of fine lines, her eyebrows slightly raised. She can't place me. I lean down, feeling like a giraffe next to her, touch her shoulder, and say softly, "I'm Emily. I worked for Dick at the journal."

"Of course," she answers, taking hold of both of my hands. "He spoke so highly of you, Emily." Jane is so short that if she were looking straight at me, she'd be staring at my chest. She has to tip her face up toward mine, which makes her look even more vulnerable than a seventy-year-old woman would normally look at her husband's funeral, and I have to press my lips together to keep from crying again.

"I'm so sorry," I finally manage.

"We were married for forty-nine years," Jane says. "We would have celebrated our fiftieth anniversary this June." She says it with more wonder and pride than sadness. "He was always a surprise to me." Her voice is startlingly low and gravelly for someone so tiny. She looks radiant for a split second; her eyes widen and the darkness over her face just seems to lift; it's as if she's watching a movie in her head, watching one of the good parts flash by. Then Elizabeth takes her by the elbow and gently leads her away, toward the next set of people waiting to comfort themselves by comforting her, eventually toward the door. Richard, who had been standing next to his mother the whole time, looks at me and smiles.

"Dad really was so fond of you," he says. "I've wanted to meet you. I'm only sorry it has to be under these circumstances." He waves his hands around vaguely, then drops them to his sides. Up close, Richard doesn't look nearly as much like Dick as he did from afar, I notice. His eyes are hazel, not brown like Dick's, and his mouth—wide, with full lips—is completely different. I decide then that telling a thirty-seven-year-old man that his father was proud of him would be condescending, better suited to a bar mitzvah, so I just smile back, and then, impulsively, I hug Richard. At first he's surprised—I feel him startle, his back stiffen—but then almost immediately he hugs me back. I take a big breath—he smells good, like vanilla—and draw away.

"I'm so sorry." That's all I seem to be able to say today, but really, it *is* a funeral, after all. Richard nods, looking sort of bemused. I'm still thinking about what Jane said, "He was always a surprise to me," as I head toward the exit.

Kevin is waiting for me outside, near the edge of the parking lot, away from the mourners. He looks anxious. He's probably eager to get back to work. "You okay now?" he asks. He's ready for me to be okay, ready for the waterworks to have dried up.

"Fine." I take his hand. What will I say to him if I'm pregnant? How do you tell your husband, who has been trying to convince you to start a family, that his wish has come true, but, *woops,* the baby might not be his? Jesus.

It turns out that the church is only a few blocks from our apartment, but I'd never noticed it, tucked back on a side street behind a thick hedge cover, like a secret hideaway only Presbyterians know about. We duck through the bushes and walk up to Oakland Avenue, the busy street of stores and cafés, packed with midday shoppers and workers on their lunch breaks. Kevin is staring at his feet as we walk, as if he's never seen them before. *Oh, look, feet! So useful!* On the sidewalk, he lets go of my hand. We're trying to cross the street, but no one will slow down. We can't find a break in the traffic. He looks up from his shoes and squints, fixes his gaze on the rush of cars zooming past. He takes one tiny, tentative step off the curb, then immediately backs up again. "Emily," he says softly, so that I have to lean in to hear him underneath the noise of a nearby delivery truck. "Do you still want to be married to me?"

I have brought Kevin to this sad, sad question; all these weeks, he has been watching my receding shadow and wondering, *Is she gone for good?* What's left of my heart—that drained, sickly creature, that brown, dying insect—crawls up through my chest cavity, into my throat, and lurches out of my mouth. There it is, on the sidewalk, skittering away, looking for a better home. There's nothing but hollowness inside me now, nothing but a vacant lot, a patch of dead grass, maybe a FOR RENT sign rotting in the ground.

What is the answer? My brain is frozen. I still want to be married to you, but I might be carrying someone else's child? I don't want to be married to you, but I don't want to cause you pain, either, so let's just stay together and nobody will get hurt? Will you want to stay married to me after you find out what I've done—what I'm still doing? *I'm so sorry.* My skin—all of it, the entire outer layer of me—seems to tighten, as if someone is pulling on me from the back. I do the only thing I can possibly do under the circumstances. I pretend I didn't hear him. "Come on," I say, spotting a small space between cars and stepping into the street. "Now's our chance." Without waiting for a reply, I dash halfway across, with about two inches to spare between me and a speeding Geo Metro. I pause for a second on the yellow dividing line in the middle of the road. I can feel the hot whoosh of wind from the oncoming traffic. I calculate fast whether I can make it ahead of the blue minivan that's barreling down Oakland, or whether I should wait. I glance back at Kevin, who has not followed me. He's still there, on the sidewalk, watching me, cautious, waiting. The steady stream of traffic between us shows no sign of abating. I turn away from him and decide to make a run for it ahead of the minivan. In the blink of an eye, I go. I run so fast my feet barely touch the ground. I run so fast I fly to the other side.

IT'S BEEN A WEEK SINCE DICK'S FUNERAL, AND I'VE HAD a million opportunities to take the test—which I bought last Saturday, which lurks in the back of the linen closet, scary-monster-like, waiting for me—but I haven't done it. I keep feeling like I'm about to get my period: I'm bloated, my boobs are sore, and I'm irritable as hell. But, according to my stealthy online research, these are signs of early pregnancy, too. "Hey, if you're a few weeks pregnant and you feel like crap, don't worry," YoMama.com advises. "Things will only get worse!"

It's Friday, and David and I are meeting at White's. He e-mailed last night and suggested the café, rather than our usual rendezvous spot, his bed. "I'm still swamped with work," he wrote. "But I need to see you." So here I am, sitting at the same table where we had our first date, watching the same people in their colorful coats hurrying in breathlessly for their midmorning coffees, feeling the same way I felt on that fateful Friday two months ago—like vomiting—but quite possibly for a different reason.

I'm biting my nails again, too, just like last time, when David ducks in the door. When I see him, I quickly pull my thumb out of my mouth, and a bit of cuticle rips off; I stare for a second as blood oozes out.

"Hi," David whispers, pulling a chair up close to mine. He looks overworked and grim. I hadn't decided ahead of time what I was going to say to him. On the one hand, it's probably better to offer up potentially life-changing news when you know for sure that it's true. Why torture him with, *David, my period's late,* when I could go home and find out in a matter of minutes what that means—when all it might mean is that my period's late? On the other hand, it's as much his problem as it is mine. At least, it ought to be. Is it? I don't know. If there's a rule book for this kind of situation, nobody's shown it to me. It's probably in that aisle at Walgreen's. Now that I see David, his tired eyes, his unshaven face, sympathy for him suggests that I should spare him the uncertainty. But something else, stronger, tugs at me to tell him quickly, *now.*

"David, I—"

"I need to say something to you," he interrupts, reaching for both of my hands and setting them gently on the table, covering them with his. I love his hands. They're broad, almost square, but with long, surprisingly delicate fingers. Just the feel of them, on top of mine, makes me shiver.

"Okay, well, I need to tell you something, too," I say. He pulls his right hand away and I notice the blood from my cuticle smeared on his fingertip. I'm about to point it out to him, but something in the way he's looking at me turns my words into ice.

"What I need to say is," he starts, pulling his left hand away, too, leaving my poor hands naked on the table, "I can't. Because you're . . . I mean . . ." He's got his palms squeezed up against the sides of his head now, as if he's physically holding his skull together. He sighs. "I practiced saying this, believe it or not."

"I don't know what you're trying to tell me," I say quietly, even though I'm beginning to.

He waits for a long time, and then he says, "It's that you're *married,* Emily."

I can practically feel the porcupine quills poke out through my skin. "Well, that's not exactly—" *breaking news,* I'm about to say, but he interrupts again.

"It's that you're married, and I'm not the kind of person who has an affair. With someone who's married. That's not the kind of person I am." David hasn't taken his jacket off, I notice, as if he wants to be able to make a fast escape. "Well, it's not the kind of person I thought I was." This is the man I've been having an affair with for the past six weeks. This is the man I ate chocolate pudding off of a few days ago. "I'm . . . I was . . . crazy about you," he says, "but." He lets go of his head. *What about the pudding? Didn't that pudding mean anything to you?* "Really crazy about you. But," he says again. He's become very repetitive all of a sudden. I would like to mention this to him. *You've become quite repetitive,* I would say, in the immortal words of Len Ross, *and you're repeating yourself!* "You're married," he continues, a doctor giving bad news to a terminal patient, "and this feels wrong. It's felt wrong the whole time, Emily. Don't you think it has?" He says it like it's an urgent request. If I feel the same way, then David is off the hook. I don't, though. I don't! But before I can answer, he barrels on. "I love being with you, in a lot of ways." My stomach lurches again. I press my fingers onto the surface of the table and swallow hard. What I want to do most right now is throw up. "But more and more, as time goes on, I just feel guilty. Morally compromised." I'm just looking at him, memorizing his face. I wonder if he practiced that phrase, "morally compromised," on the way over. It sounds a little bit mean.

"Well," I say. It comes out a croak. Later, I'm sure, I will have a million responses to David's breakup speech—and this, clearly, is what I am on the receiving end of, a breakup speech—but right now it's all I can do to keep the contents of my stomach approximately where they should be, to breathe, not to let David see me cry, and to keep my heart from exploding into shards in my chest. That's one good thing, I suppose: it turns out I still do have a heart.

Just my luck. "I guess you're a better person than I am," I say in the most sarcastic voice I can muster. But then, as I say it, we both realize that it's probably true, and David flashes me the most sympathetic, hangdog look, such a striking admission of our ethical inequality, that I practically gasp. *Morally compromised,* he said.

I get up so fast, I knock my chair over. He might have his jacket on, but I'm going to be the one to leave first. That'll show him! I pick up my chair with a clatter and shove it under the table. "Hey, buster," I say too loudly. "If you're so hung up on *ethics,* it wasn't very *ethical* of you to break up with me in a coffee shop!" Any second now, my head's going to spin all the way around. I know I'm not making sense. It just strikes me as a bit unnecessary to break up with someone in a coffee shop. In my favorite coffee shop! Who's morally compromised now? "Who's morally compromised now?" I'm going to leave on a high note, albeit an insane one. I'm going to leave on a note so high it shatters glass. I hurriedly shove my arms through the sleeves of my coat, realizing in a muddle that it's upside down. I wrench myself out of it and try, in a last-ditch effort for a dignified exit, to drape it over my shoulder.

"Emily, wait." David is standing up now, too, and not knocking anything over in the process, either. Damn the jacket that he never took off.

"No," I say. "Wait for what?" In about two seconds, I'll be crying. I need to get out of here.

Now, finally, David looks as sad and confused as I feel. He grabs me by the wrist as I'm trying to flee. "Shouldn't we talk about this?"

I freeze in my tracks. "Talk about it?" David holds on to my wrist and pulls me slightly nearer. I'm suddenly aware of the other people in the coffee shop. If I glanced around, I'm sure I'd see them staring at us. I'm going to have to find a new favorite coffee shop. "Outside," I hiss.

I manage to get my coat on and maneuver around the tables and out the door without tripping over my shoelaces or falling

over a chair. The November air—back to normal now and cold—
is a shock in my lungs. David is a half step behind me as I hurry
away from White's.

"Stop, please, Emily," David says. If he grabs me again, I'm
going to clock him. I do stop, though, and I turn to him. We're a
half block from White's, away from people, in front of Metropoli-
tan Bank. "Can we sit?" he asks, motioning to a green bench. I
want to flee, but I have to stay. A tiny, hopeful voice in my head
whispers: *Maybe he's going to say he doesn't mean it. Maybe he already
regrets this fiasco.* So I sit, knowing that that high voice lies. Away
from the scene of the crime, at least, I no longer feel quite as much
like crying. We're out of the sun, in the shadow of the bank's
awning, and I realize just how cold it is. David sits next to me,
close, and I inch away, hugging my arms around me.

I shake my head. "You're breaking up with me. Honestly,
what else is there to talk about?" My words wisp away in the air.

He leans forward, his elbows on his knees, and looks straight
ahead. I glance at the profile I could draw in my sleep: the dark hair
that falls across his forehead, his slightly crooked nose, the lips that
are almost too gorgeous to belong to a man. "I don't know. I guess
I just wanted to explain."

My emotions are swinging back and forth so fast they could
create their own energy source. I'm terribly sad. I'm calm and
resigned. I'm furious. I'm definitely furious! I hear a snort come
out of my mouth and I sit straight up. "David, you've already indi-
cated that our relationship has weakened your value system. What
now? Do you want to describe just how dreadful you feel about
sleeping with me?" I dig around in my purse for a pen and hold it
up to him triumphantly. "Do you want to draw me a graph?"

But David just sits there. He won't take the bait, won't give me
the satisfaction of a good argument. At least if we were shouting at
each other, we'd be in it together. "I'm really sorry," he says. He's
still staring straight ahead, and his voice is low and quiet. He's
speaking slowly, carefully. It's as if he's searching inside himself
to talk to me. Even in my heartbreak and confusion I can see that.

"I was so excited when we got together. So excited about getting to know you. You know, because we were . . ." He brightens for a second. "But then things started to go south for me. As much as I . . . maybe I . . . loved you . . ." He takes a deep breath, exhales fast. I feel my eyes start to sting, and I swallow hard. "I just, I started to think about what we were doing. I mean, this is really wrong, Emily. Don't you ever think about that?" Without waiting for me to answer, he continues. "It started to feel sour. I started to feel awful. And that's how I've been feeling."

"For how long?" I ask.

"A few weeks."

I want to say, "But I don't love Kevin! I love you!" I want to fall down at David's feet and cry, "I'll do whatever it takes to make it better. I'll leave Kevin." But even as I'm thinking them, those words feel fake and hollow, scripted, what Spurned Lover tragically exclaims in the breakup scene, because even as I'm thinking them, I'm getting over this, in a weird way, like I can see myself two months from now, and I am not still mourning David. But at the same time, my throat is closing up and tears are pricking my eyes, because, right now, Jesus, this hurts. And then I remember that I could be pregnant. I'm married, I've been cheating on my husband, I'm possibly pregnant, and I've just been dumped. I think I'm actually laughing from the sheer horrible absurdity of it when I turn around, toward the bank, and that's when I see Kevin standing against the building, about six feet from our bench. From the look on his face, he's been there for a while.

"I've never seen anyone so calm," I say, my head buried under the covers. "Never." I think I've said the same thing five or six times now, but it just keeps coming out of my mouth. I'm in the freshly painted guest room at Meg and Steve's, huddled, freezing, under four heavy blankets. I can't get warm. But I'm going to have to emerge from this nest before too long; the oxygen is running out.

"What did he *say?*" Meg asks patiently, wearily. She's sitting on a hard-backed chair next to the bed. I hear her shift, hear the rustle of fabric. She's been trying for the last hour to get the story out of me, but I've been incapable of narrative. All I can do is hold out shards of my shattered life to her to glimpse, from within my increasingly poisonous little cocoon.

"Okay," I say, shoving my head out into the air, breathing, finally. The room smells of paint. The walls are dark green, a color called "Reverie." I helped Meg pick it. I wonder what color "Infidelity" would be. Probably red, or fuchsia. Something jarring. Something compelling, something with repercussions; ultimately you'd know every time you looked at your walls: a mistake. "Here's how it went." I look at my overnight bag lying open in the corner. After the episode in front of the bank with David and Kevin, I staggered home, threw what I thought were a few essentials into my suitcase, and headed over here. I must have been in a trance: all I managed to pack were four pairs of underwear and three sweaters I never wear anymore. No bras, no socks, no shirts, no pants. "I turned around, and Kevin just glared at me. There was hatred in his eyes. And ice. He was so calm." Oops, I already said that. I take a big breath again, then a sip of water from the glass on the nightstand; the water tastes vaguely like paint. "He said, 'I thought so.' *I thought so.* He knew. And you know, I knew he knew, and a part of me must have wanted him to know, because I obviously didn't have the guts to tell him, so I'm almost glad he knew, glad he *knows,* even though I'm not sure if I really wanted him to know or not, you know?"

"No," Meg says, shaking her head. "Sweetie." She rests her hand on the lump under the covers that is my knee. She shakes her head again. "I'll tell you, I'm at a loss."

"And David," I say with a gulp, reliving the whole squalid scene again. I must have started when I saw Kevin; I must have moved or tensed or jerked, because just then I noticed with horror that David was moving toward me on the bench, like he was about to comfort me; he was reaching out for me, and I heard myself say, quietly, sternly, "Please don't hug me in front of my husband."

And then David looked at me, a cartoon of himself, his features practically rearranged from the shock, and he swiveled around, and his eyes met Kevin's, and then he looked down, flushed, and right then I knew: that was it for us; it was all over, because nobody can feel that much naked shame and still have desire left over, or even much affection. He whispered, "Oh, my God," but it wasn't directed at me; his dismay wasn't meant to be shared; it was private and horrible, and we were separate.

Meg is silent for a minute, then suddenly smacks her hand against her forehead and says, "Ohhh!"

"What?"

"I never understood quite why it was so awkward when you ran into David in front of the school back in October! Now I get it!" The look of comprehension on her face fades and turns back to incredulity. "I can't believe you didn't tell me."

I can't quite believe any of this, the mess of my life, the aftermath of the hurricane. I'm not even sure if there are any survivors, including myself. Kevin stood against the bank building, his hands shaking, his nostrils slightly flared. There were no other indications that he'd just overheard me, just the subtle, contained variations of Kevin. But he had heard. He stared at David for a long time as if David were somebody he thought he recognized. And then Kevin looked at me and he said, "I thought so," and then he turned and he left. "He left," I say to Meg. "He didn't even wait for any kind of explanation; he didn't yell at me or hit David or do any of the things you might think a betrayed husband would do." "Cuckolded," is the word. What color would that be? An awful orange. A color you could hardly even look at. And at the thought of that, I finally, finally start to cry.

Meg once told me that sometimes, at her school, one student will deliberately hurt another one, hit or bite or scratch another kid, and then, unaccountably, the malicious little rug rat who caused the injury will start to cry. And when that happens, Meg will take that child aside and gently tell her that she has to stop crying, that she hurt someone, and so she has to be a big girl, and stop crying, and say she's sorry. Because, Meg told me, if you're the one who inflicts the pain, it's not fair to start crying. It's not fair to weep for sympathy when it's apologizing that you ought to be doing. That's what I'm thinking about now, as I'm bawling uncontrollably, as I'm sobbing on Meg's sympathetic shoulder, drenching her pretty pink shirt with my murderer's tears.

I wonder where Kevin is now, if he's gone home, if he's still wandering the streets. If he's packed his bags and headed back to Oregon. Meg loves Kevin. She'd probably rather be with him, comforting the one who deserves it. But she's my best friend, so she holds me, she rocks me back and forth a little bit as I cry and cry. After a few minutes, during which the only noise in the room is my pathetic hiccupping and wheezing, Meg gently pulls away from my soggy embrace, then climbs into the bed next to me. "Okay, sweetie," she says softly, her arm around my shoulder. "It's going to be okay."

It's probably not. But what else can I do but try to believe her?

As much as I'd like her to, Meg can't babysit me for the whole day. She's meeting Steve at the doctor's office for her first ultrasound. And despite the thundercloud over my head, she can barely contain her excitement at the prospect of hearing the baby's heartbeat for the first time, of seeing an image of the tiny black-and-white blob that will, months from now, be her baby. After another sympathetic half hour, during which she doesn't tell me that I'm a faithless slut and I don't tell her that I'm a faithless slut who might be pregnant, she leaves me to get ready. She hugs me again and asks if I want to come to the appointment, but of course I don't. I can't imagine injecting my vile self into Meg and Steve's beautiful moment. Meg's been waiting for this ultrasound for weeks. Although the thought does occur to me that maybe the doctor could just glide that contraption from Meg's belly to mine, and I'd have an answer.

When she leaves, I pick up the phone to call Heather. Luckily,

Heather had transplanted herself from Kevin's and my apartment (is it still Kevin's and my apartment?) to our parents' house two days ago. So at least she wasn't propped up on the couch fixing her gimlet eyes on me while I flew through the place gathering my things. At least I didn't have to face her questions and recriminations, what would surely have been her judgmental response to my situation, born of her newfound monogamous and maternal zeal. I can just picture her steady, passive-aggressive gaze; I can hear her saying, "You must feel really bad about yourself, Emily. That's how I felt when *I* used to cheat on my boyfriends." My finger hovers over the last nine in my parents' phone number, and then I put the phone down abruptly. Ambivalence is the only constant between Heather and me. Sometimes she's the first person I want to talk to, sometimes the last. I can't deal with her now. And if Len or Barbara were to answer the phone, I just might break into a thousand tiny pieces. Thanksgiving is in six days, anyway. When I show up at my parents' door with a bottle of wine and no husband, I'll have plenty to answer for.

I rub my freezing-cold feet together under the blankets and consider my options. On the surface, I feel like a blind, miserable bottom-feeder crawling around in the sludge. Deeper down than that, I feel like a shameless, guilty wretch who leaves a toxic wake wherever she goes. But deeper down than that? I feel sort of calm. Not good, certainly not good, but steady. For someone whose entire web of relationships has just unraveled, I feel surprisingly un-alone. I still don't know what I'll do if there is a baby. But right this second, I don't need to know that. Right now, there's only one thing I need to find out. So what else is there for me but to take the test? Meg's gone; I have the house to myself. I don't have to work today. And my social calendar is wide open. A small shiver wriggles through my body, up and down my arms and legs: my first sad wave of unrequited desire for David. But the voice in my head that has been, up to now, fairly unreliable, has changed pitch, become recognizable. *Proceed,* it says. *Face this.* If Meg has any pregnancy tests left over from before, I know exactly where they'll be. She showed me, back before her miscarriage, before everything. She kept them upstairs, in the bathroom cabinet, behind the toothpaste. So I grab a sweater—baggy, with pink and orange stripes and a huge hole in the elbow; I couldn't have dreamed up an uglier sweater—from my suitcase, wrap it around myself, and trudge upstairs.

Meg and Steve's bathroom is the best room in their house. It's huge and inviting, with an enormous claw-foot bathtub and a big purple plush rug a person could sleep on. Hell, maybe I will. Maybe I'll move into their bathroom, make it my new home. With a hot plate and some new curtains, I could be very comfortable here. I dig out some apple bubble bath from Meg's side of the medicine cabinet and turn on the water. Then I root around a bit more, and sure enough, there's an unopened package of Easy One-Step Early Pregnancy Test. As the room fills with steam, I peel off my clothes. The last time I undressed in the middle of the day, it was for a different reason. Naked, my clothes in a heap on the rug, I sit down on the toilet. The test instructions are complicated, or maybe my brain is just frozen, but it takes me a few minutes to figure out exactly what to do. Hold the indicator stick under the stream? What stream? I picture a babbling brook filled with tiny swimming babies gurgling and clamoring to be noticed. Here I am! Pick me! I'm the one! If Kevin had written these instructions, they would be simple and elegant, clear but with respect for the enormity of the task. If Kevin had written them, I believe I would know exactly what to do. Finally, after reading the same three sentences a dozen times, I understand. I maneuver the little plastic stick under myself. It's an ignominious way to determine a pregnancy, really: a whole new life announces itself in the splash of urine. The test is supposed to be "mess free!" but of course in one second my entire hand is wet, and the tester stick, which is supposed to stay dainty and dry except for the tip, is dripping. With my dry hand, I grab a tissue and spread it out on the edge of the tub. Carefully, I lay the wet stick on top of it, and I climb into the warm water. A song we played on the ancient record player the day

I helped Meg at school pops into my head, replete with cheery bells and whistles: "Engine, engine, number nine, rolling down Chicago line. If that train goes off the track, do you want your money back? *Yes! No! Maybe so! Yes! No! Maybe so!*" Of course you would want your money back if your train derailed. What kind of idiot wouldn't want her money back? *Yes! No! Maybe so!* The Easy One-Step Early Pregnancy Test requires three minutes for the results to appear in the "indicator window." *Yes! No! Maybe so!* Three minutes. I'm not wearing a watch, but I am determined not to stare at the stick. I close my eyes and start counting. I lean back against the tiles and sink as low as I can into the deep tub. One Mississippi, two Mississippi, three. Dr. Miller has already offered me full-time employment, in the wake of Dick's death. So I know I'll be okay financially. I suppose I could move back in with my parents for a while. Barbara would surely get over her disappointment in me when she holds her grandchild in her arms. I can picture Len in the early morning, the baby resting against his shoulder. "Look here, little baby, out the back window, at the maple tree. Did you know that the earliest settlers in Wisconsin, approximately two hundred years ago, used the same technique for procuring sap that maple syrup manufacturers use today?" Thirty-three, thirty-four, thirty-five. Is it really over with David? I can practically feel the texture of his skin, his thick hair, taste him as if I'm running my tongue lightly over his lips. Did Kevin actually find out? Jesus, was he really standing there? The hugeness of this reality explodes like a volcano in my brain, creating an ugly new landmass there. Kevin *found out*. Forty-eight, forty-nine, fifty. There's a billboard on Capitol Drive that advertises DNA testing for the general public. "Daddy, Daddy, Where Are You?" a fat cartoon baby pleads, in bold black letters. I've always scoffed at this sad, bizarre advertisement as I've driven past it. What kind of mother needs a DNA test to determine her baby's paternity? Seventy-four, seventy-five. The bubbles make white peaks like frothy waves on my knees and my stomach. One hundred two, one hundred three. There's no way I'm pregnant. Surely I'm the kind of woman who will need complicated hormone treatments to get pregnant someday, injections and patches and petri dishes, not the type who accidentally gets knocked up when she's not looking, not the type whose body wantonly gives up its eggs to the highest bidder. I straighten my legs, rest my feet against the tiles. I'm starting to feel a little bit relieved. One hundred forty-four, one forty-five. This is just the last hurrah of the dream that was David. I'm such an idiot. I miss Kevin. I've been married to him for five years; I've loved him for nine. And now, my God, I've *ruined* him, ruined us. One hundred eighty. My eyes are still closed. Two lines mean yes, one means no. Yes, no, maybe so. Three minutes are up. One hundred ninety-two, one ninety-three. I have to stop counting now and open my eyes. I squeeze them shut, try to take a snapshot of everything this moment holds: the heat of the water on my body, the lingering apple scent of the bubbles, the pulsing in my veins. My eyes don't want to open. I breathe, and breathe some more, and then I open them. Eight lines dance in a blur as I try to focus—eight? The instructions said nothing about eight—and slowly the eight dwindle to four, then to two, and then one, but then two again, and two lines squirm in and out of focus, yes, no, maybe so; two lines, two lines like tiny pink minnows swimming toward me, yes, no, maybe so, yes, yes, yes.

When the phone rings, probably no more than ten minutes later, but I don't know for sure, since I stopped counting at 193, it doesn't even occur to me to answer it. I'm still submerged up to my chin in water that has grown tepid. I'm thinking about nothing. I'm thinking about the chipped grout on the bathtub tiles and the way the apple scent of the bubble bath is beginning to make me nauseous. I'm thinking that I'm going to have to emerge from the tub soon, at the very least because Meg and Steve will be home before too long. So I'm only half-listening when the machine picks up.

"Hey, Emily." Meg's voice is crackly and distorted. "Are you there? If you're there, could you please pick up?" Is she calling to tell me that they found out the baby's sex? Is it too early to know that information? I can't remember. For the first time, and surely not the last, I imagine the tiny tadpole swimming around inside of me. A boy, I think, and then, *Oh, crap,* because I don't want this, my God, I don't want this. I realize I have no idea what he might look like at this moment, just a few weeks from his sordid beginnings. I'm picturing a tiny, fully formed, fully clothed little man, a homunculus, a small sprout of a human wearing a top hat and tails and twirling a miniature cane: Mr. Peanut. A tiny flame of tenderness lights in me; I douse it, fast. I hoist myself out of the bath, wrap a towel around myself (it's slightly damp; I decide not to think about it), and grab the phone just as Meg is saying, "Okay, I guess you're not there. . . ."

Is she calling to describe the sound of the heartbeat, the feeling of hearing it for the first time? I don't want to steal her moment, but I'm going to have to tell her my news, too. I won't be able to wait. "Don't hang up! I'm here!"

Meg bursts into tears immediately. It's a full minute before she can get any words out, but even as I'm waiting for her to speak, my heart sinks, and I know. "There's no heartbeat," she says finally, still sobbing. "They couldn't find a heartbeat."

"Oh, Meg."

"The baby's gone. It's dead."

"Oh, sweetie."

"Again," she whispers. She cries, the most racking sobs I've ever heard. I can make out Steve's low tones in the background, a soothing murmur. I'm sitting on the edge of their bed in a towel, marveling at the small-scale meanness of the universe, its banal cruelty. Meg is not pregnant, but I am. In seventh grade, Amelia Huber, the prettiest, most cold-blooded, and, not coincidentally, most popular girl in our class, asked me if I wanted to eat lunch with her and her friends. The entire day I was giddy with anticipation. When I finally sat down with them, she and her friends gig-

gled, gathered their trays, and got up and moved. The universe is
Amelia Huber. "I wasn't expecting this," Meg says after a while.
Her voice is high and small.

"No," I say. "I know."

"Emily, what am I going to do?"

"It'll be okay," I say stupidly, an echo of her words to me just
an hour ago. They sound as wrong coming out of my mouth as
they did coming from hers. "Where are you now? Are you at the
doctor's office?"

"No, we're in the car," she says. "We're on our way home."
Meg used to call me in the car on her way home from school to tell
me all the silly details of her day, and she loves to annoy Steve by
phoning from the passenger seat when they're heading somewhere
together. "We're going to a movie!" she'll say happily. "Steve's
wearing that awful shirt his mom got him for his birthday!"

"Is there anything you need? Do you want me to be here when
you get home?" I ask.

Meg confers with Steve for a moment; I hear their muffled
voices. "Actually, maybe could you go to your parents' or something for a while? I'm sorry. I think I'm going to need to go to
bed . . ." She and Steve need to be alone, but she's too polite to say
that. Meg, poor Meg.

"Of course. I'll get out of here."

"Call me later, okay?" Meg sounds like she's about five
years old.

"I love you," I say, and think, *which is worth very little in today's
market.* After we hang up, I quickly towel off, put on my ratty
clothes, and gather my things together. I could go to my parents', and I might even be able to make up a plausible lie so as not
to arouse suspicions—the heat's out in the apartment; there's a
mouse infestation; all of my possessions have mysteriously been
incinerated—but the fact is, I need to go home and talk to Kevin.
He deserves that, at the very, very, very least.

.　.　.

In the car on the way back to the apartment, I wasn't thinking about the fact that I was pregnant; not exactly. The news I had just learned felt strangely like something I had known for years, for my whole life. I felt a weird tingling in my limbs. I was alone, and pregnant, and I didn't know who the father was. But I was anesthetized. There was so much to freak out about, I couldn't pick just one thing, so I somehow abstained completely.

As I merged into three lanes of light traffic, I convinced myself that Kevin would not be there. I figured that he would have fled, that he would have hastily packed his bags, a rerun of my actions earlier today, and booked the first flight back to Oregon. Simultaneously, I came to believe, as I was driving over the Hoan Bridge, that Kevin would in fact be home: that he would be holed up in the living room with some canned goods, a flashlight, and a few blankets, vowing never to leave, and that he would have chained the door, and maybe propped some heavy furniture against it for good measure. Why would he want to see me? I wouldn't want to see me. I would knock on the door a few times and then turn away in resignation, allowing Kevin time, the one thing I could give him. I even started to relax a little bit, believing that I was about to receive a stay of execution, a snow day on the morning of a math test I hadn't studied for.

"Hey, kid, your mom's a coward," I said out loud to the fetus. "But starting today, I'm going to try harder." I nodded and gripped the steering wheel. Then I thought that those words might have confused the fetus: try harder? Try harder to do what? To be a coward? The fetus hasn't had any experiences yet in the world. For all he knows, being a coward might be something to aspire to. I tried to explain. "What I mean is, I've behaved terribly. Maybe I'll tell you about it sometime." I was gesticulating, and rambling, and when I flicked on my turn signal to change lanes and glanced out the window, I noticed that the man in the green Honda in the next lane was staring at me as if I were crazy. I gave him a little wave.

Now, trudging down the hallway to our apartment, I see

Kevin's shoes lined up neatly on the doormat—even in crisis he remains steadfastly tidy—and I know that the lock will not have been changed and the door will not be barred, and that this, to put it mildly, is it. "Brace yourself, kid," I say to the fetus, and I slide the key into the lock and open the door.

I sense Kevin's presence before I see him. If this were a horror movie, all the ten-year-olds in the audience would be shouting at the screen, "Don't turn the corner! Don't turn the corner!" But, just like in a horror movie, the girl never heeds the warnings. I plod through the empty, darkened kitchen to the living room. The only light is coming in through the half-open blinds, dim and diffuse. The first thing I see is my collection of colored glass bottles smashed, the carpet littered with pretty shards of red, blue, yellow, and green. I swallow thickly. I deserve this, and more. The next thing I see is Kevin, sitting primly on the couch. His hands lay folded on his lap. He looks up at me, as pale as I've ever seen him, which is saying quite a lot; he's as white as a mushroom, and the skin under his eyes is an alarming shade of gray. He looks like a corpse. This is how I've made him feel.

Kevin gestures at the wall and the broken glass. "Sorry about that," he says, no trace of irony in his voice.

I nod, swallow again.

"Why are you here?" he asks politely, as if he's never seen me before.

"I thought you—" I have to clear my throat. "I thought you might want to talk. Or yell at me. Or throw things at me." I smile wanly.

Kevin shakes his head. "No."

"Okay. Um." I clear my throat again, hug my arms close to my chest. "How are you? How's it going?"

He looks at me calmly, icily. "It's going fine. It's going great." He lifts his hands and thrusts them into the air as if he's about to conduct a symphony, then just as abruptly drops them back into his lap, defeated. "It's going fucking swimmingly, Emily. How's it going with you?"

"Oh, um, okay. Okay." I survey the living room again, wonder if I should gather up the few things I feel attached to—my grandmother's candlesticks, the potted begonia, Aunt Mimi's blanket—to protect them from Kevin's wrath. But he seems pretty wrathed out; he seems to have wreaked what wrath he had. "Okay," I say again, stupidly. I look away from Kevin; I can't bear his gaze. My eyes land on our wedding album, displayed neatly where it always is, on top of the bureau. At least he hasn't destroyed it. I probably would have. I have the urge to grab the pretty white photo album and run. Our apartment suddenly seems like an archaeological site, the foreign habitat of a lost civilization, and I want to flee with the most important relic. My favorite picture in that album is a candid one of the two of us, taken just after the ceremony. After the guests had descended upon us like pleasantly scented preying mantises, had bestowed their good wishes and kisses on us, and had moved on to embrace our families, Kevin and I sneaked off behind the big maple tree, to where we thought no one could see us. One of the guests, armed with a disposable camera, caught us there, holding hands, our foreheads together, leaning into each other. In that photograph, I look giddy and keyed up; Kevin looks relieved. We look happy. I remember feeling at that moment that Kevin and I had blended together, that our wedding ceremony really had created something new and better out of us, a lovely sculpture from two hunks of clay. I think of that photograph now, and it's a picture of somebody else's life. We'll never have a moment like that again.

I walk over to the wall opposite Kevin, where the broken glass is strewn over the carpeting. I kneel down and start picking up the bigger pieces, placing them carefully in the palm of my right hand. They're like tiny daggers, and I'm slow and deliberate as I try not to slice my skin. I avoid the tiniest shards; when I've cleared up most of the bigger pieces, I'll use the mini–vacuum cleaner we keep in the bathroom closet for the smaller ones. I pile bits of glass into my hand. I reach for the thick, intact bottom of the green bottle my mom got me for my birthday, the razor-sharp edge of my favorite, delicate, pink one that I found at a garage sale. For a second, I feel unfairly, unaccountably angry for what Kevin has done to my bottles. Then that feeling disappears. Mixed together in my palm, the broken pieces look like little, lethal Christmas ornaments, or precious jewels.

"You don't have to do that," Kevin says softly. It's all ahead of him, all of the ugly cleanup work, how he'll have to navigate the terrain of despair and recovery and the way he'll finally shape his life without me. Just like Meg and Steve, who will have to stumble through their own new, familiar grief: it's all just beginning. I suppose there are emotional minefields ahead of me, too. Along with other things.

"I don't mind," I say. I pull a longish segment of the neck of a blue bottle from the carpeting. My hand is full of broken glass now. I can picture exactly how Kevin did this, exactly how he destroyed these bottles: not in rage or bitter passion, not blinded by the image of my face as he hurled the glass against the wall in uncontrollable fury. That's not Kevin. Kevin, I'm certain, considered his actions for a full ten minutes before lining up the bottles in a careful row on the coffee table, one by one pitching them deliberately, precisely at the wall as if he were trying to win a giant teddy bear at the fair. *Step One, lift bottle in hand and aim at target. Step Two, extend arm back and behind head for maximum velocity.* Kevin, I'm sure, winced as each bottle shattered and fell, beyond repair, to the floor.

"Kevin," I say, still kneeling, surrounded now by only the most minute shards of glass, still gingerly holding the larger pieces in the palm of my hand. "I'm going to vacuum the rest of this, but don't walk around in bare feet for a while, all right?"

He nods, absently fiddles with the corner of a couch pillow. *What a mess, what a mess, what a mess.* I could turn things around here; in an instant, just by squeezing my hand shut, I could initiate a sequence of events, a reaction: Emily feels pain, sees blood, cries out. Kevin jumps up. Together, Emily and Kevin discard glass, clean and rinse wound, apply bandage. Kevin would tend to me with sympathy. He would wash away my blood, watch with me as it mixed with water and flowed down the sink. Kevin would hold my hand and carefully wrap it in gauze. He would do this, tenderly, whether he wanted to or not; unlike me, he always rises above his worst instincts and obeys his best ones. And I would stand there, inelegant and dripping, letting Kevin comfort me. I would ease into him, let him cradle my hand in his. Maybe then I could inflict the final injury.

Instead I stand, walk over to the kitchen garbage can, and let the pieces of glass drop from my hand into the pail. *See, kid? I didn't manipulate this one. I'm getting better.* I stand there, looking at the contents of the garbage pail: coffee grounds, take-out containers, dirty napkins, onion skins and spinach stems from a dinner I made two nights ago. I stare at the debris, trying to divine my future. A stink rises up to meet me. How will I do this? How exactly will I say to Kevin, "I'm pregnant, but it's quite possibly not your baby?" *Hey, fetus, any suggestions? Now's your chance.*

I hear Kevin move in the other room: there's the soft thud of his feet on the floor; there's the creak of the squeaky floorboard next to the rocking chair. "Go," he says from the living room, just loudly enough for me to hear. I'm still standing in front of the garbage can, my feet glued to the ground. I let the lid drop, but I don't move. "Forget about vacuuming," he says, more loudly now. "Just leave." I'm immobile. After another minute, I hear Kevin start coming toward me. I'm still frozen where I stand. "Emily, just *leave!*" he shouts from the hallway just a few feet away. "Why can't you *listen to me?* Just LEAVE, JUST LEAVE, JUST LEAVE!"

He's behind me now as I turn away from the garbage can. "Leave," he says again, this time almost a whisper. I turn to him. His face looks pinched, as if I repulse him, or he's bracing himself, or both. He stands there for a minute, studying me. We're close enough to kiss. I'm seized with the urge to look away again, but I don't. Kevin's hair is greasy and sticking up in strange places, and he's unshaven, although, since he is not a hairy person, only the most observant viewer would recognize this. He looks like he hasn't showered in a week, even though he learned about my infidelity just a few hours ago. He looks like he's aged five years in one morning. He presses his lips together so hard they disappear. "Did you love him?" he asks finally. "Was it worth it?"

It's an amazing thing to wrap your life around someone else's. It's mind-boggling, really, to choose one partner, a single mate, from so many, many men: men who may have been boyfriends or lovers or flings or one-time dates, or just harmless, brief flirtations; men who passed by on the sidewalk and smiled, men who were just a moment of eye contact. There are so many of them, on airplanes and in classrooms, living in apartment buildings across the street, inhabiting neighboring offices. So many fish in the sea! That's what my mother always said when one of those eligible men turned out to be a loser, or not interesting enough, or plainly not interested in me. It really is quite a thing to pick one person from the throngs, to be picked by him in return, and to say: *you, forever.* And it's even more astonishing to wield the power to devastate that one person with nothing more than a broken promise. Did I love David? Was it worth it? *Yes, no, maybe so. Kid, was it worth it?* The fetus is unhelpfully mute, as usual. *David wasn't really the point,* I think, but I don't say it; I just hold out my empty hands to Kevin, palms up, an unanswerable question, a wordless apology, a plea.

It's not entirely true that I'm homeless, I think, as I sit in the car around the corner from my apartment building, wiping nonexistent tears from my face. After I left Kevin dazed and alone and staring at the garbage can, I managed to get into my car and drive a half block to a side street so that he wouldn't see me if he moved from where he was rooted and glanced out the window. Then I pulled over, turned off the engine, let out a loud, weird moan, and tried to cry. Nothing came. I rested my head on the cool steering wheel. *I'm alone, I'm pregnant, David dumped me, I've destroyed Kevin, and I'm homeless,* I thought. *A tear or two would not be out of line here.* I took another deep breath. "Ohhhh!" I said out loud, forcing the air from my lungs. "Unnnnhhhh." Then, in a last-ditch effort, I bit the inside of my cheek, hard. My cheek began to throb, but my eyes were dry as stones. I raised my head and looked around, licking the pinched skin on the inside of my mouth. I was parked on Edgewood Avenue, a street of small bright bungalows and trees on both sides that are so big and vibrant their leaves meet overhead, like they're shaking hands. A woman wearing a long flowered dress and mittens was unloading shopping bags from a nearby car. A few houses over, some children jumped in a pile of leaves. "Fuckers!" I said, from the privacy of my car, for the hell of it. "Fucking happy normal people!" Just then one of the children in the pile of leaves caught my eye and waved shyly. I waved back.

Now I pull a map out of the glove compartment and pretend to study it so that nobody calls the police on the strange, ranting lady in the red Toyota. True, I can't go to Meg's at the moment, and I can't go back to the apartment that may or may not still be mine, but I can always go to my parents'. Just not right now. The idea of staggering into my family's warm, judgmental, loving embrace is about as appealing as heading back upstairs and asking Kevin if he has change for a twenty. I consider checking into a motel. I contemplate driving somewhere secluded and huddling up in the backseat with the ratty picnic blanket we keep in the trunk. But in the end, I follow the time-honored tradition of uninspired women everywhere with time to kill: I head for the mall.

I grew up with a girl named Linda Payne. She was in the year between Heather and me in school and, aside from being called Window Payne throughout grade school, she mostly flew under the radar. During my junior year of high school, though, the amazing rumor circulated that she was having an affair with Mr. Giesler, the boys' gym teacher and girls' basketball coach. Baypoint High School, noted statewide for academic excellence, was a hotbed of nothing much. So the idea that a student was involved with a teacher ignited the place. Mr. Giesler must have been in his mid-twenties then. He had acne scars but he was thick-haired and handsome; his lightly pocked face made him seem worldly, like he'd lived through something. He was the kind of teacher who knew not only the names of the boys who'd had him for gym class, but all the girls' names, too, even the ones who didn't play basketball, which, in retrospect, is creepy. But it didn't seem creepy then. Back then, when he said hi to you in the hallway or patted your back as he passed you in the cafeteria, you felt special: for a moment, his coolness alighted on you; in a blink, it drifted away. The idea that Linda Payne and Ted Giesler were sleeping together was so titillating that for a while, Linda carried an exotic cachet, and Mr. Giesler seemed admirable instead of what he really was, which was criminal.

Linda, of course, got pregnant. Mr. Giesler got fired and divorced, in that order, and the next year, instead of going back to high school, Linda ended up working at Sugar's Shoes in Shorebrook Mall.

Sugar's Shoes is tucked away in a dark corridor of the mall and barely does any business. In the '80s and '90s, the store occupied a trendier, higher-rent location in Shorebrook. Since then, it's moved two or three times, farther and farther away from the main foot traffic. If it has to relocate again, the store will be a small kiosk in the parking lot. Even I can see that Sugar's footwear is four or five years behind the times: the clunky wooden heels and cutesy pastel flowers that adorn most of their shoes do not achieve the funky retro look they're going for, but instead seem sad, tired, like shoes that are trying too hard and, at the same time, not trying hard enough, shoes that get into trouble for passing notes, shoes that do not pay attention to current events. I suddenly feel a great and surprising affinity for Sugar's Shoes.

I used to see Linda Payne once in a while during my senior year (what should have been her junior year), the last time I had occasion to spend much time here. I've always hated shopping, but when I was in high school, I would sometimes allow myself to be dragged on aimless trips to the mall with my friends, friends who were like rechargeable shopping batteries, gaining more energy in each store, while I slowly dwindled. After an hour or so, I'd gasp dramatically and tell them to go on without me, and I'd park myself on a bench somewhere out of the way with a book and a soda. On her breaks, Linda would usually lurk in one of the vestibules or, if it was warm enough, outside on the concrete, smoking and pulling at her eyelashes. She'd taken on this eyelash-plucking habit, as far as I knew, after she'd had her baby. As a result, her face looked vulnerable and alien, with big pale blue irises and protruding eyeballs behind blinking, naked lids. I'd always say hello to her, and she'd wave back solemnly from the midst of a cloud of cigarette smoke. Even then, when I didn't know anything, I knew that sex had ruined Linda Payne. And even then, I knew it didn't have to be that way.

I plunk myself onto an empty plastic bench across from the shoe store. It's the same bench, or its replacement cousin, that was here thirteen years ago, and probably much longer. The cigarette burns dotting the edges could be Linda's, for all I know. Two slim, gray-haired ladies in track suits march past me at a surprising clip, arms swinging. I scan the mall and it occurs to me that I am look-ing for her, that I have come here looking for Linda. But what on earth would I say to her if I found her? *How did you manage it, Linda?* I knew she gave up her baby for adoption, and rumor was that it had been a boy.

Restless, I stand and make a quick pass of the few flounder-ing stores in this dark section of the mall: a cheap no-name per-fume store, a shop that sells only sugar-free candy, and, improbably, Santa's Warehouse, a store that sells Christmas items year-round. Someone has seized the obvious opportunity and scrawled "Santa's Whorehouse" over their sign. I wander into Sugar's Shoes; a young girl wearing great gobs of blue eyeliner looks up from the counter and fires at me, fast as an auctioneer, "Welcome to Sugar's Shoes. MayIhelpyoufindsomethingtoday?" I shake my head, and she bends back over her magazine without another glance. I make my way slowly up and down the aisles, feigning interest in a pair of thick-soled Mary Janes, some high-heeled plastic flip-flops. My life is a train wreck. How is it that I'm shopping for shoes instead of perched on the ledge of a tall building? Why am I okay? My future has derailed. Everything I love, everyone I have loved, is piled up around me, twisted and unrecognizable. I pick up a pair of brown boots from the shelf. Actually, I could use a pair of boots. I run my hands over the soft suede, scan the shelf, and find a size eight. I did this, though. I drove this train off its tracks. *Yes, no, maybe so.* I engineered this disaster. So maybe there's comfort in having no one to blame but myself. I sit down, slip my shoes off.

Here's a question for you, Linda Payne: Why did you let things get so out of hand? You could have done it differently: no one would have had to know. I imagine her still-puffy body next to mine on the little mirrored shoe-store seat. Why didn't you have an abortion, stay in school, graduate? You didn't have to do it this way.

"Hey," she would say, her left hand tugging at the few remaining lashes clinging to her eyelid. The smell of cigarette smoke would waft from her hair. "I might have, you know, done it differently. But I didn't even know until, well . . ."

I pull on first the left boot, then the right, understanding then that she wasn't thinking about a couple of missed periods, a bit of inexplicable nausea, a slight weight gain. Stress, she would have thought, if she noticed at all. And then a swelling, growing, the sudden knowledge, much too late.

"Do you have regrets?" The brown boots are comfortable, cushiony. I stand up, admire them in the floor-level mirror.

Imaginary Linda looks up at me from the bench. "There's no right answer," she says, wistfully. "Regrets?" She wriggles a pack of cigarettes out of her back pocket and lights one.

"Are you allowed to smoke in here?" I ask. She shrugs. "I bet you wish you hadn't smoked while you were pregnant," I say. "Somewhere out there a fourteen-year-old asthmatic probably resents you." Linda looks at me blankly and blows a big puff of smoke in my direction.

It occurs to me that I could just walk out wearing these soft boots. The *Cosmo*-reading girl at the counter hasn't looked up in five minutes. If she notices, she might not even say anything. And if she does, I'll just say I wasn't paying attention; I was distracted. I wander around the store wearing the boots, casually regarding the merchandise. Imaginary Linda trails behind me.

"So, what are you going to do?" she asks. She takes a long drag on her cigarette.

"Possibly shoplift these boots," I say. The idea of it, the thought of such a pointless, reckless act sends a thrill down my spine.

"That's not what I meant," Linda says, yanking away at her eyelashes with her free hand. "About the baby."

"Yeah, I know." I make my way quietly to the front of the store. My old sneakers are where I left them in the middle of the floor. This will be a tip-off to *Cosmo*-girl, but who cares? I'll just never come back here. "Seeing you . . . I haven't thought about you in years," I say. "I'm going to do what you should have done. I'm going to make an appointment, fix things, maybe go back to Kevin. I know he'll forgive me eventually, if I try hard enough. He never has to know about this." Yes, this is what I'll do. Clean up this mess.

But suddenly, like a sucker punch, imagining my life with Kevin takes the breath out of me. The heady confidence I was feeling a moment ago flies away, snickering. I collapse onto the nearest footstool. Do I really want to spend the next months, years, repentant, tiptoeing carefully around the man I have injured, trying desperately to repair the marriage I deliberately destroyed? And my other, imagined possibility? It no longer exists: David has taken himself out of the picture. And then, what about this pregnancy? Almost imperceptibly, as I sit here in Sugar's Shoes wearing brown suede boots that are not mine, something moves through me, settling, shifting. I'm not Linda Payne; I'm not a misguided fifteen-

year-old with no resources, no options. I'm a thirty-year-old pregnant woman who just came within an inch of shoplifting a pair of
boots. I kick them off and plod back to my shoes.

"There's no right answer," Linda says again, her bare eyelids
like tiny clamshells closing and opening over the pale pearls of her
eyes, closing and opening. She takes another puff of her cigarette.
"I will say this, though," she says softly. "Don't start pulling out
your eyelashes. That, my friend, is the road to hell."

The pumpkin pie makes no sense. The pumpkin pie is like a drag
queen at a charity ball, high heels at a bowling alley. There is no
reason for me to be assembling this pie from scratch: my mother
is purchasing absolutely everything for Thanksgiving dinner fully
prepared and loaded with preservatives from her local grocery
store, including the turkey, stuffing, cranberry sauce, corn bread,
two kinds of sweet potatoes, and two pies: one apple and one pumpkin. What I am doing is redundant and excessive, and, although the
store-bought turkey will be tasteless and dry and the yams will be
cloyingly sweet, the pies, I know from experience, will actually
be quite tasty. This pumpkin pie is a waste of my time, which is
exactly why I'm making it.

I came here, to my parents' house, last week. I left Sugar's
Shoes and drove halfway to Madison just to clear my mind. I sped
down I-94. My arms and legs felt like blocks of ice, but inside I felt
hot, as if I were metabolizing my own organs. The fetus was a
dream I couldn't quite remember, nudging and bumping at the
corners of my brain. I missed David: the thought of him was a
phantom limb, a ruthless ache where something important had
once been. And I missed Kevin. I missed Kevin with actual, physical impact; I missed him with a sour, acid mix of guilt and canyon-
sized loss. David and Kevin swirled around in my head, and after a
while, I could no longer outline the borders of my pain. When I
almost got sideswiped by a merging truck, I realized that driving

wasn't going to accomplish anything good. So I turned around and headed here.

Heather met me at the door. The lights blazed in the hallway, and she looked flushed and warm. The house I grew up in seemed to me a bright sanctuary, and I exhaled, for what felt like the first time all day. "Did we have plans?" Heather asked sleepily, scratching her head and squinting at me.

"Did you just get up?" I asked her. It was almost 7:00 p.m.

"You know how Mom and Dad keep the house so warm," she said. "I fall asleep like nine times a day." She smiled and rubbed her eyes.

All of a sudden I felt hungry and not-hungry at the same time. "We didn't have plans," I said, gently moving her aside and setting my overnight bag on the floor. "Do you think Babs and Len would mind if I stayed here for a while?" I was still numb and not ready to explain things. I didn't know what I was going to say.

Heather grabbed my elbow. "Did you and Kevin have a fight?"

"Sort of," I said. "Yeah. We did."

"What happened?" She practically bared her teeth at me, she was so eager to gobble up this tasty morsel.

I thought fast. "You know how he's always cleaning up after me, and how I'm always begging him not to, in case he throws away something important?" Heather nodded. "Well, he threw away my journal."

She yelped sympathetically and clapped her hand over her mouth. "Your *diary*?" she exclaimed, from behind her hand. We were still standing in the blindingly bright entryway.

"Yep."

"Where is it? Did you get it out of the garbage can? Was it already in the dumpster?"

"Worse," I said sadly. "The garbage had already been collected."

"So you *left*!" She was relishing this. I felt guilty, making Kevin the bad guy. But the truth would out.

"I left." I slipped my coat off and hung it on the hall closet doorknob. We went and found my parents; Len was watching TV in the den, and Barbara was in the living room poring over the current issue of *Home Decor* and casting ruthless, appraising glances at her furniture. When I told them this concocted story, they acted appropriately sympathetic and concerned. My mom hugged me and asked if I wanted her to talk to Kevin (*"Oh, God, no!"* I barked, surprising us both), and my dad went out and got doughnuts. They both reassured me, told me that marriages survived such things, that I would cool off and forgive Kevin and be back home tomorrow or the next day. "Stay here as long as you need to," Barbara said, "but don't let it go too long. Kevin loves you. He made a mistake." *He* made a mistake! Kevin's only mistake was to love me, to trust me. Barbara's words were like hands closing around my neck. I was a fraud for allowing my family to believe my lie and, what's more, letting them dote on me because of it, but I had decided that Thanksgiving was my deadline for telling everyone what had really happened, and so I accepted their ministrations; I let their love prop me up. Heather just stuck close to me, the way she used to when we were little. Her hands fluttered near me, trying to help. She watched as I unpacked my bag and she successfully restrained herself from commenting on the bizarre contents of my suitcase. She even followed me into the bathroom and stood next to me at the sink as I washed my face. She rested her head on my shoulder and fiddled with my hair. It felt good to stare at our similar reflections in the mirror; it felt reassuring. We all played Monopoly at the kitchen table that night, the first time the four of us had sat together and played a game in fifteen years. The light above the table cast a bright glow over my family. They let me win.

"Mom," I say now, wiping flour on my jeans. "Do you have any Crisco? Does anybody even buy Crisco anymore?"

Barbara is sitting at the kitchen table while I make this pie, sizing up me and her cupboards with equal concern. It's been almost a week, and I haven't gone back to Kevin, haven't even spoken to Kevin, which of course my parents don't understand since I haven't told them the truth; they think I'm being a drama queen, and as much as they're trying to stay sympathetic, their impatience is starting to show. But today is Thanksgiving. "I still don't understand why you're making the *crust* from scratch," Barbara says, as if I've just informed her that I will no longer be bathing. "Also, I believe I've changed my mind about the cabinets. I no longer think that light wood will coordinate with my granite countertops." She clicks her tongue. "I'm afraid that combination would be *gauche*."

Heather hands me a tub of Crisco that looks like it was purchased in 1977, and may have been. She's trying to help me—*I was the manager of a bakery,* she insisted, and I decided not to remind her that she was fired. She keeps bumping into me.

There will be seven of us tonight, but we're setting the table for eight: Rolf Larsen is driving in from Minneapolis this evening, Meg and Steve are coming over, and my parents, Heather, and I make seven, but everybody still thinks Kevin will show up, too. They've been talking about it so much, I'm beginning to believe them.

"Okay, sous-chef. Don't use your grubby hands to mix this." I hand the bowl to Heather. "It says here that the heat from your hands will melt the shortening, causing the crust to come out heavy, not light and flaky." As I read these instructions, I realize how very much I want this crust to be light and flaky. "I mean it," I say, as I see Heather removing her engagement ring.

"Batter matters," Heather says, then smiles goofily and jams a wooden spoon into the mixture.

"Crust is a must!" I say, opening the cupboard.

"Just buy the pie!" my mother pipes up. She sighs dramatically, then stands. "Dears," she announces. She places her magazine carefully on top of a pile of other decorating magazines that crowd the countertop, which doesn't matter since this countertop is so rarely used for cooking. "I'm going to go pick up our dinner."

She bustles around, looking for her coat and purse. "It's just lovely to have you both here." She kisses Heather on the top of her curly head, then me.

I pull the ginger and cinnamon from my mom's spice rack, sugar and vanilla and evaporated milk from the pantry. I have to call Meg this afternoon, before she and Steve come over. We've spoken a few times since I left her house last week. I've tried to follow her lead about the miscarriage: I always ask her how she's doing, but most of the time she doesn't want to talk about it, so I blather on about other things. She's been solicitous to me, curious about what I'm going to do next, and helpful but not pushy with her advice. She's offered to accompany me on my apartment search, which I think is my next step. But Meg's sadness, this time around, is slowing her down, pulling her under. Once in a while, in the middle of a conversation, she just drifts away. "Sorry," she murmurs after a minute or two. "What were you saying?" Sometimes she starts crying, but she says she doesn't want to hang up, so I wait, quietly, listening to her sob. I haven't told her that I'm pregnant. I need to, I've tried to, but the thought of how she'll feel when she hears the words stops me in my tracks. But I have to tell Meg before I announce it to my family. (Happy Thanksgiving, everybody! I'm pregnant and unsure just exactly who the father is.) Tonight's the night: we'll all be together, celebrating, and hopefully a little bit drunk, and maybe, just maybe, on this glad evening, they'll find it in their hearts to be happy for me. In any case, Meg needs to be forewarned.

"Now what?" Heather asks.

"I know," I say, nodding. *Now what?*

"Huh?" Heather pushes the mixing bowl toward me. "It's all mixed. What do you want me to do now?"

"Oh. Here." I dump three tablespoons of ice water into the dough. "Mix it with a fork and then mush it into a ball and then flatten it. Can you do that?"

Heather scowls at me. "I don't know. I've never used a fork before."

"Sorry," I say. "Then we'll cover it and stick it in the refrigerator." I hand her the plastic wrap. "You know what? I'm going to leave the piecrust in your capable care. I have to go make a call." I leave Heather in the kitchen, happily balling up a mound of dough.

I close the door to my old room, sit down on the edge of the bed, and dial Meg's number. She answers after seven rings, just as I'm about to hang up. "Hello?" She sounds like she's underwater.

"It's me."

"Hi, me."

"What're you doing?" I ask.

"Watching . . . um . . . a tennis match." Meg hates sports.

"Where's Steve?"

"He's actually out buying flowers for your mother."

"You know my mother's not cooking anything, right?"

"Still, she's the hostess."

"*I'm* making a pumpkin pie," I say. "Those flowers should be for me."

"You can have one of the daisies," Meg says. She sounds a little bit perkier. "We'll pull one out of the bouquet especially for you. Or maybe a lily." She knows I don't like lilies.

"I'm making it from scratch," I say. "Isn't that weird?"

"Yeah, Betty Crocker." Meg agrees. "Didn't you fail seventh-grade home ec?"

"I got a C. And it, like, so *totally* wasn't my fault. That sewing machine had a mind of its own! Anyway, my mom is appalled that I'm not just going to the bakery counter at the grocery store and picking up a nice pie," I say.

"Sure, and we'd all be just as happy with frozen turkey dinners tonight." Meg has been a guest at my parents' house many times; she's been served everything from take-out Chinese to Alfredo's pizza to single-serving TV dinners. Meg knows that a frozen entrée for Thanksgiving is not entirely beyond the pale.

"Wouldn't that be funny?" I say. "Lean Cuisine turkey and mashed potatoes? Only three hundred calories."

"I'll tell Steve to buy a bouquet of plastic flowers instead."

"They do last longer."

Meg laughs. "Yeah."

My leg has begun to shake; I steady it with the hand that's not clutching the phone. I could just end the conversation here. I could make a few more frozen dinner jokes and then say, "Gotta get back to my pie now! There's pumpkin filling to be made!" I dig my bare toes into the purple pile of the carpeting. "So, Megabyte, I have to tell you something," I say finally. Then I'm silent, because the words absolutely will not come.

"Okay," Meg says, and I still don't say anything, and it's starting to feel cruel, like I'm playing a trick on her, making her wait for this. I straighten my back and uncurl my toes.

"I'm pregnant," I say finally. There is a certain incongruity about making this announcement in my cotton-candy-colored childhood room. My fingers dance on the polka dots of my old bedspread. The other end of the line is quiet. I can hear the pop of a tennis ball hitting a racket and the polite, muffled cheering of the crowd. "Meg?" Still nothing.

Meg's voice, when she finally speaks, is tiny and constricted, as if her larynx has squeezed shut. "You're what?" I hear a deep, ragged breath, and the TV goes silent.

"Pregnant. I found out last week. I didn't know how to tell you."

For a long time, Meg is quiet. I think briefly that she's hung up, but I know, whatever her response, it won't be that. So I wait. Will she tell me that she no longer wants to come over for dinner? That she no longer wants to have anything to do with me? Will she cry?

"Is this . . . good news?" she asks faintly.

"I'm not sure."

Another pause. "It is good news," she says. "Trust me, it is."

"Yeah."

"It's okay, Emily," Meg says. I don't know what she means: it's okay that I'm suddenly single and pregnant and somehow this will all work out, or it's okay that she's just had her second miscarriage of a wanted pregnancy and I've just found out that I'm carelessly, haphazardly, *unjustly* knocked up? "Um," she continues, in a more recognizable facsimile of her own voice, "you know, I hate to ask this, but who's . . ."

"I don't know!" I say too loudly, cutting her off.

"Oh, Jesus," Meg says. "Oh, Emily." She inhales with a gasp, and I realize with a start that she's laughing. "Did you skip your adolescent rebellion or what?"

"I know." I wiggle my toes in the soft carpeting. "I should have smoked a lot of pot when I was sixteen instead."

"Oh! Oh, boy!" she yelps, then catches her breath audibly and descends into more laughter, but somehow, from Meg, this hooting is not unsympathetic.

"Hey," I say, relieved. "Hey, now. It's not nice to make fun of someone else's catastrophically bad judgment."

"Em," she says after another minute, suddenly serious. "I promise you, you'll survive this. And you know, I'm always, always here for you."

The choices I make about men may be apocalyptic, but my taste in best friends is impeccable.

Late in the afternoon, during the post-preparation, pre-celebration lull, the doorbell rings. It's too early to be any of our guests, my mom is napping, and Heather and my dad are playing gin rummy in the den. "Did somebody order a pizza?" I holler, and then pad, still barefoot, to the front door. I've been sitting in my bedroom as the afternoon has begun to sink into early evening, trying to figure out a way to tell Kevin and David that I'm pregnant. And although I've been having imaginary conversations with him for the past two hours, I'm unprepared for the thin, familiar figure standing in the late-autumn shadows of my parents' front porch.

"Hi," Kevin says.

"Hey!" I say happily, in the moment before I remember that

I've destroyed our marriage and that he hates me. He's wearing the dark blue coat that his parents sent him for his birthday last year. I want to hug him. A rush of cold air blows in through the open door. "Will you come in?" I ask.

"Just for a second," he says evenly. He waits for me to take a few steps back into the hallway, careful to leave plenty of space between us.

"What on earth are you doing here?" It pops out of my mouth, and I'm immediately sorry, afraid of alienating him, of scaring him away, as if he were an injured bunny who's shown up at the door. "Oh, I didn't mean," I say, flustered. "I mean—"

"It's fine," he says. His voice is neutral, almost—but not quite—friendly, definitely not laced with the icy bitterness I would have expected. "I'm on my way to Doug and Wendy's." I briefly consider what the Pretzels must be saying about me, and I wonder whether they've invited any single women to their Thanksgiving dinner. This is the new psychological scenery of my post-affair life. Kevin takes a deep breath and glances past me at the expanse of my parents' front hallway. "I wanted to tell you something." It's been a week since we've seen each other, a week since we've spoken. I have the urge to pull him into the living room for a game of gin with Heather and my dad, to drag him into my bedroom, sit him down, and regale him with stories of the last week spent with my family. I feel like my best friend has returned to me after a summer away.

"Okay," I say, tucking my hands behind my back to keep from reaching out to Kevin.

"I want to give up the lease on the apartment," he says, and I am reminded of the time Kevin and I were walking near his parents' house and I stumbled across an electrical fence and, without thinking, touched it. I should have known better, then, but I didn't, and the painful shock of it made me leap back with a yelp.

I take a wobbly, involuntary step to the side now, steady myself against the wall. "Okay," I say again, trying to keep my voice under control, but it comes out shaky. Of course we should get rid of the apartment.

"I can't live there, you understand."

"I do," I say, and then I look down, because one of the phrases you should not say to your husband when you've cheated on him and he's telling you that he's going to make a new life for himself is "I do." "I get it," I say to the tiled floor.

"I'm going to stay with Doug and Wendy for a while," he continues.

"And then?" I lift my head to meet Kevin's eyes. They ought to be cold, piercing; by all rights, he should be looking at me with blunt rage or grim anger, but he's not; he's just looking at me, openly, intently. He stretches his hand out and touches my face, and I understand, as his cool fingertips brush my cheek, that this gesture is the most generous gift anybody has ever given me.

"And then I'll keep looking for a house," he says, as if there could be no other answer. He drops his hand back to his side and shrugs. "I'm thinking, actually, that I might see what's available in the city. Expand my options."

"That's a good idea," I say, and it *is* a good idea, although I feel a prickle of frustration, too: the irony is not lost on me that for months I tried to convince Kevin to stay in the city, and only after I've wrecked our lives does he decide that I may have been right. "Yeah," I say. "That sounds like a good plan." The floor is cold beneath my feet. I squeeze my eyes shut for a second. Kevin is moving on—slowly, sanely, peeling himself from me. Even though I'm entirely to blame for the sodden, stinking mess of us, and even though I can't honestly say I wish for things to be the way they were two months ago, and even though I have no right to be, I am, at this moment, the saddest I have ever been. Right here, right now, in the foyer of my parents' house, with the smell of pumpkin pie wafting over us, I have never felt more bereft.

"Well," Kevin says, after a long moment. "I should probably be going."

All of the "I'm pregnant but" speeches I've been practicing suddenly clamor in my head. Now is the time. I owe it to Kevin to supply him with this knowledge. This child I'm carrying may be his. And if it's not, well, he needs to know that, too. He stands before me now, on the brink of leaving, his face and his posture still, remarkably, open to me. Kevin is standing here, close, and I can smell his shampoo, I can see the tiniest speck of dried blood on his chin from where he nicked himself shaving. Probably not even thirty minutes ago, he was standing naked in the shower in the bathroom that used to be ours. Now he's on his way to a Thanksgiving dinner where he won't quite belong, making the best of things. I suppose there is a fine line between cowardice and kindness, a small distinction between respecting Kevin enough to arm him with important knowledge and suffering this burden alone for just a little while longer. I shift my weight from one freezing foot to the other. "Happy Thanksgiving," I say.

Kevin turns and reaches for the doorknob. "Same to you," he says over his shoulder, opening the door, and another icy breeze blows in as he is about to step outside.

"Wait!" I say suddenly. Is it my own latent sense of decency that spurs me forward, the deep and sudden understanding that sometimes it is profoundly uncomfortable to do the right thing? Is it my irritation that Kevin has decided to look for a house in the city? Is it the same impulse that compels a person to rip a Band-Aid off a scab? Whatever it is, I clench my fists at my sides and force myself to look him in the eye. "No, Kev, there is something else." He stands, half in and half out of my parents' house, looking very old and tired. Kevin's papery skin has never responded well to stress. "So, I'm, um, I'm, um," I stutter. Kevin nods. My fingernails bite into my palms. "Pregnant. I am pregnant."

For one second, for just the briefest flash, a flicker of joy moves across his face. And then he realizes what I'm saying, everything I'm saying, and that is the moment that I know I have stabbed him in the heart. He turns quickly away from me and stares out at the front lawn, but not before I see humiliation and

despair sink into him. Then he looks back at me, Kevin again—
poker faced, impenetrable. He's still clutching the doorknob. A
breath like a hiss escapes from his mouth. "Do you even . . . ? Am
I . . . ?" He twists the doorknob back and forth, back and forth; it
makes a squeaking noise beneath his fist.

"I don't know," I say, swallowing hard. Wind chimes tinkle in
the distance. I can feel myself starting to shake a little. I wrap my
arms tightly around my body. "I'm sorry."

"*Don't,*" he says, the word like the low, fearful growl of a
wounded dog. *"Don't tell me you're sorry."* Kevin is a Tupperware
container of rage and pain. His emotions are sealed, locked in so
tightly they'll probably stay there, preserved, forever. "Emily," he
whispers, so softly I can barely hear him; I'm really shaking now,
squeezing myself hard to still the trembling, and I hear my own
breath coming fast and sharp. "Emily," Kevin says again, moving
away from me and onto the front step. His face is contorted now,
barely recognizable as the face of the man who was my husband,
my best friend, my beloved. He begins to back away. A dry rustle
of leaves rattles across my parents' front yard, and I have to strain
to make out his last words to me. "I wish I'd never met you."

Sometime later, maybe ten minutes, maybe an hour, my father
pads past me, whistling, on his way to the bathroom. I'm sitting,
huddled against the wall next to the front door.

"Emily!" he says with a start. "What are you . . . ?" and then he
sees my face and stops. He bends toward me and unwraps my arms
from my sides, takes my hands in his, pulls me up. "Come on,
honey," he says, and leads me to my old bedroom, offering me the
sweet and timeless Ross family cure for whatever ails a person:
"Why don't you lie down and take a little nap?"

So I climb obediently into my childhood bed. My dad tucks in
the covers, kisses me on the forehead, and shuts the door. I hunker
down low, pulling the heavy blankets up to my eyes the way I used
to, only now my toes hang off the edge of the bed. The bulky digi-

tal clock radio that I got for my twelfth birthday casts a gentle green glow in the room. I close my eyes and lie there in the dark, trying to remember what it felt like when I was little, safe in this house, in this bed, when my biggest mistakes were on math tests and science quizzes, and everything ahead of me was brilliant and bright.

THERE'S A HUSHED ATMOSPHERE IN THE HOUSE I GREW UP IN on the morning after Thanksgiving. There's a feeling, almost a smell, of stillness. Everyone but me is still asleep, and the house is warm and quiet. Snow started falling early last night, just after Rolf arrived and before we sat down to dinner, and apparently it snowed all night, because this morning there must be seven inches on the ground, all soft and bright and puffy. I'm standing at the picture window in my parents' living room, staring out at the rolling white landscape of their big backyard. It's as if the world is covered in marshmallow fluff. Which makes me hungry. For marshmallows. In an instant I'm as hungry as I've ever been, so I move away from the window and set about finding myself some leftovers. I would have thought that my confrontation with Kevin might have killed my appetite, but it didn't, not last night and not now. Our grocery-store Thanksgiving dinner, it turned out, was surprisingly tasty, or maybe my newly insatiable appetite just trumped my old, persnickety taste buds. In any case, I have no post-Thanksgiving food hangover this morning, none of the usual groggy, overstuffed bloat, and I try not to make any noise as I carefully assemble a huge

plate of turkey, mashed potatoes, cranberry sauce, and sweet potatoes (topped, fortuitously, with marshmallows) for my breakfast.

The quiet in the house this morning, though, may be as much
a result of the blanket of snow outside as a consequence of the fact
that pretty much no one inside is talking to me. Well, I suppose
Heather is talking to me, if shriekingly accusing me of ruining her
special day counts as talking; yesterday, apparently, was supposed
to be her shining moment, the big introduction of Rolf Larsen,
fiancé.

"I didn't ruin it," I told her, immediately wondering if in fact
I did. We were in the bathroom again. We had left my father, Meg,
Steve, and Rolf sitting around the dining room table, awkwardly
staring at their dessert plates. Just after my announcement, my
mother had quietly retreated into her bedroom, murmuring something about a headache. Heather had waited a few moments, the
steam practically pouring out of her ears, before she slammed
down her fork and stormed off. In the bathroom she faced me, her
hands on her hips. I saw her in front of me, and I saw our reflection
in the mirror behind her. I wanted to point this out to her and say,
"Look! You're an Emily sandwich!" Instead I repeated, "I didn't
ruin anything," the fervor of the moment making up for my lack
of conviction. "I had to tell everyone. I'm sorry if my life is happening at the same time yours is. I'm sorry if the timing of my
pregnancy inconveniences you."

"God, Emily," she said. "You can never just let me have a
moment. You always have to take everything from me." We had
slipped right back into our familiar adolescent skins. In a weird
way, it felt kind of good. "You could have waited to tell everybody until tomorrow, until after Mom and Dad had had a proper
chance to meet Rolf," she continued. "Now whenever they think
of the day they met my *husband*"—she drew the word out as if it
were the name of some kind of exotic tropical fish—"they'll think
of the day their other daughter announced that she screwed up her
marriage and got pregnant by some guy she was fucking around
with!" Her face was red. Heather blushes when she's angry, just

like I do. "Rolf thinks you're a jerk!" she said, then looked at the floor.

"No, he doesn't." I didn't think Rolf thought I was a jerk. And how would Heather know?

"God, Emily!" Heather snorted again.

"You know," I said, heat rising to my own face, "you don't have to be happy for me, but you don't have to be such a spoiled brat." I felt protective of the fetus. I wanted to cover his ears; luckily, I was pretty sure he didn't have them yet. He didn't need an aunt who couldn't even acknowledge, even a little bit, the good fortune of his presence. Ever since my conversation with Meg earlier in the day, I'd been feeling less and less ambivalent about the pregnancy, more and more like this kid was nothing but good luck, whoever his father was. I wanted someone in my family to be happy for me.

"God, Emily," Heather said, for the third time. Then she whirled around and stomped out of the bathroom. I heard her bedroom door slam, a comforting echo of the late 1980s, when I could turn Heather into a tiny ball of tongue-tied fury just by looking at her.

I made my way back into the dining room to the uneasy silence at the table. I slumped into my chair next to Barbara's empty place. She was still in her room. She was going to be next on my list, but I needed to regroup. Meg, Steve, and Rolf were nibbling on my pumpkin pie, which had turned out perfectly. My dad was scratching his bald head. I helped myself to a large slice of pie. "This crust is light and flaky, if I do say so myself," I said, shoving a forkful into my mouth.

"Mmmm," Steve agreed. A lump of pie fell onto his shirt collar. He genuinely seemed to be enjoying the dessert, for which I felt a surge of gratitude.

Rolf Larsen folded his napkin, then neatly set it and his fork down and looked around the table. He was a nice, nondescript kind of Minnesotan, or at least that was the way he seemed. It was true; I hadn't had much of a chance to talk to him. I thought I would probably like him, once I got to know him. He was pale and thin, and he wore his hair so short it was almost a crew cut. I suspected it felt soft to the touch, like a pony. He seemed a little overwhelmed, but who could blame him? He hadn't said much, but he had eaten his dinner with gusto and, in between bites, had frequently reached over to Heather and touched her neck or her back. He reminded me of Kevin. Someday I would mention this to Heather; someday it would give us both a good laugh. "I should go see to Heather," he said formally, sheepishly. "Will you all please excuse me?"

After Rolf left the table, we ate our pie in silence. I really was very hungry, in spite of everything. The pumpkin filling was dense and sweet, a perfect complement to the delicate crust. I could just make out the ginger. As I was considering a second piece, Len, who hadn't said a word since I'd made my fateful announcement, placed his hand just above my elbow. "Emily," he said. "We love you and we're here to support you, sweetheart." He squeezed my arm gently. "We'll support you, whatever you do." Did he think I was going to have an abortion? Give the child up for adoption?

"Dad," I said defensively, pulling my arm away, "I'm going to have this baby." I felt tawdry saying it; I felt like he could picture me having sex.

"I know, sweetheart. That's not what I meant." And I realized my dad gave me more credit than I gave myself. "I'm going to go talk to your mother," he said, and I nodded gratefully.

And then it was just me and Meg and Steve, and we could all finally make eye contact. Meg stuck her tongue out at me and waggled her eyebrows. Steve smiled. As usual, bits of food were stuck in his teeth. How, I wondered for the millionth time, could a dentist not notice this? Sweetly, he extended his arm across the table to pat my hand but missed, softly banging on the table instead. My parents were in their bedroom, Heather and Rolf were in Heather's old room. Through the thin walls of the house, I could hear deep tones and higher, louder, more urgent exclamations, followed again by reassuring low voices: two reasonable men comforting their distraught women. Not that I had looked too far beyond the first part of my plan, the making of the actual announcement, but this wasn't how I had wanted things to go. Somehow, I'd thought that my family might all come together, heroically—that, yes, naturally they would be upset at first, but they would be upset *for* me, not *with* me, and then they would quickly acknowledge my situation, recognize the flaws and the drama, and then understand that there would be beauty in the outcome. Maybe someone would even make a toast! To life! To grandchildren! To incredibly irresponsible behavior! I had thought that I would ultimately find myself floating in a sea of their acceptance, their love, and that because I was coming to terms with things, they would intuitively, deeply, and *quickly* understand what Meg herself had articulated earlier: everything was going to be okay. Instead, and I saw now that there really had been no other possibility, just as I'd decided to grow up and make things right, all this strife erupted, all this chaos, all these terrible feelings, all because of me. I sighed and slumped even lower in my chair. Another few slumps and I'd be under the table entirely.

"So, that went well, huh?" Meg said, pointing her fork at me for emphasis. Steve elbowed her.

All I had now was a sense, deep down and intermittent, that there had been a shift, that I was on the other side of all of my stupid choices. All I had now was the knowledge that I had sunk to the bottom of my life—this was it, right here, the bottom; there had to be some small comfort in that—and if I could hold my breath long enough, I would eventually emerge on the surface, probably gasping for breath, but alive.

"Who's for more pie?" I asked, and Meg and Steve lifted their plates.

I'm scooping the last bit of reconstituted cranberry sauce onto my spoon. Cranberry sauce is just jam, really, and Thanksgiving just happens to be the only occasion on which it's okay to eat jam like this, straight up, or spread over turkey. It occurs to me that I might want to implement this combination more often. Who says it's not acceptable to spread jam—strawberry, I think, but even grape jelly would do—on your run-of-the-mill baked chicken in the middle of February? It sounds incredibly appealing to me right now.

My family is stirring. I can hear my parents laughing—are they laughing?—in their room, and I heard Rolf click the bathroom door shut a few minutes ago. I'm acutely aware that these are my last moments of peace before things get messy again. This warm, satiated feeling I have now, this slow calm, just me, here, at the kitchen table at my parents' house, it will all be broken in an unseemly collision of personalities and emotions, in just a few minutes. I can't imagine what the crash site will look like. Will Heather still be furious? Will she start in on me, stomping her feet and flailing her arms about, before she's even poured her cereal? Will my mother talk to me at all? Will she sulk disapprovingly, glare at me from behind her sequined reading glasses, as if I've deliberately sullied her carefully honed reputation? Will my dad defend me? Or will he give me a wink, grab a bagel, and retreat into the safety of his den? Fleetingly, I wish Kevin were here. He's always run interference in my family; he's mediated every Ross conflict with unflappable courtesy. ("Barbara, I think that when Emily compares you to a charging rhino trying to take over her wedding plans, what she's trying to say is that she loves and respects you, but that she doesn't think that releasing one hundred doves into the air at the conclusion of the ceremony is entirely necessary.") Then I wish David were here. Go to hell, you judgmental jerks! My lover and I are going into my room to have steamy, unpredictable sex.

I hear Heather, still in her room, calling for Rolf, asking him if he would bring her a cup of water from the bathroom. I hear my dad grumbling about never being able to find his slippers—his house slippers, he calls them—my mom telling him that they're where they always are, under the bed. *Hey, kid. Hey, little friend.* I pat my belly. *Hello. Here we are.* "No, nope, they're not under the bed, Barbara!" Len calls. "Oh, yes, sorry, here they are!" There's more indeterminate thumping from that end of the house. I should sneak back into my bedroom or, better yet, out the side door. *Head for the hills,* my brain is urging, but I feel petrified, rooted to my chair by some faulty electrical impulse in my flight-or-fight mechanism. Whatever is about to unfold, I guess I'll be seeing it through to the end.

I turn my gaze to the kitchen window, to the transformed face of my parents' front lawn. The snow outside, it strikes me, is really a lie. It's just a half foot of cold deception. It may look innocent, like a soft blanket, but it's hiding its own dark secrets, all the muck and trash of autumn buried beneath it; stinking, decomposing leaves and gum wrappers and cigarette butts, everything that will reappear; it's all there, on the placid streets and the sidewalks and in the parks and backyards, just waiting. The snow is not just gently concealing the sleeping buds and shoots of spring: it's covering up all the world's crap, too. When Len and Barbara and Heather and Rolf finally emerge from their bedrooms, all sleepy and smug, their morning rituals completed, they'll say, *Oh, look, look at the snow; it's so pretty!* And they won't even think about shoveling the driveway or brushing off their cars or the leaky garage roof, or about how, in a few days, the snow on the curb will turn filthy with soot and dog piss; not at first: they'll just gasp at the beauty of the world draped in white.

"Hello there." Rolf's appearance jolts me out of my reverie. His resemblance to Kevin is disorienting; for a second, I forget where I am.

Before I can fully collect myself, Heather shuffles up behind Rolf and wraps her arms around his waist. Her hair is half-straight and matted on one side of her head. She looks rumpled and tired and she burrows her face into Rolf's neck for a moment, then peers over his shoulder at me. "Hey, Em," she says, no trace of last night's rage in her voice. She and Rolf two-step together, attached, over to the cupboard, where Heather reaches above him for a box of Raisin Bran. A minute later, my parents show up, first Barbara, then Len. My dad walks over and ruffles my hair, then does the same to Heather. "Dad!" she says. "It took me hours to achieve this style!" Barbara doesn't look at me, but she doesn't look at anyone else, either; she moves directly to the coffeemaker and busies herself spooning coffee into the filter. This is how she starts every morning, sullen until she's caffeinated, so I can't gauge her mood, but everyone else seems normal; they're not ignoring me or hurling invectives; no one, it seems, is going to slap a scarlet *A* onto the front of my T-shirt and send me out into the cold.

"Look!" Barbara exclaims sharply. "Look at all that snow!" She sounds slightly mad at it, but awed, too. "My goodness!"

"Well, that settles it," Heather says, craning her neck to see out the window. "As soon as breakfast is over, I'm going back to sleep."

"Ah," Rolf says, "and that's because of the *snow*."

But Heather has the right idea. I have the overwhelming desire, suddenly, to rest, to gather my strength. My head feels heavy and precarious on my neck, a boulder balanced on a spindly stick. Len and Barbara and Heather and Rolf step around each other, reaching for bowls and mugs and sugar. I'm perfectly still, but inside everything is changing. I close my eyes. For now, just for right now, I'm content to be here, in this chair, in my parents' kitchen, letting the easy, happy chaos of my family shore me up for what's ahead, for after I sleep, for the rest of my life, when I will have to be brave.

Postscript

A FEW DAYS LATER, WHEN THE ROADS HAVE BEEN PLOWED but the inevitable weariness and grime of the long Midwestern winter have not yet settled in, I decide that I need to go for a drive.

During the strange days immediately after Thanksgiving, my family dealt with their post-traumatic stress in uncharacteristic silence. I would have preferred the intrusive questions I know they wanted to ask: Had I thought ahead to full-time employment? Where was I planning on living? Had I spoken to Kevin? Were we talking about divorce or was there any hope of reconciliation? I would have loved nothing more than to have shouted, "None of your business!" and stomped off, only to return five minutes later and answer their nosy queries. But instead my parents and Heather and even Rolf, the gentle alien in our midst, kept their distance. They tiptoed around me as if I were an exotic panda just shipped in from China: Do Not Upset Our Zoo's Recent Acquisition, or She May Behave in an Immature and/or Aggressive Fashion. I would wander from my bedroom into the kitchen or the living room and there they would all be, talking and laughing, and then they would see me and fall silent. My dad rubbed my back every time he passed me. My mom kept bringing me sandwiches I hadn't asked for. Heather started a dozen stilted conversations with me about people we used to know, and Rolf just nodded at me, practically constantly, like a bobble toy. This morning I woke up and I knew I needed to get out of the house.

I keep the radio off as I drive through the quiet streets of my parents' neighborhood. I let this silence form a soft padding around me, instead of a thinly frozen lake under me. I aimlessly circle the lazy streets for a while and then find myself heading north, toward the road that runs parallel to the highway. *I'm finally alone!* I think. But then I quickly realize: not anymore. I can distract myself from the idea of the fetus for a time, but it doesn't matter: he's still here. This knowledge settles into my stomach, and I feel queasy and hot. I have the desperate urge to run away. But wherever I go, he'll be there. The hum of the road is suddenly oppressively loud, and I am in a tin can hurtling through space. Beads of sweat break out on my forehead and upper lip. Unbidden, I recall a detail I skimmed from one of Meg's books: if a pregnant woman doesn't take in enough calcium, her fetus will leech it straight from her bones. I feel my skeleton suddenly weakening, growing soft and porous beneath my skin. I'm trapped, stuck inside my own, rapidly deteriorating body, as this beast sucks the life force from me. Good God, I can't breathe. I need vitamins! I force myself to take a sip from the bottle of water I brought with me. I turn down the heater and unzip my jacket. I take a breath and focus on the road. I clear my throat; I'm still here. I wiggle my fingers on the steering wheel, shift my hands from 9:00 and 3:00 to 10:00 and 2:00.

Okay, I think. *Get a grip. Fetus, can you help me out here?* I picture him nodding gravely, giving me the thumbs-up. I turn the heat off completely, open the vent, and let cold air fill the car. I begin to feel a little bit better. I think I can breathe now. Every light I come to is green, and there are few other cars around. After a while, the hiss of the road under the wheels becomes a soothing sound again. I start to feel peaceful, in a way that seems like it might last for a while. Without my knowing it, the fetus has begun to turn into a quiet comfort, my tiniest companion, not to mention my best audience. I may be stuck with him, but he can't exactly leave the auditorium, either. So maybe what holds you back is also what holds you down, a necessary thing, like gravity. "The fetus" begins to seem like a less than acceptable term with which to refer to him. I squirt some washer fluid onto the windshield and turn on my wipers. I drive past a strip mall, then a series of fast-food restaurants. I pass a moving van with a gaudy orange depiction of Montana splashed across its side panel. I decide to call the fetus Monty, at least until he's born. We drive together, Monty and I, and I'm okay again, and I know that I have something I want to tell him.

"All your actions have consequences, Monty," I say, and the surprising croak of my voice is loud in the car. "Well, maybe not yet, but they will." That isn't quite what I wanted to say. "You have to make good choices," I try again, "all your life, because if you don't, you'll end up doing something rash and destructive and hurting other people." That's not quite it, either, although it's closer to the mark, for sure. I can't put my finger on what it is I want him to know.

I veer off at Adams Avenue and I see where I've been headed all along: Jupiter's Palace of Cheese. I slow and pull into the parking lot. I've never seen it from this angle before; I've never seen it from a full stop. It's flat and uninspiring. It looks like a motel. The sun shines dimly on the few cars in the parking lot. What do I have to offer a child, anyway? I've screwed up so badly, I don't even know who his father is! "I'll probably tell you a lot of stupid things during your life," I say, as the engine clicks a few times. "Everything I say is wrong. Whatever I tell you, do the opposite." But that doesn't seem fair, either. I unbuckle my seatbelt and zip up my jacket.

The air is thin and sharp on my face as I walk across the pavement to the Palace. There are patches of ice on the ground, and I have to walk carefully in my sneakers. I almost forget the momentousness of this occasion, of my crossing the threshold into

Jupiter's Palace of Cheese, and then, by nothing more than my own forward motion, I'm through the jingling door and I'm inside. Years of contemplation, and all it took was a turn signal, Adams Avenue, a simple slowing down, and then me, making my way toward the door.

The first thing is warm air and the heavy, foot-ish but not unpleasant aroma of a complicated mix of cheeses. I breathe in, look around. A few people mill about. It's nothing in here, and it's everything. I begin to explore. There are some peripheral displays of specialty foods, seasoned crackers, and canned asparagus spears and sweets your aunt Minnie would serve while you sat on her plastic-covered sofa—watermelon-coconut strips and butter biscuits and marzipan bars. But mostly there is cheese, counter after counter of cheese, all the cheeses I knew about and some I've never heard of: Swiss and Gouda, Babybel and Beaufort, brick, cheddar of all ages, Colby and Gruyère and Monterey Jack. It's just one display after another of cheeses, of choices, utterly predictable and yet the most unexpected collage of one thing, one prosaic thing, made glorious by its unashamed excess. The possibilities are endless. There will be things I can show my child, galaxies.

"Oh, Monty," I say softly, full of wonder. "Just look at all this cheese."

Acknowledgments

Many people helped guide *Still Life with Husband* toward completion. I am grateful to Julie Barer and Jennifer Jackson, my agent and editor, for their equal measures of wisdom and kindness. This book wouldn't exist without their care and expertise. Thanks also to my publicist, Sarah Gelman, for her patience and professionalism.

My deepest appreciation to my friends Erica Ackerberg, Judy Bernstein, Carolyn Crooke, Peter Kafka, Mimi Kleiner, Elizabeth Larsen, Jim Moore, Daniel Riseman, Deb Rosen, and the members of the Wednesday night writing group, especially Jon Olson, for their keen editorial vision and encouragement.

Special thanks to Carly Yiannackopoulos for being such a wonderful friend to my daughter. My family have been endlessly helpful and supportive in every way, and there aren't enough words to express my love and gratitude. And finally, to Andrew and Molly, my thanks for everything, and my love.

A NOTE ABOUT THE AUTHOR

Lauren Fox earned her MFA from the University of Minnesota in 1998. Her work has appeared in *Utne, Seventeen, Glamour,* and *Salon.* She lives in Milwaukee with her husband and daughter. *Still Life with Husband* is her first novel.

A NOTE ON THE TYPE

This book was set in a version of the well-known Monotype face Bembo. This letter was cut for the celebrated Venetian printer Aldus Manutius by Francesco Griffo, and first used in Pietro Cardinal Bembo's *De Aetna* of 1495.

The companion italic is an adaptation of the chancery script type designed by the calligrapher and printer Lodovico degli Arrighi.

Composed by Creative Graphics, Inc.,
Allentown, Pennsylvania

Printed and bound by R. R. Donnelley & Sons,
Harrisonburg, Virginia

Designed by Soonyoung Kwon